Angelique

A Transitional Age Youth Novel

DEENA SAUNDERS-GREEN

ISBN: 0-9981835-0-4
ISBN-13: 978-0-9981835-0-3

Cover photographer: Otis G. Sanders
Cover Model: Kat Branchman
Cover designer: Tunisia Johnson

For information about special discounts for bulk purchases,
please visit www.GreenPinesMedia.com

For those impacted by foster care.

Acknowledgments

I don't have the space to list everyone who inspired me to write; however, this book would not have been possible without a number of amazing people and organizations.

To my husband, Terry: Thank you for being supportive and encouraging me to pursue my dreams—especially the unconventional ones.

To my father, Lindsey: Thank you for pushing me when things got too easy, and for being the voice of reason when things got hard.

To my mother, Elois: Your kindness has been a blessing to more people than you know. Thank you for unconditionally accepting the kids in our home. And thank you for your wonderful BBQ!

To Tyler Malachi: My very first reader! Thank you for your feedback and labor. You're my biggest cheerleader.

To The Greens (Lakewood and Long Beach): Thank you for welcoming our kids and making them feel like part of the family—disappointments and all.

To Christina Brown: Thank you for your prayers, and for helping me give Angelique a voice.

To Otis Sanders: Thank you for your guidance, and for showing me that dreams can and should be pursued.

To Flo Jenkins: I wish I would've known about your amazing editing skills in grad school. I wasted a lot of time researching drug addition. Thank you for your keen eye and for your words of wisdom.

To Mashanti, Shamontia, Darren, Desiré, Melissa, Ashley, and Mihret: You have strengthened my prayer life more than you will ever know. And to Bumble-Bea, Ni-Ni, and RJ, thank you for reminding me that kids have a unique voice that should be heard.

To Kimberly Guerrero: You weren't obligated to read or even like my stories—and yet you did. Thank you for being gracious enough to read the screenplays, and bless you for not telling me how awful they were.

To the Stipend Sisters: Thank you for allowing me to vent, for making me feel normal, and for being the most amazing social workers on the planet.

To Olive Crest: Thank you for going above and beyond when it came to our kids; and for setting such high standards for foster parents.

To Aspiranet: You're not simply running programs, you're changing lives. Thank you for your phenomenal work—particularly with TAY in Transitional Housing and Aftercare Services.

To Chris Abel and the staff at Spurr & Associates: Thank you for taking a chance and providing housing (and hope) to the young adults under our care.

To Kim Carter: You challenged me to think differently and inspired me to become a more compassionate social worker. Thank you for being the inspiration behind Kim Carson, and for the wonderful work you're doing at Time for Change Foundation.

To Victor & Eileen Marx: Your obedience is helping people heal all over the world. Thank you both for being so transparent and sharing your stories. Vincent Marks would not have been possible without you and All Things Possible Ministries.

And to my Heavenly Father: Thank you for Your Son, for giving me life, and for giving me purpose.

Summer 2012

1

ALL I WANNA DO IS SLEEP, but here I am staring at a useless alarm clock before it even goes off, again. I hate waking up early. I heard somebody say that we all have an internal alarm clock that works better than one from the store. I don't know if that's true, but I wish I could turn both of 'em off. Waking up at seven in the morning is bad enough, but lately, I can't even sleep past five. I don't know what's going on. I feel tired all the time, but as soon as my head hits the pillow, my mind starts racing. I can't rest. I tried telling Liz how I felt once, but all she said was, "Angelique, you're only eighteen, you're too young to be tired." I stopped making an effort to have any real conversations with her after that. I mean, seriously? She's my case manager, did she even bother to read my file? But even if she didn't, how are you gonna tell somebody who's been in foster care that they're too young to be tired?

I stare at the clock for so long that the digital numbers blur. After a while, my mind tells me that it's not just a clock, but part of some red-eyed creature lurking in the dark. I know it's crazy, but my heart starts pounding like the thing is real. I have no idea why I'm freaking out, but I do know that it's too dark in here. I turn over on my futon and pull open the curtains so the lights from the courtyard can shine through. When I turn back, the creepy feeling is gone.

My eyes wander over to the collage of pictures taped to the wall and the pounding in my chest turns into a dull ache. The biggest one is a grainy eight by ten of my grandparents from back in the eighties. They couldn't have been more different. My grandma was short and pudgy with green eyes and skin so pale that she couldn't tan even if she wanted to. At least that's what Mom used to say. She had a slight smile on her face and her honey-colored hair was cut into a typical eighties style— feathered into a helmet in the front, but long in the back. My granddad stood next to her with his arm draped around her shoulders. He was tall and lanky with chocolate eyes and the smoothest ebony skin that I'd ever seen. His Super Fly mustache was so long that it framed his chin, and he had one of those old-school curls that was in desperate need of moisturizer. They were an interracial couple from a small town in East Texas, and even though segregation had ended way before they met, the tension between the blacks and whites never really went away. I googled their town a while back and found an article about how the people in charge had voted to keep the cemetery segregated—in the name of tradition. No wonder they moved to Southern California.

I can't help but smile when I look at the picture of me in the arms of my dad—the infamous Tavio Lopez. It was taken when I was around three, back when I used to see him on a regular basis. His shaved head and goatee made him look hard and dangerous—well, *that*, and his tatts. He had so many that it looked like he was wearing some kind of long-sleeved shirt under his wife beater. When females (and even a couple of guys) visited me for the first time, they always stared at that picture. "Is that your dad?" they'd ask with their mouths hanging open. At first, I thought they were asking because they didn't know I was half Mexican, and then I thought it was

2

because my dad was a cholo. When I finally asked my neighbor Dani, she stared at me and shook her head like I was clueless, "It's 'cause he's hot!" Then I'd have to explain that he wouldn't be visiting because he was serving a twenty-five year sentence for attempted murder.

There was a picture of me when I was four with my baby sister Brianna (although everybody called her Bribee for as long as I could remember), and our mom, Angela. My mom was such a liar. She used to tell people that Quincy Jones was her biological dad—and they believed her because she kinda looked like one of his daughters. She had her mom's green eyes, that "good" hair and skin color that always kept people guessing. She was, and still is beautiful—but she's crazy as hell. Bribee got a lot of Mom's features and a hint of her color, but everything else—especially the blonde hair—came from her dad. Mom always said that he was just a psycho sperm donor, and since Bribee was born during one of their many separations, she ended up with Mom's last name, Bailey.

There were a lot of other pictures on the wall, but my favorite one was of me, Bribee and our foster sister Kimi. We all had on birthday hats because I had just turned eight. I loved that picture, but it also made me sad because it reminded me of how fast bad things can happen.

I notice something move out of the corner of my eye. *Please don't tell me it's another roach.* I can't stand bugs of any kind, but roaches are the most vile thing on the planet. Even killing them is disgusting, but I know that if I don't take care of it now, I'll see even more of 'em later on. I force myself out of bed, grab a flip-flop and smash the nasty thing against the wall. My skin crawls and a sour feeling makes my stomach turn. I can taste the bile rise up in the back of my throat as I wipe off the wall and my sandal with a handful of tissues. *Ugh.* It's a struggle, but I manage to keep my gag reflex under control. After I flush the filth down the toilet, I grab a rag and some bleach spray from under the bathroom sink. I need to make sure nothing nasty was left behind.

When I'm done, I scrub my hands with soap and water so hot that I can barely stand it. *What else had that nasty thing crawled on before I even saw it? There could be germs and filth and roach eggs all over my apartment! I should just move everything and do a deep clean - but if I do that, I'll be late for class and I can't be late. This professor don't play, and she's already given me a warning. If I'm late again, I could get kicked out the class, and if I don't take English this summer ... I'ma have to push my whole plan back! No, I gotta stick to my schedule and finish on time.* I feel a tightness growing in my chest and suddenly I'm so light-headed that I have to hold onto the counter so I don't fall. I feel like I'm having a heart attack, but I know it's all in my mind, so I just close my eyes and take a few deep breaths. I inhale through my nose; hold it for a few seconds and then exhale slowly through my mouth. This was the only useful thing I ever learned from all those therapists – that deep breathing actually helps with my anxiety.

Once the feeling passes, I look in the mirror and check myself. "Keep it together Angelique. You're okay, just breathe and keep goin'." As usual, my hair is a tangled mess but I don't need the mirror to tell me that. I already know that I should be wearing a scarf at night, but I hate having to do one more thing. *Why didn't I get hair like Bribee and Mom?* All they have to do is wet their hair and it falls in place. I ended up with the poofy stuff that I have to fight with a comb, a brush, water, sprays and conditioning creams. And then there's the dark circles under my eyes. Last week, a sales lady at a makeup kiosk in the mall asked me if I was going, "heroin chic." I thought she was calling me a dope fiend, so I cussed her ass out. I felt really bad after Dani told me that it was a popular style from the nineties. It was just the lady's way of saying that she thought I was stylish or something. I tried to apologize, but I could tell that she was too scared to hear me. Plus, it seemed like the whole mall stopped and stared.

The alarm clock gives off a loud buzz letting me know it's finally seven. If I didn't misplace my phone so much, I'd get rid of the annoying thing, but I have a schedule to keep and I can't risk getting off track. I know I don't need to deep clean everything, but I do need to tidy up. I fold my sheets and comforter making sure that all the corners are perfectly lined up, and then put them inside of the chest that doubles as my coffee table. Once my pillows are stacked on top, I close the lid and push the futon back into a couch position. I feel better once everything is in the right place. I even pull my custom-made toss pillows out of the closet so that I have something nice on the couch. They're my favorite decorations because I made them myself from old t-shirts of the groups and bands that I used to listen to back in the day. Some of these Independent Living classes we have to take are stupid, but that sewing one was cool. It gave me a whole bunch of ideas on what to do with some of my old clothes.

In the kitchen, I grab an oversized salad bowl and a box of Captain Crunch out of the cabinet. This is one of the best things about living on my own. I can get whatever kind of cereal I want, and I can eat it whenever I want to. I know it's not the healthiest thing, and it's probably why I'm starting to get fat, but I don't care. When you've had other people telling you what to eat and when to eat it your whole life, having Captain Crunch for breakfast, lunch, or dinner is like heaven. As the cereal falls into the bowl, I notice two almond-looking things tumble in with it. It's not until they crawl out of the bowl and run for cover that I realize what they are.

"Dammit!"

My first instinct is to jump back, but then I grab the can of bug spray that I keep on the counter. I know it's a weird place to keep it, but you never know what you're gonna find when you turn the lights on in this place. I hose down the entire kitchen from top to bottom, choking on fumes as I do. My heart starts pounding again, but this time, it's not from anxiety.

Do I change out of my pajamas or put on shoes? Nope. I march across the courtyard to the office, poofy hair and all. The sign next to the door says Perdido Transitional Housing Program: Empowering Foster Youth Since 1998, but everybody knows that this program is a joke. It should've said running roach motels since 1998 because I don't feel anything close to empowered.

The office opens at seven and I'm hoping the new Director will already be here. Unfortunately, the only person inside was Vanessa, one of the so-called Resident Advisors. That's another joke. The last Director had a thing for some of the girls in the program, so he made up those R.A. positions to keep them here after their time in the program was up. Of course he had to hire one of the guys so it wouldn't be too obvious. The three of them were supposed to be mentors and advocates who kept an eye on things after the staff went home, but that didn't happen. They only thing they did was turn into narcs with paychecks and discounted rent.

I can tell from the reflection in Vanessa's glasses that she's online socializing instead of working like she should be. I stand there getting more and more pissed because she doesn't even bother to look up at me.

"Good morning Angelique," she finally says with an attitude. "How can I help you this time?"

"There were roaches in my Captain Crunch." I'm trying my best to keep my temper under control. "I know that has to be some kinda health code violation. Plus, I don't get free food like some of the people in this program, so somebody needs to pay me back for my cereal." I cross my arms and stare at her.

She pushes herself back from the desk and walks over to a nearby cabinet. After unlocking the door, she fumbles around for a while and comes back with small box. "Here." She puts a box of foggers on the desk in front of me and then goes right back to the computer.

God if you're real, please keep me from jumpin' across this desk and chokin' her ass out. I close my eyes and take a deep breath before I say anything. "Vanessa, you've lived here for what - almost three years? I'm sure you know this problem is way beyond foggers."

"What?"

She barely looks at me, and she's not even listening! "Foggers won't work if all the apartments around me are filthy!" I yell. "What's the point in having rules about cleanliness if staff won't even enforce it? We shouldn't have to live like this!"

She shakes her head like she doesn't even care—like I'm inconveniencing her or something. "Bring it up in group tonight," she says and then shrugs like it's not a big deal.

"Vanessa, what exactly is your problem?"

She tears her eyes away from the computer like she's about to say something, but then she looks me up and down and shakes her head.

"Angelique, this is a place of business. When you come into this office, you need to be dressed appropriately."

I'm about to die from some roach disease, but this chick is worried about how I'm dressed? Whatever. She's useless. I leave, slamming the door behind me in the process.

The fumes in my apartment are still strong so I open all the windows and go into the bathroom to take a shower. I've always loved long hot showers, even when the heat would make me light-headed. In foster care, the shower was the only place that I could go to get away from all the craziness. Sometimes I'd even take two showers a day, which usually got me in trouble. My cheap-ass foster parents were always complaining about the water and how high the bills were—as if they weren't getting paid for me being there. Hell, that's what they signed up for. Although I have to admit, I did cut down on my shower time after I got my own place. Fifty-seven dollars, I smile just thinking about it. I thought I was being overcharged when I got my first bill, so I called the water company to complain. I just knew they were crooks tryna run a scam, but when the electricity bill came a couple of days later, I realized that some of my habits were costing me money. I nipped my shower habit in the bud three days later.

After a short shower, I wipe the steam off the mirror and pull my hair back into a poofy ponytail. *Dang, when did I turn into the thick girl with the pretty face?* When I was little, I used to love having people tell me that I was pretty because it made me feel special. But that was before I learned that being pretty wasn't always a good thing. It could bring unwanted attention, especially when there wasn't anybody around to supervise. Sometimes being pretty meant having your stuff stolen and getting into fights, or having chunks of your hair cut off or tied into knots while you slept.

I get dressed in my favorite jeans and a polo shirt with River Beach RYA embroidered on the chest. I hate uniforms and dressing up, so I'm glad this job has a casual dress code. They even encouraged us to wear running shoes in case we have to go after a kid. I grab a deli-made turkey sandwich from the fridge and head out the door with my backpack flung over my shoulder.

On my way out of the complex, I see Melinda making her way in. She always looks like the CEO of some big company instead of the Director of a non-profit agency. She's so short, I wouldn't be surprised if her pantsuits were custom-made, and I can see those stilettos peeking out. She's only been running the program for few months but I can tell she knows how to handle her business. I like the fact that she actually talks to us instead of relying on all the case managers and R.A.'s for information. She's nothing like the last Director. He seemed to care more about making himself look good than taking care of our needs.

"Angelique, I was hoping I'd catch you before you left. How are things going?" she smiles.

"Honestly … this complex is infested with roaches, and it has been for a long time. I'm tryna work and go to school, but I can't even have a decent breakfast because there were roaches in my Captain Crunch!"

She holds up a manicured hand with a disgusted look on her face. "I heard there was a problem, which is why we're having an exterminator come out this week. I just didn't realize it was that bad. Notices are going up today."

"Seriously?" I can't help but look at her a little crazy. "I've been filling out service request forms since I moved in, but nothing ever happened. The last Director just handed out foggers. With him, a clean apartment was a suggestion, not a rule."

"Well I definitely don't want any hitching a ride home with me," she shivers. "Plus, foggers are just a short-term solution to a bigger problem—which we'll be going over in group tonight."

That makes me smile, until I remember that she was looking for me.

"Wait, what did you wanna talk to me about?" *Aw hell, what did I do?*

"I'm helping a colleague do a foster parent training on Friday, and I was wondering if you'd be interested in going with me to share your story."

"Me?" I can't even hide my shock. "Do you know how I feel about foster parents? I might say something inappropriate."

"I'm not worried," she smiles. "I think foster parents need to hear from young people who've gone through the system. Plus, it'll give you some practice. I heard you're majoring in Communications."

Dang, she got me. "They may never invite you back," I warn.

"Like I said, I'm not worried," she says. "Meet me here at six and you can ride over with me. Better yet, I'll pick you up from the Youth Academy."

"I see somebody's been reading files around here." *Wow, she actually knows where I work, and what my schedule is?* "Okay, I'll put it in my calendar."

"I appreciate that. Let me know if anything changes," Melinda says as she walks toward the office. "Have a good day."

I pull out my phone and unwrap the earbuds that I keep coiled around it. Once they're in place, I start my favorite playlist and make my way toward the bus stop. I can't help but smile. Speaking in front of crowds always makes me nervous, but I love it; especially when the subject is something that I'm passionate about. And I will tell anybody that listens—I hated my time in foster care with a passion!

2

THE BEST THING ABOUT BEING in Perdido's THP is the housing, of course. It's free for the first three months of the program because they want us to focus on getting a job and getting into school. But even when we do have to pay, it's crazy cheap because we all get a $500 credit towards the rent. Sometimes we can even choose our own apartments. Most residents start out in a two-bedroom because they're broke, and if you share an apartment, $500 from each person will cover all the rent. Once we start working, we can move into our own place—if space is available. We just have to do a budget and show our case manager that we can afford it. A one-bedroom is $725 a month; but with the credit, it really only costs $225. That may not sound like a lot, but for somebody that's been homeless or struggling, that's a big deal. If you don't have that kind of money, you can get a studio like me and Dani. The rent is normally $575, but with the credit, we only pay $75. That's pretty easy to swing with a part-time job.

The second-best thing about this THP is the free transportation. Residents with a car get a $50 gas card every month, but the rest of us get a 30-day bus pass. Some people won't ride the bus because they think it's beneath them; or maybe they're really just scared 'cause you never know what can happen.

I remember one time, me and one of my friends were on the bus and we saw this guy having a full-on conversation with himself. When his stop came, he walked down the aisle as if he was leaving, but then he walked up to my friend and started punching him in the face! Luckily, some older guys pulled him off. But it was crazy. They had to call the cops and everything.

But then you have the lazy, unrealistic folks, the ones who won't even look for a job until they have a car. I'm still tryna to figure that one out. How are you gonna get a car if you don't have money? Hell, I'm grateful for my free bus pass. *That's $50 that I can keep in my pocket.*

I swipe my pass through the fare box near the driver and make my way down the aisle, checking out the other passengers as I go. Once I slide into an empty seat in the back, I sigh and silently curse myself for taking a class at nine in the morning, during the summer. Especially a three-hour English class that makes me drowsy the minute I take my seat. *The faster you finish your general ed's, the faster you finish school,* I remind myself. *Just stay on schedule.*

On a good day, River Beach Community College is only a twenty minute bus ride, but I have to get there half an hour early to make sure I get to class on time. I hate to admit it, but I still struggle with my time management skills every now and then. I'm learning, but sometimes I'm learning the hard way. During the first week of the summer session, I was dropped from class because I kept coming in after roll was taken. I wasn't trying to be rude to Professor Lau, but it seemed like she was picking on me. I'll never forget that conversation.

"You see me here every day!" I told her after class. "Why would you drop me?"

She looked at me and raised one of her eyebrows. "Ms. Lopez, I'm teaching three classes right now. Each one has thirty students enrolled and nearly a dozen on the waiting list trying to get in. I have no idea of who is in this classroom, and I have no idea of who is serious about staying in this class. That is why I take attendance."

"But my bus don't get here until 8:57! I can't walk all the way across campus in three minutes!"

She lowered her head and stared at me over the top of her glasses. "Then apparently, Ms. Lopez, you need to take an earlier bus."

I stood there with my mouth hanging open like a fool. I had heard that students could be dropped for not attending class during the first week, but I didn't think it would apply if I was only a few minutes late because of the bus. In high school, the teachers didn't care. Once they found out that I was in foster care, they were just happy I showed up at all. It was obvious that Professor Lau wasn't having it. It was also obvious that my time management problems were about to throw my whole school schedule off.

"Please, is there any way I can get back in this class?" I pleaded. "I swear I'll get here on time from now on."

She stared at me for a while, but then she pulled a form out of her briefcase, signed it, and handed it to me. "Fill this out and take it over to Registration. And be advised, I do not give third chances."

The class was so boring that I had to take notes and eat candy just to stay wake, but I'd been early ever since.

After lunch, I study in the library for nearly an hour, and then board the bus to my job at the River Beach Residential Youth Academy. I never understood why people came up with fancy sounding names for things instead of calling them what they are. Residential Youth Academy, RYA or The Res ... it's all just another way of saying "group home". It was nice and well-supervised, and most of the staff was cool, but it was still a group home.

The Res was a single-story building at the end of a cul-de-sac on a street that I'd passed by tons of times, but I never even knew it was there. Based on the pictures hanging in the office, the front of the building hadn't changed much since its days as a convalescent home. It was so quiet and clean that the neighbors usually forgot that it was a place for messed-up kids. During the new employee orientation, the vice president told us that the rec room and more bedrooms had been added in the early 90's, turning the place into "a 36-bed, level 14 facility for girls between the ages of 11 and 17". It was all just a fancy way of saying that it was a place to keep the kids that nobody wanted to deal with. I was all too familiar with these kinda facilities 'cause I'd been sent to places just like it—more than once.

If somebody would've told me that I'd be working at a group home six weeks ago, I would've thought they were crazy. But that was before their director came to THP to talk about their job openings for Youth Partners.

"It's a part-time position, specifically designed for former foster youth who are willing to mentor, supervise, and advocate for kids at our facility," Kathy explained. "You need to be goal-oriented, have good communication skills, and be willing to learn about how the system works." I couldn't believe that jobs existed specifically for folks like me. They didn't even require a college degree. I filled out an application and got called in for an interview two days later. I'm not gonna lie, I was brutally honest when I sat in front of their interview panel.

"I've been in group homes like this before," I told them. "I think a lot of them are used as a place to warehouse kids when social services is too lazy to find them good homes." I also told them about my experiences with group home staff members who were clueless, negligent and even dangerous.

"That's one of the reasons we're hiring former foster youth," one of them said. "You've seen bad facilities and you can help us maintain high standards. You can also relate to a lot of these kids because you've had similar experiences."

I liked what they were tryna do at the Res, and even though I was skeptical about working at a group home, I was secretly hoping that I'd get the job. Luckily, I didn't have to wait too long. I was offered a position three days later. The timing of the whole thing was perfect because I was sick of flipping burgers.

I pull open the door of the main entrance and walk down the deserted hall to the staff offices. It's quiet so I know that the kids are still in the rec room having their free time. When I get to my desk, I notice one of the counselors typing away on her computer with a frown on her face.

"Hey Zoila." I pull my lanyard badge out of my backpack, hang it around my neck and stuff my personal items into a locker.

"Guess who got into another fight today," she sighs. "And now I get to write another report." She turns to me with a worried look on her face. "Her county social worker told me that if she gets into one more fight, they're sending her to juvie. Can you talk to her?"

"Where is she?"

"She's waiting for you in the rec room."

I sign-out a two-way radio and clip it to my waist. As I walk down the corridor towards the rec room, I make sure that I speak to everybody along the way. I'm not gonna lie, sometimes it's hard working here because there's a lot of drama with girls (and sometimes with the staff, too), but it feels good knowing I can help. Like what I'm doing is important, and maybe all of the crap that I went through can actually benefit somebody.

When I get to the end of the hall, I push open one of the heavy double doors and scan the rec room for Max. About twenty girls are scattered around the place doing different activities, but I don't see her anywhere. One of the younger girls in the back looks up from the bracelet she's making and waves at me with a crooked smile. When I wave back, she points to the corner behind her and slowly shakes her head. That's when I see the figure sitting on the floor. I can't help but smile. Even the eleven-year-olds are tired of that girl acting up.

Her knees are drawn up to her chest and her head is down as if she's trying to hide from the world. I can hear the angry sounds of screamo music blasting from her earbuds two tables away. She looks up like she's pissed, but once she sees me, her

14

anger fades. Her face is bruised; there's also a scratch on her neck, and her lip is busted.

"I don't condone fighting … but dang! Did you even get a chance to hit her back?" I joke.

"Don't make me laugh," she winces. "It hurts when I smile."

"You wanna go for a walk?" I reach out my hand and she lets me pull her to her feet.

Max reminds me so much of Bribee—or at least what I imagine she looks like now. We weren't always the happiest kids because of all the stuff we went through, so I could see Bribee being emo just like Max. Who knows, maybe she dyed her hair black and has piercings, too. Of course, the fact that they're both Scorpios who'll be turning fifteen this year is another huge factor.

We stroll around the property for quite a while before I finally decide to say something. "So, I hear your next trip is to juvie. Are you *trying* to go?"

"I don't know. I'm just sick of being here," she sighs. "The staff is always on me, and I'm tired of these chicks talking trash all the time. I can't wait 'til I'm eighteen so I don't have to deal with this crap anymore."

I stare at her because she has no clue. "That drama doesn't stop when you turn eighteen. People will always be on you, and folks will always talk trash. You know that, right?" She doesn't say anything. "What's really going on?" I finally ask.

She walks over and sits at one of the nearby picnic tables. I follow her, but I don't press. There's nothing worse than having somebody hounding you to talk when you're tryna get your thoughts together. We just sit and watch some of the girls shoot hoops at the other end of the property. When Max finally does say something, I can tell she's close to breaking down.

"You know that new girl who got here on Friday?" she asks.

"The wannabe chola with the bright red hair and crazy eyebrows … looks like she's surprised all the time?"

She nods and laughs even though she has tears in her eyes. "She used to live up the street from us. She's been telling everybody about my mom. They keep messing with me, so we keep fighting."

My heart sinks. Every kid at the Res has a file. Sometimes it's missing a lot of stuff and sometimes it has everything in it. Either way, reading about stuff on a piece of paper is a whole lot different than having a kid actually tell you about their abuse. And that's exactly what Max did shortly after I started working here. I liked the fact that she trusted me enough to open up, but I'm not gonna lie, it was hard to hear because we had a lot in common.

"Did I ever tell you how beautiful my mom was?" she asks. "I saw pictures of her from back in the day. She seriously could've been a model."

I feel a lump growing in my throat.

I sit on the edge of the tub watching as she leans close to the mirror and puts makeup on her already-beautiful face. Her skin is perfect, but she uses a brush to put powder on her cheeks, chin, and forehead. I hold my breath when she applies the black liner because I'm scared that it'll slip and poke her in the eye. Her dark-brown hair hangs to the middle of her back in slight waves.

A love song plays in the background and she sings a few lines as she puts on her eye shadow. I pull my stepstool next to her and climb up so that I can look in the mirror, too. I wonder if my face will ever be pretty like hers. When I pretend to put on eye shadow, her reflection smiles at me.

"You want some lipstick?" she asks.

I nod, but I remember the last time she let me wear lipstick, it caused a fight. Daddy had stopped by to visit, but when he saw me, he got really mad.

"She's only three!" he yelled, "You keep that shit offa her face!"

Then Mom screamed at him and they went back and forth until she threw his VCR out the window. They screamed at each other some more, but then he stopped. She apologized and they started kissing. After they came out of the room, she promised not to put makeup on me until I was older.

"Daddy's gonna be mad," I tell her.

"Well, your Daddy's not here!" she snaps. But then she smiles. "And, who says he's gonna be mad?"

She pulls out a tube that I already know is called Deep Mahogany and applies a lot of it to her lips. When she's done, she presses her lips to my cheek. After she pulls away, she grabs my chin and moves it around to inspect her work.

"See ..." She turns me toward the mirror and I smile when I see the perfect imprint of her lips on my face. "You get to wear lipstick, and your daddy gets to keep his damn mouth shut."

⋙⋘

"Everybody loved my mom," Max says with a sad smile. "She was always happy and guys were always trying to take care of her. We didn't have to worry about anything."

⋙⋘

There's a knock at the door. When she opens it, I see a man in nice clothes. He's holding flowers. I don't know who he is, but I know I don't like him.

"Beautiful flowers for a very beautiful woman," he tells my mom.

"Aww, thank you." She kisses him on the lips and it makes me mad, because she's only supposed to be kissing Daddy.

"I have something for you, too, Babygirl," he tells me. I don't like him calling me that.

He pulls five dollars out of his pocket and hands it to me.

"Jason, you don't have to do that," Mom says.

"Hey, you know I like taking care of pretty girls." He pulls her close and they kiss with their tongues. I'm not a baby anymore, but I wanna cry.

"Babygirl, what do you say?" she asks in a way that I know is a warning. If I don't take it, I know I'll get my butt whipped.

I take the money from him. "Thank you," I say quietly.

17

"I don't know what happened." Max shakes her head. "All I know is everything changed. It's like, she just gave up one day."

❧❧

My heart is pounding. I put my stepstool in front of the kitchen sink next to Mom and climb onto the top step.

"I can help rinse," I tell her as she slowly scrubs a plate. She doesn't look at me, but she hands me the plate and starts to wash another one. Bribee's in our bedroom crying again. She has been for a while, but I don't think Mom hears her anymore.

"You want me to go check on her, Mom? I know how to make her bottle," I tell her, but I don't think she hears me anymore either. She's been really tired ever since Bribee was born.

"Can you shut that kid up!" Jason yells from the couch. "I can't hear the goddamn game!" He finishes his beer and pulls another can from the cooler near his feet.

"I'm trying to do the goddam dishes," Mom yells back. "Why don't you get your ass off the couch and pick her up once in a while? She is your daughter!"

"Yeah, whatever," he says under his breath.

Mom throws a soapy bottle into the sink in front of me and walks over to him. "What the hell's that supposed to mean?"

There's a prickly feeling on the back of my neck. I want to be invisible, but somebody needs to feed Bribee. If I'm quiet, they usually don't see me, so I climb off my stepstool and carry it over to the pantry. I pull out a can of formula and take it over to the sink.

"How do I know that kid's mine?" Jason yells, "I know Tavio still comes over here!"

"He's Angelique's father! You expect me to stop talking to him just because your dumb-ass is jealous?"

I add a scoop of formula to the bottle in the sink and fill it with tap water. There's a sour smell coming from the nipple, so I wash it and screw it on as tight as I can. The formula clumps up inside, but that's okay. I just cover the top of the nipple with my hand and shake it like Mom does.

On my way into the bedroom, I see Mom stand in front of the TV, and I know bad things are about to happen.

The smell of Bribee's dirty diaper hits me as soon as I open the door, but I know that feeding her is more important than changing her diaper. I drop her bottle into the crib near her feet and climb up the side rail so I can pull myself inside. "Shh, shh … It's ok, Bribee," I whisper as I pull her into my lap. I try to support her head like Mom showed me, but it's kind of hard to do. "Poor baby, you hungry?" I ask as I try to feed her. She moves her head around so much that it takes me a couple of tries to get the bottle into her mouth. When she finally quiets down, I sing a song so we don't have to listen to Mom and Jason scream at each other.

When she's done eating, I slide her off my lap. She starts crying again but she's okay as soon as I give her her pacifier. "I'll be right back." I climb out of the crib to look for diapers; but then I remember—there's a new pack on the table, in the kitchen. I don't wanna go back in there, but I know that babies aren't supposed to stay in dirty diapers for too long.

"All you ever do is drink beer and sit on your ass watching TV all day. You're a grown-ass man, but you don't do shit around here!"

"Do you ever just shut the hell up? You bitch and complain about me not being here, but then you bitch and complain the whole time I am! Can I just get some goddamn peace and quiet?"

I don't make a sound. Once I'm in the kitchen, I open the pack of diapers and pull one out as quiet as I can.

"Angelique!" I jump when he yells at me. "What the hell are you doing?"

"Bribee needs her diaper changed," I tell him, trying my best not to cry.

"You wanna talk about me?" He laughs. "A four-year-old is doing your job because your psycho-ass pops pills all day. You're pathetic."

"Oh, I'm pathetic?" she yells. She stomps into our bedroom and marches back out with Bribee in her arms. I hold my breath waiting to see what she's gonna do. I wanna run over and take my sister away from her because she's being too rough, but I can't move.

"This is your child!" Mom yells and Bribee screams. "But your sorry-ass can't even keep a job, so Tavio is taking care of his daughter—and yours! You wanna call me pathetic? Who do you think is payin' for the rent and the groceries? It sure as hell ain't you!"

19

He stares out into space like he doesn't care. But I know that he's getting really mad, because I've seen him look like that before. She should stop, but she doesn't.

"Yeah, that's right," she laughs. "You got another man payin' for the roof over your head and the food you eat."

Jason jumps up from the couch and hits Mom in the face so hard that she falls back and almost drops Bribee.

⤙⤚

"When she started getting high all the time, things really got crazy. Guys were always coming in and out of the house ..."

⤙⤚

It's late and Bribee's finally asleep. I look around at all the stuff on the floor of our bedroom and try to ignore the empty feeling in my stomach. I need to tell Mom that there's no food in the house, but when I knocked on her bedroom door this morning, some guy told us that he would beat us bloody if we bothered them again. We try to stay away from Mom's friends because a lot of them are scary, but she hasn't come out of her room since yesterday morning—that's when we ate last. I can usually handle it, but Bribee's only two and she still cries a lot. Sometimes being hungry makes it hard for me to sleep, but right now, it just makes me brave.

I don't make a sound when I walk down the hallway. Once I'm in front of her door, I can hear them arguing, and I have to stop myself from running back to our room where I know it's safe. I wanna see what's going on but I don't want them to see me, so I turn the doorknob super-slow. When I can't turn it anymore, I push the door open to a tiny crack and peek inside. Mom's leaning back against her headboard in a tank-top and panties. The man is in his underwear, but I can only see his back so I don't know what he's doing. I can tell that he's really busy with whatever it is.

"Where do you want it?" he asks. Mom looks over both of her arms just like Bribee does when she's trying to show me her ouchies, but then she pushes her foot towards him. The man puts something that looks like a pencil box on the table next to the bed, and that's when I see the needle. My heart beats really fast. I can't see everything that's happening, but I

20

know it's bad. A little while later, Mom looks sleepy, but she's smiling. It's the first time that I've seen her smile in a long time.

❧❧

"After a while, she didn't care how she got money. She was so messed up ... she told me that guys wouldn't look at her anymore—but they liked *me*." Max wipes away her tears. "Back home, everybody used to look at me crazy because they all knew. Now everybody here knows. What kind of mother pimps out her own daughter?"

3

AFTER WORK, I make my way to the bus stop with a heavy heart and knots in my stomach. I hated leaving Max there to be picked on, but the best thing I could do was let her talk and offer her some words of encouragement. I even told her a little bit about Dani's story. I'm not gonna lie, my mom was crazy and got high a lot, but even she had her limits. If she would've even thought about putting me on the streets, no joke, my dad would've probably killed her.

When we finished talking, I filled out a report and told the night staff to keep an eye on her, but I wanted to do a lot more. I could see myself going back and busting through the door of the rec room. *Pack your bags*, I'd tell her, *you're coming to live with me.* I'd help her get her stuff, and the two of us would walk right past that red-headed bitch and out the door, leaving everybody with their mouths hanging open. But then reality set in.

What am I gonna do, get bunk beds for my studio apartment? Not to mention the fact that this THP doesn't even allow overnight guests.

After I take a seat in the back of the bus, I think about Bribee and my heart feels even heavier. I haven't seen my sister in six years. I don't know if she's safe. I don't know if her adopted family is treating her right. I don't even know where she lives, but that's gonna change in three and a half years. Once she turns eighteen, nobody can stop us from seeing each other, and she won't ever have to worry about a place to stay. *I'm gettin' my shit together so she can stay with me.*

When I look up, I realize the bus is driving past the complex.

"Dammit!" I yell, getting stares from everybody around me.

I hit the buzzer to get off at the next stop and check my phone for the time. I'ma probably be late for group. *Oh well, it's not like I did it on purpose.* Some residents are always showing up late for meetings and events because they don't take this program seriously. That's not me.

When I finally get to the complex, I punch in my security code and walk inside the gate to find Vanessa talking with Liz. They stop talking and watch me as I walk by.

Why are people always talking trash? I don't even wait for them to say anything.

"I just got off of work!" I snap. "Instead of lookin' at me crazy, why don't you do something about the residents who sit on their asses all day?"

Liz frowns and shakes her head, but of course, it's Vanessa who opens her mouth. "You need to watch your language before you get written up."

I ignore her and walk across the courtyard to the common room. That's when I see that people are still hanging out. Group hasn't even started yet. I think about checking my email before we start, but all eight computers in the back of the room are being used. Normally they're off limits from 6:45 to 9:15 on Tuesday and Thursday nights. It's basically so people won't disturb—or avoid—group, but it looks like the late start time is too much of a temptation for some folks.

The common room was always supposed to be the social center for residents, but everybody avoided it until Melinda came. When I first moved in, there were a couple of computers and a printer in here, but they were slow as hell; and it felt like the folding table and chairs would break if you typed too hard. They also had some inspirational posters and books about stuff like chicken soup and moving somebody's cheese. Nothing about this place made sense, especially the way it was

23

decorated. There was wood paneling on all the walls, so the whole place looked like a basement—which wouldn't have been so bad if the lights were decent. Unfortunately, the staff never bothered to replace the burned-out bulbs, and the ones that did work were always flickering. The checkered tile seemed new, but it didn't even cover the entire floor. If you walked past the boxes stacked near the back of the room, you could see the mustard-colored tile underneath.

After Melinda got here, she told us that the place was getting an extreme makeover. "Give me some ideas on what you'd like to see in here," she said during that first meeting. Everybody was quiet at first, but once she said it was going to be a place for us to have program activities and hang out, the ideas started flowing real quick. It started out with simple things like getting rid of the musty smell and all the boxes. And I know it sounds bougie, but nobody wanted to hang out in an ugly spot, so we had a lot of ideas on how to make it look nicer. After that, somebody suggested better computers with faster internet, and then they started getting kinda crazy. All of a sudden, they were asking for things like big-screen TVs, surround sound, gaming systems, and recliners. Omar even asked for a treadmill, as if his conceited-ass couldn't just run around the block a few times.

When they closed the common room down, we didn't know what to expect. "I'm not going to make any promises," Melinda told us, "but I can tell you that it will look and function much better." We watched workers come and go for about a month before they announced the grand re-opening, which ended up being a really big deal. The CEO of Perdido came out with administrators from the County and a bunch of business people who had donated stuff. They even had reporters and a film crew here.

I'll never forget the first time I saw this place after it was re-done. Three of the walls were the color of beach sand, and they had a bunch of framed inspirational quotes from people like Gandhi, Michael Jordan, and even Dr. Seuss. They also had bulletin boards with announcements and important phone numbers, but it was the other wall that stole the show.

Apparently, a former resident was a really talented painter, so they hired him to do the artwork. The edges of his mural were the same color as the other walls, but he had painted cracks around the entire thing. It looked like the regular wall had been chipped away to show a brick wall hidden behind it. That in and of itself was pretty cool, but the amazing thing was the realistic group of young people that he had painted. They were busting through the bricks with sledgehammers and crowbars. Some were even on ladders using their bare hands. It looked like they were all on a mission to get to an island paradise that had been painted in the background. Looking at it made me feel like I could climb through and walk to that island myself.

When I finally pulled my eyes away from the mural, I saw all the other cool things. We had new computers and a laser printer—on real tables, with real chairs. If we didn't feel like staying in our apartments, we could do homework, eat, or just hang out at tables near the computers. We could also lounge on one of three couches on the far side of the room. That was the most popular spot, not because it's where we'd be having group, but because that's where they had hung the 60-inch flat screen TV. We were so excited about it that nobody cared about the recliners, treadmills, or gaming systems that we didn't get.

I see the couches are already occupied by people and placeholders, so I drop my backpack into an empty folding chair and make my way over to the food. Thank goodness Melinda doesn't believe in a "cookies and punch" kind of meeting. She always says that real discussions happen around real food, so our meetings are always like feasts. I can't help but smile when I see the three-foot long burritos. Like always, one is chicken and one is vegetarian. There's also a giant bowl of tortilla chips and two types of salsa. I can handle the mild one, but the spicy one makes my eyes water and my nose run like crazy. A second table has the fruit and vegetable platters, a tray of cookies, and a few rows of bottled water.

"Wus up, Angelique?" I hear as I slide a slice of chicken burrito onto my plate. I look over to see Omar staring at me with a sly grin on his face. He grabs a plate and follows me a little too close. Omar is fine with his caramel skin and sexy eyes, and lifting boxes all day definitely didn't hurt his muscle situation. The problem is he knows he's fine, and he takes a lot of pride in hooking up with as many chicks as he can. I don't have time for that kinda drama; plus, this program has a really strict no-fraternization policy, so most of us just ignore his flirting. Hell, a hook-up is not worth getting kicked out and being homeless—but that don't stop him from trying.

"Omar, I don't even feel like dealin' with you right now." I make my way down the line and add some strawberries to my plate.

"Hey, I'm just tryna be social," he says, "but you know it's hard when I got a weakness for thick girls."

"I thought you had a weakness for skinny girls," a voice behind us says. We both turn to find Dani staring at him with her bony arms crossed. Her auburn hair is hanging over one of her shoulders in a cute Katniss braid, and her eyebrows are raised, waiting for him to respond.

I can't help but laugh and shake my head. "Busted once again."

"Hey, you can't blame me for tryin'," Omar says with a guilty smile. He strokes his goatee and walks away to stalk somebody else.

I step off to the side and wait for Dani to get some food on her plate.

"Do you know why group is running late?" I ask when she finally joins me.

"You don't remember? Last week, we voted to have some of the applicants sit in. We're starting a little later because the case managers had to go pick them up."

That entire discussion had completely slipped my mind. *Dang, I gotta get some sleep.*

"Are you okay?" I know she's worried, but I honestly can't answer. Luckily, Melinda and Vanessa walk in with the visitors so I don't have to.

I can read all three of them without even trying. The girl is pretty, but her makeup is not doing her justice. Her foundation is way too light for her dark skin, and she's wearing too much of everything. She seems over-the-top from her weave to her heels. *Somebody's on a mission to find a man.* One of the guys has a wild, curly afro and a skin tone similar to mine. *He's probably mixed, too.* He's scruffy, his clothes are wrinkled, and he's wearing some Chucks that've seen better days. There's a grin plastered to his face and he's looking around like a kid at an amusement park. *He's definitely spent some time on the streets.* The other guy is wearing Dickies with sharp creases, and Cortezes so white they practically glow. He has on long sleeves—in the summer—and I can see a flesh-colored bandage on the side of his neck. *He's hiding gang tatts.*

Vanessa points in my direction and says something to the three of them. I feel myself tense up as they walk over. *What now?* I hold my breath and wait for the drama to start, but it never comes. I can't even explain how stupid I feel when they grab plates and stand in line behind me. Scruffy-dude has some serious B.O., but other than that, they're not harming anybody. *Why do I always think the worst?*

"Let's go get our seats," Dani frowns. We make our way over to our chairs and chat until Melinda gets started.

"Good evening, everyone!" she yells above the noise. Everybody quiets down and she starts to talk in her regular voice.

"Before we get started, I want to go over a couple of things. First, I want to remind all of you that we do not have maid service, so please clean up after yourselves. And second, enjoy the food, but please be considerate so that everyone can have something to eat," she turns to Scruffy-dude and smiles.

"My bad," he grins with his mouth full. He has two plates, one on top of the other. The lower one is lined with cookies, two layers high, and the top one has at least four slices of burrito on it. A few residents laugh, probably remembering how greedy they were when they first got here.

"As we discussed last week, we have some visitors joining us," she nods toward the greedy dude. "You've already met Orlando."

"What-up?" he says, with food still in his mouth.

"This is Ashley ..." Melinda gestures toward the girl. She gives a fake smile and a Miss America wave. "... and this is Ernesto."

"Sup," he says with a slight head nod, but he keeps a hard look on his face.

"They've all passed their first interview ..." We all clap and the three of them look around like they've never heard applause before. "... but we decided to do something different and invite them to group before the final decision is made." Turning to the three of them, she says, "Every transitional housing program operates a little differently, and we wanted to give you an idea of how things work here. Some of you may decide this program isn't for you." *Was she talking to Ernesto when she said that?* "So here's my question for the group." She looks around the room and asks, "What do you think they need to know to be successful here?"

It's quiet for a little while, but then Monet speaks up. "Well ... the staff is cool, but I think we learn more from each other." She always looks so tiny in those baggy boys' clothes. "I would say, just don't be scared to talk to people, 'cause we've all been through it." A lot of us nod. Monet's cool as long as she's on her meds, but when she's not ... aww man. I'm talking about serious breaks with reality. I guess it makes sense if the rumors about her dad are true. Until I met her, I'd never really known any Indians—or I guess I should say, Native Americans. Of course almost every Black person I know claims to have "Indian blood" in their family, but you know they're just talking.

"Okay, what else?" Melinda asks as she scans the group.

"They need to know that hearing complaints all the time just brings everybody down," Dani adds. "We need to talk about the good things that are happening, too."

"Yeah, but it's not about bragging," Amanda says. "It's about encouraging. Like, if you reach a goal and you talk about it, it might help somebody else feel like they can do it, too."

Amanda's a chunky white-girl with mad style and a lot of attitude. Lately, she's been into that whole fifties rockabilly thing and it looks really good on her. She looks completely different from her brother, and roommate, Rodrick. He's slender but crazy muscular because he's into dance. He also has brown skin and curly brown hair that he got from his dad who's Black.

"You need to know that you can and will get kicked out for not following the rules." Vanessa warns. "There's only forty-five spaces in this program and a long list of people trying to get in. If you can't do what it takes to make it here, step aside and let somebody else have a chance." Quite a few people agree, and it pisses me off so much that I can't keep my mouth shut.

"How can you expect people to follow the rules when they're not even enforced like they should be?" I ask. All of a sudden, everybody's talking at once and arguments break out. I know I shouldn't gloat, but I'm glad I'm not the only one who's sick of the fakeness here.

"Okay, okay," Melinda says loud enough to get everybody's attention. "We've definitely fallen short when it comes to enforcing policies in this program, and that's not fair to residents or staff. We'll discuss some changes in more detail tonight." She writes something down on her notepad. "But right now, there's a lot of tension in here. Why don't we change the energy with some praise reports?"

Luis is the first to share. He's a stocky Latino dude with a preppy look and a very mellow personality. He's also the unofficial repairman around here. A while back, I noticed that him and Dani are always sneaking looks at each other when they think nobody's watching. I hope they get together after

29

they leave THP because they're both cool people—and they're both really short.

"Remember that interview I had a couple weeks ago?" he grins. "Well, they finally called me back. I start my new job on Monday." Almost all of us clap to show our support.

"Why would you leave a good-paying job to work at a hardware store?" India asks. She looks all annoyed, as if he's messing up *her* money situation by wanting to change jobs. She *needs* to be annoyed that her boobs are about to fall outta that tank top.

"How do you know what his job pays?" Dani snaps.

India glares at her. "I'm not stupid. He got a car *and* he got his own place—and it's not even a studio. You can't get a one-bedroom unless you makin' some money. Plus, have you seen his apartment? It's laid-out, and I *know* the program didn't pay for it."

"Luis, would you like to talk about why you're changing jobs?" Melinda asks.

He shrugs, but he looks a little embarrassed. "So ... right now, I'm basically doing side jobs and working as a handy man. The money's not bad," he smiles, "but it's not steady. I'm twenty-three, I only have a few months left in the program, but I'm still not as stable as I wanna be. I don't even have insurance. They're supposed to be changing things so we can keep our medical insurance until we turn twenty-six, but that doesn't help me right now. If I get hurt, I'm screwed. I'm just now getting serious about school, so I need a job where I can work at night. And I need benefits—even if that means making less money for a while."

I notice quite a few people nod with a faraway look in their eyes, and I wonder if they're all thinking the same thing. Two years seems like a long time, so it's easy to forget that this program won't last forever. When it's over, there ain't no guarantees of free, or even discounted rent. I mean, I know there's Section 8, but those waiting lists can be crazy. On top of all that, there won't be case managers, and there definitely won't be financial help when things get rough. That's why I'm all about staying on schedule and sticking to my plan. I'ma finish all of my general ed classes in two years and then transfer to a state university that's cheap enough for me to live off of my financial aid. But I'ma work, too, that way I can take care of my sister.

"Thank you, Luis," Melinda says. "Anybody else?"

"I'm about to get my GED," Chris says. He's our Mac Miller look-a-like. "I gotta go to adult school, but now that I got my car, I ain't gotta worry about transportation."

I clap loud to show him extra love 'cause he's like a brother to me. We spent some time in the same foster home before he got kicked out for selling and smoking weed. I always tell him he needs to write a book or something because his story would be a bestseller. Russian-born, adopted, re-homed, and almost beat to death, foster kid ... that alone is a lot. Add being raised in the hood and a love for Black culture, and you got a crazy combination.

My mind starts wandering, and I tune out the other residents as they share. I think about Chris' background and how it had changed everything I used to believe. I always thought being adopted was the happy ending to the nightmare of foster care, but Chris had opened my eyes to the fact that adoptions could fail. I never knew there were people who'd spend thousands of dollars to adopt a kid, just to throw them away when things got rough. From then on, I couldn't stop worrying about my sister.

When I bring my attention back to the group, I hear that India's reconnected with her family, but it's not going like she planned. " ... They comin' out the woodwork now that I'm in this program and got some money comin' in. They tryna make me feel guilty, talkin' about 'we family.' But where was you when I was homeless? ..."

Dang, do we really need to have another discussion on boundaries and unrealistic expectations? She had the same issue with some of her friends. It's not that hard; just say "no" and quit being stupid!

Omar talks about his attempt to get a credit card, but that didn't go so well either. "... I found out my credit is messed up. If they would've just asked for ID or a birth certificate, they would've known that it wasn't me—I was only fourteen at the time! Now, everybody's lookin' at me like *I'm* the criminal."

"Has anyone else experienced identity theft while they were in foster care?" Melinda asks. Hands go up and it looks like the majority of us have been through it.

Why can't we ever have straight good news without a bunch of shit thrown in? I sigh louder than I mean to.

"Would anyone else like to contribute?" Melinda glances at me with a raised eyebrow.

"Well, since we're not really giving praise reports anymore, I got something that needs to be addressed." My tone is harsher than it should be, but right now, I don't care.

"We have residents here who are living in nastiness. Normally, I don't care—but when people are nasty, they get roaches and roaches travel. When I open my Captain Crunch and find roaches ... it pisses me off. That shit's *nasty!*" I hear laughter and sounds of disgust around me.

"Excuse my language, but when other people's nastiness starts messing with my money, I got a problem. I don't get EBT, I gotta buy my own food. So the first thing I wanna know is, why do we have rules about cleanliness if they're not enforced. And second, I wanna know who's gonna reimburse me for my Captain Crunch?"

"This problem has become a safety issue," Melinda says as she looks around. "We'll be doing our part by having an exterminator come out, but spraying alone won't solve it. You all have to live together, so I'm curious, how do you think this should be handled?"

The room is quiet and everybody seems to be looking at each other.

"The rules need to be enforced or dropped. It's as simple as that," Amanda eventually says. "Personally, I think people should get their warnings, but if they don't fall in line, they need to *go*. Hell, kick 'em out!"

There's a lot of agreement, and a lot of people suddenly looking very uncomfortable.

"All I know is, some of us grew up in dirty houses," Monet says in a soft voice. "I keep my crib clean 'cause I don't wanna live like that no more.

Most of us agree.

"Okay, and what about compensation for Angelique?" Melinda asks. Once again, all I hear is dead silence.

"People, this is a no-brainer," Rodrick suddenly says. "If your apartment is dirty and you have roaches, just assume some responsibility and buy the girl some Captain Crunch! We don't need to know who you are…You know you're nasty. Just leave it in a bag by her door."

I can't help but smile. "Thank you, Rodrick!"

"Girl, I gotchu," he says in his over-the-top, drama-queen way. The group's response reminds me that he has a gift for making people laugh, especially in uncomfortable situations. I just hope they're not laughing at him.

Melinda smiles and scans the room. "So what do you all think of Rodrick's idea?"

Almost everybody agrees. Those who don't will keep their mouths shut, because they're probably the ones with the dirty apartments. I'm glad Rodrick said something. It's nice to feel like somebody's finally on my side.

"So, just to be clear," Melinda continues, "if your apartment is dirty on a regular basis and you've ignored the critters that you've seen, you owe Angelique a box of cereal."

"Captain Crunch." I have to clarify, 'cause I'm not tryna end up with some generic knock-off.

"If you have objections," she adds, "you can speak up now, or see me privately; but this needs to be taken care of before we meet next week." She takes more notes and flips back a couple of pages. "It looks like that brings us back to policy enforcement." Suddenly she looks real serious. "Each one of you signed a contract before you moved in. I strongly suggest you review it, because starting tomorrow, all parts of those contracts will be honored. That includes the policy of unannounced apartment inspections."

Almost everybody starts groaning and protesting. Even I'm a little nervous, and I know I have nothing to worry about.

"We'll make sure you're prepared," Melinda says above the complaints. "Each R.A. will be opening up their own apartment to demonstrate cleaning techniques. That means you have three different opportunities to attend this training. If your job or some unforeseen event prevents you from attending, you may schedule a one-on-one with your case manager. But this is a mandatory training."

"Hold up," Ashley glares at Melinda. "You think we have to be taught how to clean? I'm not stupid...I know how to clean up!"

Vanessa jumps in before I have a chance to respond. "Let's be real," she tells Ashley, "I know kids who had never even seen a toothbrush before they went into foster care. And not everybody had foster parents who taught them that type of stuff. You may already know how to do everything, but I guarantee there are people living here who do not know how to clean."

"We're not making any assumptions about you personally," Melinda adds. "The County expects us to have life skills trainings, so that's what we're doing. If you already have knowledge about what we're covering, just think of it as a reminder. Also, you're free to offer suggestions of your own— if it's appropriate." Melinda checks her watch and looks at the clock. "Let's take a fifteen minute break. When we come back, maybe we can have some of the current residents talk about their experience in the program. After that, we'll give our visitors a chance to ask questions."

Everybody scatters the minute she stops talking, but I sit there lost in thought for a while.

"Don't tell me you're worried?" Dani says. "Your place is always spotless."

"Yeah, but having people just show up ... I don't know about that." I can't explain the uneasy feeling in the pit of my stomach. All I know is I don't like surprises. "I'm gonna see if there's any food left. You want anything?"

When she shakes her head, I make my way back to the snack table to see if anything good is left. Nobody ever wants the vegetables, so of course, that platter is almost full. Rabbit food. It's not that bad though, especially if you put enough ranch dressing on it. As I pick over the remnants, I hear Omar tryna hook up with Ashley.

"You know what?" he says in a low voice, "We would make some pretty babies. Let me see your phone." He pulls her cell out of her hand and basically takes a selfie that she just happens to be in. When he starts typing, I already know he's setting things up for a late-night booty call. He tried the same thing with me, and apparently a whole bunch of other females, when we first moved in. Luckily, Dani and Amanda were looking out for me, so I knew about him from the get-go. We usually try to look out for each other here, but every now and then, you get chicks who think you're just a hater. If they wanna look stupid and risk being homeless, that's up to them, but at least we tried.

Omar whispers something to Ashley as he gives her phone back. She giggles like it's the funniest thing in the world, and I realize something—she's about to look real stupid. His phone vibrates and he checks it with that sly grin on his face.

"I need to go take care of something," he says, looking her up and down. "Don't go nowhere." When he steps outside, Ashley stands in line behind me and picks through the vegetable platter.

"Try not to get caught up with the dudes in this program," I tell her. "They have a 'No Fraternization' policy."

"What does that mean?" She frowns.

"It means we can get kicked out if we hook-up with somebody in the program."

"Why do they even care?"

I shrug kinda casually, like I don't know what's up. "Too much drama, jealousy, and fights, I guess. Plus, they don't want nobody havin' babies up in here."

She was quiet for a while, "What happens if somebody gets pregnant?"

Dang, she's already schemin'. "It depends. They usually help out with one kid, but a second baby means they gotta go to a family shelter. This place is all about being independent. I guess they figure that's not gonna happen if folks are havin' babies and gettin' money from the County."

We spend the rest of the break making small talk, mostly about the staff. She even asks about my experience in THP. I'm not gonna lie, I'm surprised she even bothered. She doesn't strike me as a "program" type of girl.

"All right, people, let's finish up," Melinda announces. Everyone returns to their seats and quiets down. "Do we have any residents who'd like to talk about their experience in the program?" She scans the group and Dani raises her hand when no one else volunteers. "Can you tell our guests your name, age, and how long you've been in the program?" Melinda asks.

"My name is Dani. I'm twenty-one and I've been in the program for a year and a half," she sighs. "I love it here ... I mean ... I know it has its problems, but it's nothing compared to what I dealt with when I first left foster care." Most of us nod in agreement. "My case manager's pretty cool. She helped me with all the paperwork I needed for college, and even showed me how to find a job on campus doing something I love. I'm not gonna lie though— it's hard. When I first moved in, my mind wasn't right, and it took me a while to really get involved; but once I did, things took off. School led to a job, and a job led to me getting my own place ..."

"Your own place?" Ashley interrupts. She turns to Melinda with attitude—once again. "That's the second time somebody talked about havin' their own place. I thought you said everybody had to have a roommate?"

What the hell is her problem? "New residents do need a roommate," I say with just as much attitude as she's giving. "Especially if they don't have a *job*." I stress the job thing because she already told me she's not working right now.

I almost laugh when she rolls her eyes.

"The County pays for residents to live rent-free if you share an apartment," Melinda explains. "But if you're employed, and there's an opening, you can get a studio or a one-bedroom and pay the difference. That can range from about $80 to $250 a month."

"And I love my little studio apartment," Dani says. "This is the first time in my life that I actually have my own space. But honestly, I wish I would've kept a roommate and saved all that extra money. I only have six months left, and I'm starting to freak out because I haven't been sticking to a budget like I should. I definitely can't keep dropping five bucks a day on vanilla lattes."

"Five dollars a day for some coffee?" Rodrick asks. "Hold up." He tilts his head to the side with a frown on his face. When his lips start moving, I realize he's doing calculations in his head. All of a sudden his jaw drops. "That's over $1800 a year!" he tells Dani. "Girl, do you know what I could do with that much cash?!"

After that, everybody starts talking at once and looking at her crazy.

"I know ... I know." Dani shakes her head, and you can tell she's embarrassed. It seems like everybody's got an opinion about how they would spend $1800 in a responsible way, but I know the real deal. They are not about to make her feel stupid.

"Now y'all know she is not the only one droppin' bills like that," I say above the noise. "How many folks up in here keep spendin' money on Mickey-D's, when you can get groceries for free?" All of a sudden, it gets quiet. "Or how many people still shoppin' for clothes you don't need—every month—like you still in foster care? Better yet, how many of y'all hit the club every Friday and Saturday night?" I glance over and give Rodrick the side-eye.

"I'm V.I.P.," he mumbles and crosses his arms. "I get in for free."

"It sounds like quite a few of you struggle when it comes to making wise choices with your finances," Melinda adds. "I can tell you, this isn't something that only former foster youth struggle with. This is a national problem, but there are ways to help." She flips back a few pages in her notebook and asks, "Did anyone attend the money management workshop back in January?" Only a few people raise their hands. "Was it helpful?" The response was overwhelmingly "no". "Okay, it looks like we need to make some changes and have another workshop," she says, taking notes. "Dani, is there anything else you'd like to add?"

"Things are going good … but I still get stressed-out a lot," she admits. "Sometimes I feel like I have too much on my plate, and I don't even wanna get out of bed. Then I start thinking about my family and everything that's happened in my life. My little brothers are counting on me. They know they can't depend on my mom. She'd rather get high than take care of her kids. It's just a lot to deal with sometimes."

As she talks, I can't help thinking about my own family. I always hear people talking about bitter-sweet memories and I wish I had those. Unfortunately, my mind gets flooded with so much bitter stuff, it seems like the sweet stuff just gets contaminated.

4

Our room didn't always look junky like this. We used to have beds and a dresser where we kept all of our clothes and stuff. We even had a TV and a whole bunch of videos that we could watch anytime we wanted to. But that was before. It's not a big deal though. Even when we did have beds, Bribee always slept with me because she got scared a lot. That's how it is with little kids. And when you're a big sister, you gotta take care of them.

Everything was a lot easier before summer vacation, because we could eat at school. All I had to do was make sure Bribee was dressed, walk her to Head Start, and then get to my second grade class before the bell rang. But now that school's out, things are different. Mom stays in her room a lot, and sometimes there's no food in the house. We're not supposed to go outside because we have nosey-ass neighbors, but we can't just be hungry all day. So I just lay here looking at our junky room for as long as I can. I feel a tap on my back and I know that Bribee's awake.

"Geli, I hongry," she yawns.

When I turn over she's sucking her thumb. Her face is dirty. Neither one of us have had a bath for a while, but I guess it doesn't matter because we don't have nowhere to go anyway. We stare at each other until I reach over and pull her thumb out of her mouth. It's like a game. I pull her thumb out of her mouth and she puts it right back in. We go back and forth until she pats me on my cheek.

"Okay, stay here until I get back," I tell her.

She nods and sits up on the mattress. Our room is like a secret hideaway where nothing bad happens, but we never know what we're gonna find once we open the door. Some of Mom's boyfriends are really mean, and sometimes there's weird people hanging out in the living room.

It's quiet in the hallway, so I tiptoe to the kitchen to see if there's anything to eat. I couldn't find anything yesterday, but sometimes Mom gets stuff at night while we're sleeping. I open the refrigerator, but the only thing inside is the same old nasty-smelling stuff, and milk that went poor a long time ago. I check the microwave, but there's nothing in there either.

When I open the door to the oven, I get so happy that my heart feels like it's gonna bust open. Pizza! I put the box on the counter and use it to push back a bunch of dirty dishes that are in the way. I already know I'll find pepperoni inside because it's me and Bribee's favorite, plus, the smell is already making my mouth water. There's a giant-size grin on my face when I open that lid—but it doesn't last. Two giant roaches crawl across the pizza and run for cover into the dishes on the counter. "Shit!" I jump back. Our pizza feast is poisoned now, and there's nothing I can do about it. I don't have a choice, now I have to wake Mom up.

I walk down the hall to her room with my heart beating so loud that I can hear it in my ears. When I get to her door, I stand still for a while and listen for voices—or the sound of the bed squeaking. I don't hear anything so I open the door a crack and peek in like I always do. She's asleep with one of her boyfriends, so I go inside as quiet as I can. There's a disgusting smell, like cigarettes and musty body, and something else that makes my stomach feel sick.

A while back, Mom had left an orange colored drink on the table. It smelled bad, but I know she liked it a lot, so I snuck a sip. It was disgusting—like rotten cough syrup, and it burned worse than the time I had strep throat. After I swallowed it, I couldn't stop coughing.

"Geli, what the hell are you doing?!" She caught me red-handed and I knew I was about to get my butt whipped. I tried to say something, but when I opened my mouth a sour taste took over; and all of a sudden, I was throwing up on the carpet. Mom's eyes got really big for a minute, but then she started to smile. When I threw up the second time, she started laughing. All I could do was cry.

"Awww, come here," she stepped over the mess I made on the floor and hugged me. "Babygirl, you can't mess around with that stuff, that's a *grown-up drink." She held me tight for a while and it felt so good. "Maybe we should both leave it alone, huh?" I looked up at her and nodded because my throat hurt too much to talk.*

When I get to her side of the bed, I see the empty bottle on the floor, but this time it's not orange, it's the color of blue raspberry punch. Mom's hair is covering most of her face, but I can smell the disgusting drink on her breath and it makes me really mad. I shake her.

"Mom ... Mom." When she doesn't move, I shake her harder. "Mom, we're hungry. Mom!"

"Lemme alone," she mumbles and turns over without even looking at me. I stand there for a while because I don't know what to do. I can't take care of Bribee by myself. There's one place I know we can go, but I know I'll get in trouble. I don't even care though.

"Come on," I tell Bribee when I get back to our room. I pull her into the bathroom and we take turns using the toilet that doesn't flush anymore. When we're done, I put the lid down so Bribee can climb up on the counter. There's toothpaste in the back of one of the drawers, but the top is gone so it has hair and junk stuck to it. I know the stuff inside is still good, so I just squeeze out a glob and wipe off all the nasty stuff with a big towel.

"Here." Bribee gives me her finger and I squeeze some toothpaste on it. "Don't forget the ones in the back," I tell her while I squeeze some out for myself. We rub it on our teeth and then take turns spitting in the sink. When I'm done, I make a cup with my hands so I can rinse my mouth out, but Bribee can't do that without wasting water all over the place. She has to lean over and drink it right out of the faucet.

There's a little bit of soap in the corner of the tub, but it's melted so I can't pick it up. It's okay though; I just wet the side of the towel that doesn't have toothpaste on it. After that, all I have to do is rub the towel on the soap. That's how I make the washcloth to clean our faces.

"Don't get it in my eyes," Bribee reminds me.

"I won't if you be still."

After that, I put water in our hair and try to brush it like Mom does. I'm not that good at it, plus we both have too many tangles to make it look nice. It's okay though, I just put on a headband and use clicker-clacker balls to make a ponytail for Bribee.

"Let's go get dressed," I tell her.

When we get back to our room, we dig through the stuff on the floor. Bribee finds her Little Mermaid t-shirt and some shorts that I used to wear when I was her age. They're both a little dirty, but they're not that bad. I can't find anything clean, so I put on one of my school uniforms and some sandals.

"Where's your other shoe?" I ask when I see Bribee playing.

"I no no," she shrugs.

"You're gonna have to wear my flip-flops then."

I pull my shoes out of the closet and dropped them on the floor in front of her. They're too big but I know she needs something on her feet. Mom says that only trashy kids walk around outside with no shoes on. Plus, it's dangerous because tiny worms can crawl into your feet and live in your stomach.

"Come on," I whisper when we're dressed. I open our bedroom door a crack and peek out to make sure the coast is clear. Mom and her boyfriend are still in the room, so I grab Bribee's hand and pull her out of the apartment.

"Are we gonna get in trouble?" she asks.

"No." Sometimes I lie to her because I don't want her to get scared.

There's not a lot of people out, but pretty soon, all the kids in our building will be out playing with their bikes and stuff. Then the grown-ups will bring out their chairs so they can smoke and drink and talk shit—at least that's what Mom always says they do.

Bribee trips in my flip-flops a few times, but I hold her hand to make sure she doesn't fall down. If she skins her knee, she'll probably cry the whole way there and we have a long way to go. Every now and then, we get a couple of looks from some grownups, but nobody says anything so we just keep walking. After we cross the busy street by our school, we cross some smaller streets, and then the busy street where the train runs.

I see the house as soon as we turn the corner. It's a pretty color yellow and it has a nice porch, but the bars on the windows make it look kind of like a jail. When we get closer, I see Heina in the driveway, and I get so excited that I pull Bribee a little faster. Heina is the coolest car ever. She's just like a regular car in the front, but her back part looks like a truck. There's fire painted on her sides by the doors, and she has really cool wheels that spin around, even when she's not moving! She's been in parades, in car shows, in magazines, and even on TV!

The doorbell hasn't worked for as long as I can remember, so I just knock and we wait. I never know what's gonna happen when we get here. One time we walked all the way over here, but Emiliana didn't answer the door. We waited on the porch until Heina pulled up, and when we got inside, Emiliana yelled at us because she said we didn't knock loud enough. But then another time, she yelled at us for knocking too loud and giving her a migraine. I think she just likes to yell. The curtain moves after a little while and I hear Emiliana curse. When she doesn't open the door, I knock louder.

"Who is it!" she yells, even though she already knows it's us.

"Geli and Bribee."

She opens the door with a mean look on her face and then folds her arms over her big belly. Her robe is open but she has on shorts and a t-shirt that says 'Baby' with an arrow pointing down. It takes her a little while, but she finally steps to the side so we can come in.

"Tavio! Your daughter is here," she yells. She has a really bad attitude, but when Daddy comes out of the bedroom, there's a big smile on his face—just like always.

"Babygirl!" He lifts me up high above his head and spins me around until I laugh so hard. Bribee stands off to the side giggling because she knows her turn is next. When he finally puts me down, my head is spinning. "Bribee, you're getting too big!" he says when he picks her up and spins her, too. She squeals and laughs so hard that it makes me laugh even more. After he puts her down, she starts walking around like one of Mom's drunk friends. All of a sudden, Daddy's smile goes away. He goes over and he looks out the window. "Did you guys walk over here?" I can't look at him, so I look at the floor. "You better not lie to me," he warns, so I nod my head. "You know I don't like it when you do that."

"I know, Daddy, but we're hungry," I tell him.

"I hungry," Bribee says.

He looks at us almost like he's sad, but then all of a sudden, he rubs his chin and raises his eyebrows in a way that makes us laugh. "You're hungry, huh? Hmmm ... let's see what we can do about that." He gets a towel from the kitchen and hangs it on his arm. "Welcome to Casa de Lopez. I'll be your waiter this evening."

Me and Bribee run over and sit at the table, laughing like crazy while he's in the kitchen getting our food. Sometimes Daddy is so silly, he cracks us up, and we always have so much fun when we're with him. Emiliana's mean, but I know that if we lived here with him, everything would be okay. He would take care of us. He would make sure that nobody was mean to us, and we wouldn't have to stay in our room all the time.

"Here is your appetizer." He comes back to the table with a peeled banana that he breaks in half. Bribee stuffs her mouth with her piece because she knows what's coming next, but I take my time and eat mine slower, because we haven't had bananas in a long time.

When he comes back to the table again, we can tell that he has something behind his back. "And now for the main course …" His eyes get really big and he has a look on his face like he's surprised, but we already know what he's hiding. When he shows us the big box of Captain Crunch, Bribee gets so excited that she claps and giggles like crazy. We always laugh a lot when we spend time with him.

Emiliana's been giving Daddy a mean look the whole time we've been here, and I know she's gonna say something. He's ignoring her right now because he's making our cereal, but I already know that's not gonna last. They're always screaming and yelling at each other, especially about me and Mom.

"Geli, where's your mother?" Daddy asks after we start eating.

"Sleep," I say with my mouth full.

"Yeah, right, you know that bitch is high," Emiliana tells him. "I don't even know why you keep playin'."

I wish I could hide, but I just keep quiet and focus on my cereal while they argue back and forth. When she comes over and gets in Daddy's face, I get kinda scared though.

"That bitch been crazy from day one and your dumb-ass made a baby with her."

"Shut-up! Jealous ass—and you don't need to be worried about none of my kids except this one." He rubs her belly and smiles, but she slaps his hand away.

"Jeluz ass!" Bribee yells all of a sudden. Daddy and Emiliana stop and stare at her. Bribee's usually really quiet and scared of a lot of stuff, so when I see her pointing at Emiliana and looking mad, I'm surprised. Daddy starts cracking up, and pretty soon, Bribee's frown turns into a smile and she starts to laugh, too. "Jeluz ass!" She says it again, but this time she and Daddy are both laughing like crazy.

"Bribee, you don't say that!" I tell her. If Emiliana gets mad, my whole plan is gonna be messed up. But when she shoves Daddy and then goes into their bedroom and slams the door, I know it's already too late.

"I'm gonna put some food together for you guys to take home," Daddy says. He kisses me on my forehead and pulls at Bribee's ponytail. She smiles and drinks the milk from her cereal bowl, but I feel like throwing up. When I hear plastic bags, my heart starts beating really fast and it gets hard to breathe.

"How 'bout ... cereal and milk?" I hear him pulling food out of the cabinets and the refrigerator.

I feel like screaming. No! No! No!

"Uh-huh," Bribee answers with a big nod.

"Some bread and sandwich meat?"

"Uh-huh."

"Some bananas and cookies ... "

My sister's happy to be getting so much stuff to take home, but I'm not. I wanna tell him that I don't wanna go back, but it feels like something is grabbing my throat and I can't say anything. All I can do is cry. They both stare at me and I feel like a big baby when they do, but I can't stop—not even when Bribee looks like she's about to cry, too.

Daddy comes over and puts his arm around me. "Geli, what's wrong?" he asks, but I just hug him really tight and cry even harder. I wanna tell him that my heart hurts when I don't see him. I wanna tell him that Mom stays in her room all the time. I even wanna tell him that some of Mom's boyfriends hit us.

"Daddy, can we stay here and live with you?" I ask.

He's only quiet for a little while, but I already know what he's gonna say. My plan failed.

"That's not a good idea right now, Babygirl. Plus, Bribee has her own daddy. I can't just take her away from him."

"He doesn't care." I wipe my snotty nose with the back of my hand. "We never see him anyway."

"Geli, you're gonna have a new baby brother soon. We don't have enough room for you, and your sister, and the new baby," he says.

But I don't care. I was here first, and I didn't ask for a stupid baby brother.

45

"I'll tell you what, though," Daddy says. "When I take you home, I'm gonna talk to your mom about you guys spending more time with me. What do you think about that, Bribee? You wanna hang out over here a little bit more?"

"Uh-huh," she nods.

"See … it's gonna be fun. Plus, I'm gonna talk to her about keeping more food in the house—and giving you girls a bath 'cause you stiiiiink!" Daddy tickles Bribee's belly and she laughs so hard that it makes me smile, too.

Heina only has two seats, so Daddy puts the groceries in the back and sits Bribee in the seat with me. Once he gets in, I pull the seatbelt out and hand it to him so he can buckle it around us. I love going places with Daddy. Everybody stops when they see us, because Heina's the flyest car in the whole world. Plus, everybody knows my daddy. Whenever you see Heina, you know my daddy's close by. Sometimes, I see her parked at the apartments across the street from my school. When I do, I don't even play with my friends during recess. I just run to the fence so I can see him. The bell usually rings before I get a chance to, but a couple of times I saw him. I would yell, "Daaadyyy!" so loud across that busy street, and when he saw me, he would wave and blow me kisses and everything. My cheeks would always hurt from smiling so much. But when recess was over and we went back to class, I felt like crying.

On our way back home, we listen to a old-school song about sitting in the park. Most of the time, you can hear Heina's sounds bumpin' all the way down the street, but Daddy never turns it up that loud when we're with him. He says it can bust our eardrums and then we won't be able to hear anymore. It's kinda loud right now, but it's all good. We just listen and sing along to the parts of the song we know.

As soon as Daddy pulls up to our building, everybody stops and looks at us like we're superstars. "Watch this," he says. He flips a switch by his door and all of a sudden Heina starts bouncing up and down! At first, it's kinda scary because I don't know what's happening, but when I look at Daddy, he has a big smile on his face. I remember seeing some lowrider cars bounce like this in a parade, but I didn't know that Heina could do it. Bribee starts cracking up and it makes me laugh, too. It's like we're on a ride at the fair or something. When I see Daddy looking past me out the window, I turn and look, too. That's when I see all the people crowding around, and that's when I know that my Daddy's famous.

When we step outside, some of our friends wave at us and say hi. "Is that your Dad?" one boy asks. I nod my head like it's no big deal, but inside I feel like it's Christmas.

Some teenagers ask Daddy about Heina and car shows and stuff. "Hold up, let me take the kids in," Daddy tells them. He picks up Bribee and the groceries and we walk through the crowd into the courtyard. A couple of shit-talkin' ladies are sitting outside smoking and drinking. When they see us, they whisper to each other like me and my friends do when we're telling secrets.

"Hey Tavio, ain't seen you in a while. Where you been?" one of them asks Daddy. I remember that Mom calls her a hoochie-mama and it makes me smile.

"Been workin'... you know how it is."

"Yeah, I know." She has a fake smile on her face. "You and my cousin come up with a name for the baby yet?"

I didn't know she was Emiliana's cousin.

"Naw, not yet," he tells her.

"Well tell her I said hi." She looks Daddy up and down and then bites her lower lip. I can tell she likes him by the way she's acting. Yep, definitely a hoochie-mama.

When we get to our apartment, I push open the door and Daddy follows me inside. "What the hell ..." He looks around like he can't believe his eyes, but everything looks the same to me. He puts Bribee down and kicks a path to the kitchen. He gets more and more mad—and then I see it. I left the poisoned pizza on the counter and now there's a whole bunch of ants crawling everywhere. We had the best day ever, but I had to go and mess it up by being stupid.

"Sorry, Daddy." My eyes start to get watery, but I try my best not to cry. "I left it like that on accident." He looks at me, but I don't think he hears me. He just shakes his head and walks down the hall without saying anything. Me and Bribee look at each other and follow him to our room. We watch him look around at everything, and then he starts to use some of the really bad curse words. Bribee gets really scared and holds onto me.

47

"You and your sister sleep on this?" He yells and points to our mattress. We both jump a little. "Where the hell is your bed and all the stuff I bought you!"

"I don't know!" I yell back. I'm not sure why I'm getting mad, but I am.

I don't get in trouble or anything—he doesn't even tell me to watch my mouth. He just walks right past us. I know he's going to Mom's room even before I hear the loud knocks on her door. "Angela!" he yells.

"Stay here," I tell Bribee, and then I close the door behind me. When I look across the hall, I see Daddy trying to open Mom's door. It's locked, so I know she's inside.

"Angela!" he yells again. This time he bangs on her door really loud. That's when I hear people talking and stuff falling down in her room. And I know that if I can hear it from all the way over here, Daddy can hear it, too. "Angela! Open the damn door!" All of a sudden, Daddy steps back and kicks the door so hard that part of it breaks. That's when I get really scared. What if he hits her or tries to kill her like some of her boyfriends do?

Daddy kicks the door all the way open. I try to run over and make sure Mom doesn't get hurt, but I don't get far because Bribee grabs me and won't let go. I didn't even know she had left our room.

"You do this shit with your kids in the house ... around my daughter?" Daddy yells and then I hear commotion coming from the bedroom and the back patio. A man with no shirt on runs past the kitchen window. He must've climbed out of Mom's window, but I don't know why he's on the patio. There's nothing back there except cans and junk and spiders. There's not even a gate—but it doesn't matter, he just jumps over the fence like it's nothing.

I have to see what's going on in there, and even though Bribee panics, I pull away from her and run to the door. When I look inside, Daddy is punching on a man in his underwear, and Mom is laying across the bed with no clothes on.

"Tavio, you're crazy. Get the hell out of my house," Mom mumbles. There's a smile on her face, but her eyes are almost closed, like she's going to sleep. I look on her nightstand to see if she's been drinking, but the only thing there besides the trash is a pencil box and some foil.

48

All of a sudden, the man yells like crazy and shoves Daddy into the dresser. When he loses his balance, the man runs towards the door, but I can't move out of the way in time and he knocks me down. That makes Daddy even more mad, and he has a look on his face like I've never seen before. I watch him chase the man into the living room, and at first, it's like I can't move. It feels like everything's in slow motion. When I finally follow after them, I see the man on the floor and Daddy's stomping him, but I don't hear anything. I just stand there looking at the man's bloody face. His eyes are as big as tangerines, and I'm pretty sure he can't see out of 'em anymore. He looks like something from a scary movie—only this is real life. But then it's like the volume gets turned back on and I hear everything, especially Bribee in the kitchen screaming. I feel kind of fuzzy or something, but I'm not scared anymore. I take Bribee's hand and walk her back to our room. After I close the door, we sit on our mattress. Bribee sucks her thumb, but this time I don't pull it out of her mouth. I just put my arm around her and we listen to all the commotion.

That's what we're doing when the police get there. I don't hear everything the police man says, but after a while, a lady with a badge shows up. She says she's a social worker and that her job is to find us a safe place to live until Mom can take care of us again. She tells us some other stuff too—but I don't remember what.

"Can you help me pick out some clothes and maybe a toy for you and your sister?" She asks me.

At first I don't move, but when she starts looking through all the stuff on the floor, I go over and help her. We find four outfits for both of us, and I make sure I get the t-shirt Daddy bought me when we went to the fair. I don't need a toy, but I bring the blue monkey—for Bribee.

When we walk outside, I see police cars and two ambulances. The crowd is a lot bigger now, but this time, I don't feel like a superstar. This time, there's blood all over Daddy's shirt and he's sitting on the curb in handcuffs.

49

5

MELINDA WASN'T PLAYIN'. When she said she'd pick me up at six, she meant six on the dot. As a matter of fact, she was probably sitting in her car ten minutes before six. I'm trying to be organized like that, but I know I got some work to do. I get to school and to work on time now, but it's like I'm on CP time for everything else.

"I appreciate you taking the time to share your story," Melinda says after our small-talk dies down. "I think it's important for foster parents to hear from someone who's been through the system, but don't forget to take care of yourself."

I don't know why, but my stomach drops a little when she says that. "What do you mean?"

"Well, bringing up painful experiences can take an emotional toll. I just want you to be mindful of everything so you're not overwhelmed. Remember, they don't need to know the details—that's none of their business."

I nod because it's the same stuff she says in group, and the same thing they told me when I got hired at the Res. I know they don't want people getting all emotional and jacked-up, but sometimes that's just real life.

We pull into the parking lot of Creekside Family Services with fifteen minutes to spare. *Dang, this woman don't know how to be late.*

Inside, a receptionist welcomes us and leads us through a maze of hallways and cubicles. I swear, child welfare agencies must have agreements with each other, 'cause they have the same posters of sad-looking kids at my job *and* Perdido. When we get to their meeting room, we find a group of about thirty people, mainly couples, on break. They're reading through paperwork, socializing, and of course, eating.

"It must be a rule that says social workers have to feed people, 'cause this looks like one of your spreads," I tell her.

Melinda looks around and smiles. "Food brings people together, plus, it's hard to listen with an empty stomach. And I don't know about you, but most of us like to eat."

"You ain't the only one." I grin.

"Melinda, Angelique, thank you for coming." I turn around to find a Mr. Rogers-looking dude extending his hand to Melinda.

"It's good to see you, Aaron." She shakes his hand and introduces us. "Aaron Nelson is the Director here at Creekside, and sometimes the trainer, and case carrying social worker, and handyman and ... Didn't you play Santa Claus one year?"

Dang, he's the boss, but he has to do grunt-work? That's crazy. I guess the look on my face gives me away, because they both look at me and laugh.

"Around here, we do what it takes to get the job done," Aaron says. "Angelique, I've heard a lot about you. Thanks again for coming out." He shakes my hand and then looks at his watch. "We'll be getting started in about ten minutes. Why don't you help yourself to some refreshments while I talk with Melinda."

I make my way over to the snack table to see if I can find anything good. They have sandwiches, which is the same thing I had for lunch, but at least these were made with that good kind of croissant bread. *Ooh, and they have roast beef and turkey!* I grab a plate and get a roast beef sandwich, some grapes, and a bottled water. When I'm done, I think about going back up for another sandwich, but I don't want them thinking I'm greedy, so I just get a chocolate covered granola bar instead.

A brown-skinned lady with a shoulder-length twist-out comes up to the table and grabs a few napkins next to me. "Watch out, those are a little messy." She holds up her chocolate covered fingers. "I guess it was a little too warm in here."

"Thank you for the heads-up. I'll make sure I eat it after I talk," I tell her. "Knowin' me, I'd end up in front of everybody with chocolate all over my face."

"You must be Angelique." She smiles and wipes her hands.

"Why, yes I am." I say in my best proper voice and it makes her laugh.

"I'm Brenda. Melinda's a good friend of mine. She speaks very highly of you."

Really? "Thanks, Melinda's cool." *Why would she speak highly of me?* "Brenda and Melinda, you guys got a twin thing going on."

Brenda laughs like she's a little embarrassed, "As a matter of fact, we were known as the Thompson Twins back when we were in school."

"Why? Her last name isn't Thompson."

"Because of the eighties band ... twins, but not twins. We were both into the new wave music scene."

I just nod and grin. "I have no idea what that means," I tell her. "But okay—I'm sure it was real deep."

"Really, you don't know about new wave?" she asks. "You've never heard of Adam Ant, Missing Persons, Kajagoogoo?..."

My eyes get big with that last one and I look around trying real hard not to laugh.

"Man, when did we get old?"

I can't help but laugh now, but it's okay because she laughs, too. I can see why she and Melinda have been friends for so long. They both seem cool.

"All right, everyone," Aaron says above the noise. "Let's go ahead and return to our seats so we can finish up."

Everybody makes their way back to their seats and the room gets quiet.

"First, I'd like to thank you all once again for making this commitment," he says. "I know this has been a long journey. We ask a lot of our foster parents because we want them to be successful, but more importantly, we want our kids to be safe. The fact that you're all still here says a lot, and as a token of our appreciation, we would like to give each of you a small gift."

That's when three of his staff members come in and start handing out gift bags. I watch as people pull out a Creekside Family Services coffee mug filled with candy, a pen, a journal, and a picture frame. *I hope they're giving me a gift bag, too.*

"And it doesn't end there." He pauses and looks around the room like he's trying to figure out what to say. "At the end of each training, we invite a guest speaker who's been impacted by foster care in some way. Based on the feedback we've received, this is actually the most popular part of our trainings. Tonight, Miss Angelique Lopez will be sharing her story, and as she does, I'd like you to think about some of the things that you've learned over these past few weeks." Aaron turns to me and gestures, "Angelique?"

The group claps as he steps back so I can take his place at the front. I have butterflies in my stomach but I'm in my element. All eyes are on me and I know I got this.

"Good evening," I say as I put my bottle of water on the table. They return my greeting and I look around at all the different faces in front of me. All of a sudden, I feel myself getting heated. I'm annoyed that I'm here. I'm annoyed that they have to be here. I'm annoyed that this agency exists, and I'm annoyed that I work at a place just like it. *You have a job to do Angelique, and you're not about to let Melinda look crazy... just be real.*

"I have mixed feelings standing up here right now," I tell them. "There's obviously a need for foster parents 'cause we have a lot of kids in the system, but honestly—I really don't like foster parents." I see a bunch of questioning looks and raised eyebrows. "Now don't get me wrong, I'm sure some of you are very nice people, but I can tell you from experience,

53

some of you should not be doing this. I don't know who you are, and you might not even know who you are. So I'm asking all of you, please think about what you're about to do."

I see more questioning looks and now quite a few frowns. "That sounds weird, huh?" I nod right along with them. "You obviously put some thought into this process. You got fingerprinted, you gave up some of your evenings to come to theses trainings, you spent gas money to get here ... you even had to deal with snacks that melted and got all over your hands." I know they're following me when I hear people laugh. "Yes, all of that required some thought, but I'm asking you to think about why you're *really* doing this. As a matter of fact, I'm gonna ask you some questions. I don't need to know the answers, but *you* definitely do. Okay, are you ready?"

"Go for it," somebody says kind of loud. Other people nod and say yes.

"Okay, first of all, do you really want to help kids?" I ask. That's an easy question and I already know that almost everybody is gonna say they do. "Second, do you have the ability to stick it out when it's not just hard, but *exhausting*?" There's a noticeable decline in the number of nods, but I keep going. "Do you secretly just want people giving you props for taking in 'troubled kids'? Or, do you need some extra money but don't wanna get a real job?" A few people laugh and I take a sip of water. "I'm asking you to honestly think about this *before* kids get sent to your home. They've been through things that most of you probably can't even imagine, and if you're doing this for the wrong reasons, you could be causing them more harm than good."

I see that everybody is tuned into what I'm saying, so I take a deep breath. "Me and my sister went into foster care when I was seven and she was three because my mom was bipolar. Well, that and the fact that she cared more about drugs and men than feeding us." A few people in the group shake their heads like they can't imagine a mother doing that. I also fill them in on what happened with my dad and how he ended up in prison.

"Social Services stepped in and put us with a 'very nice Christian couple' who loved gettin' props for taking care of 'orphans'. They also loved telling me and my sister about how 'lucky' we were." I tilt my head to the side to throw in a little drama. "Can you believe that? They honestly expected us to be grateful to them for letting us live with them. We were *kids*! Never mind that we were scared and mad for being taken away from the only life we knew. Apparently that wasn't important to them, but gratitude definitely was. As you could imagine, staying there became a bit of a problem."

6

Me and Bribee sit in the backseat and look out the window while she drives past the places we use to play. She drives by our school, and the liquor store that sells water balloons. She even drives by the mall that Daddy took us to that time. When she gets on the freeway, my stomach starts to feel funny. Where's she taking us? She told me that her job is to find us a place to live until Mom can take care of us, but she didn't even ask anybody—and every single one of our neighbors was outside. We play with Miss King's grandkids all the time, we could've stayed with her.

She drives for a long time and when she finally gets off the freeway, I can't even tell where we are. All I see is a whole bunch of tall buildings and a really big mall that has a lot of stores I see on TV. I already know that those aren't good places to shop, though. Mom says that it doesn't make sense to spend money at those kinda stores when you can get the same thing at the swap meet for a whole lot cheaper. Plus, I like the swap meet because they sell the best elote there. The corn man here probably doesn't even have limes.

A little while later, she turns on a smaller street with big houses. They all look the same, and they all have big yards that look like green carpets. Everything is really nice and clean, but I don't see hardly any people. In our neighborhood, people are always hanging out and having fun, especially in the summer. All I see here is a couple of people jogging, and some guys mowing lawns.

The social worker pulls into the driveway of one of those houses and the front door opens before the car even stops. The lady who comes outside *looks like a Barbie doll. She has blonde hair like Bribee, but it's really long and kinda poofy on top. She also has on a whole lot of makeup. I don't like Barbie dolls. The man behind her looks normal though.*

"*Aww, look at them,*" *she says when we get out of the car. It's the same voice that people use when they see puppies.* "*I'm Mrs. Dorsey and this is Mr. Dorsey. What are your names?*" *She has a crazy looking smile on her face, plus she's a stranger, and Mom told me that I don't have to talk to strangers.*

"*This is Angelique,*" *the social worker tells her.* "*And this is Brianna.*"

"*No. Her name is Bribee.*" *I know I'm smart-mouthing them, but I don't care. If they don't like it, they can send us home. As a matter of fact, I wish they would.*

The social worker pulls our bag of clothes out of the trunk and we all follow the Barbie lady into the house. Everything is decorated and it smells like cleaner.

"*I wasn't able to find a lot of clothes, and what I did find needs to be washed,*" *the social worker tells them. She hands our clothes to Mr. Dorsey.* "*They likely won't have visits for a while because both parents are being detained, but I'll keep you updated.*"

What does that mean? They can't just take us away and not let us see our mom!

"*… Information about the hearing, but they likely won't need to go …*"

How long do we have to stay here? They can't just leave us here with strangers. We need to be with our mom, or Daddy. Mom told me about kids that are taken away by strangers. This is kidnapping! Kids who get kidnapped are supposed to try to get help or call the police—but the police are the ones who told the social worker to take us.

"*How does that sound, Angelique?*" *They're all looking at me. I don't know what she said, but I don't care. I'm not talking to any of them because they're all strangers, and I don't have to talk to strangers.*

"*How about I show you to your rooms?*" *Mrs. Dorsey says after the social worker leaves. I take Bribee's hand and we follow her up the stairs.* "*This is your room Angelique.*"

I hate it. The whole thing is pink and frilly and stupid, but she keeps looking at me with that dumb smile, like I'm supposed to be in love with it.

"Do you like it?" she asks. I shrug my shoulders a little because at least the bed is big enough for me and Bribee to have a lot of space. "We'll go shopping for clothes and stuff tomorrow," she whispers and smiles. She's tryna hide stuff from her husband, but I'm not keeping her secrets. I bet she's stealing money out of his wallet, too.

"I have a surprise for you, Bribee," she says, trying to act all excited. She walks across the hall and motions for us to follow her. When we get close, she opens the door and steps off to the side for us to see in. It's another pink room, but this one is kind of babyish. It has a little kid's table and chairs, coloring books, stuffed animals, and a giant dollhouse in the corner. Bribee lets go of my hand and walks inside to look around.

"This is your room, Bribee." My stomach drops like I'm going down a hill, and Bribee looks at me like she's gonna cry. That's when I know I have to say something. I have to stick up for my sister.

"We have to sleep together," I tell her.

Her smile goes away and she looks at me like I have two heads or something. Bribee walks back over to me and holds my hand again.

"Can't you at least try for one night?" She pokes out her bottom lip, like we're hurting her feelings or something, but I'm not gonna give in.

"No!" I tell her in my meanest voice, "Didn't I just tell you that we have to sleep together?"

She stands there with her mouth hanging open. If I would've talked to Mom or even Emiliana like that, I would've got beat with a belt—or at least slapped in the face. But I already know that this lady can't hit me, so I look her straight in the eye. She looks at me really mean, but she doesn't do anything.

"Babe, it's fine," Mr. Dorsey says from the hallway. "If that's what they're used to, then they should share a room." He walks in and starts pushing the bed over. "But Angelique, you have to help me move the other bed in here, okay?" I nod my head and follow him back into the ugly room. He puts pillows under both of my arms, and then puts another one under my chin—but I only smile a little bit. When I take them back to the baby room, Bribee's playing with the dollhouse. Mrs. Dorsey's moving

stuff to make room for the other bed, but I can tell by the way she's doing it, she's mad.

I wanna go home. They told us that Mom is still in the hospital and they don't know when Daddy's getting out of jail, so we have to stay here for a while. Mr. Dorsey's not so bad, but Mrs. Dorsey gets on my nerves. She acts all nice when Mr. Dorsey's around, but when he's at work, she doesn't even pretend to be nice to me. I don't care though, as long as she's nice to Bribee.

"If you were my little girl, I would make sure you were happy all the time," I heard her tell my sister. But Bribee's not her little girl, and I make sure she knows it. Like when she bought us those new clothes. I let Bribee wear the panties and the socks because we didn't have any, but I wouldn't let her wear those stupid dresses—not every day. Mrs. Dorsey kept telling us that we had to be careful, and not get dirty, and not to run or climb like a boy. All she wanted us to do was color and play with that stupid dollhouse—or their stupid cat. So I told Bribee that we were gonna start wearing our old clothes again. At least then we wouldn't have to worry about getting dirty. That next day, we didn't wear the clothes she laid out for us. I found our old stuff in the back of the closet, so we put on our pants and t-shirts.

"What are you wearing?" Mrs. Dorsey asked.

"The clothes our mom bought us." I smart-mouth her all the time now.

"Angelique, I am the adult and you are the child. I decide what's best for you and your sister ..."

"You're not our mom! And you can't tell us what to do or what to wear."

All she could do was look at me mean, but I didn't care. We wore our own clothes that whole day and we played like we wanted to. We even got dirty—a little bit on purpose. The next day, she laid out those same stupid dresses, but this time when I looked in the back of the closet, all of our stuff was gone. She wants me to cry, but I'm not gonna cry in front of her.

We still haven't seen Mom or Daddy and it's been almost two whole months. Bribee cries almost every night, but Mrs. Dorsey doesn't even care. She doesn't want us to go back home anyway. Sometimes I sneak downstairs and listen while she's on the phone with her friends.

"The oldest one is a little monster, but the youngest one is the sweetest thing," she says. "Some women would kill for beautiful girls like that ... of course it's the junkies that always get pregnant...it's so unfair ... she'll probably have more scattered all over the county in different foster homes. I hope they never see those girls again."

I hate her.

She's mad because Mr. Dorsey's working late and we have to eat dinner without him again.

"Don't forget to say thank you. We use manners in this house," she tells us. But she puts our plates in front of us and gives us juice with an attitude. She's not using her manners, so I'm not using mine.

"Tank you," Bribee says and then she starts eating.

"Angelique, use your manners and say thank you," she tells me, but I just stare at her.

"Angelique," she sighs. "Do you know how lucky you are to live here? You have a nice room, new clothes, and a lot of food so you don't go hungry. The least you can do is say thank you for what I'm giving you."

I just roll my eyes. I don't care about that stupid room or those ugly clothes. Plus, this food is nasty. I didn't wanna eat it anyway.

"Angelique, people who don't use their manners are like animals. Is that what you want to be, an animal?" She crosses her arms and stares at me like she's waiting for an answer, but I just sit there.

"You don't want to talk? Well, that's fine with me!" she yells.

Bribee jumps and I get kinda scared, too. She usually doesn't yell like that, so I can tell she's really mad—but I still don't care. She goes over and starts taking some stuff out of the cabinets. Every time she does, she slams it on the kitchen counter—a little plate, slam; a can of tuna, slam; a fork, slam. Me and Bribee look at each other and then watch to see what she's gonna do next.

She comes over, takes my food away and gives me that little plate with nothing on it.

"Since you're behaving like an animal," she says. "I guess I'll start treating you like an animal!" She dumps my food in the trash can and hits the plate on the side to make sure everything comes off. Bang! Bang! Bang! Then she practically throws the plate in the sink. We watch her peel the lid off the can, and when she walks over to me, there's a weird smile *on her face. She uses the fork to scoop the tuna onto the plate in front of me, only it's not tuna at all—it's some fancy kind of cat food. She's trying to poison me!*

My chest starts to feel like something heavy is pushing on it, and every time I breathe, the stink of the cat food makes me wanna throw up. Everything feels weird and dizzy like it's a bad dream or something. That's when I remember, Mom said we don't feel pain in dreams, so I close my eyes, and I bite my arm as hard as I can. That's how I know this is real life and we're stuck here. When I open my eyes, Mrs. Dorsey is staring at me and it makes me wanna hide.

"Stop looking at me!" I yell. I can feel the tears starting to come, but I swallow a few times and try hard to keep them in. That's when I hear the phone ring, and that's when she starts laughing at me.

"I guess I should've given you dog food," she says as she walks into the living room. "Well, when you're ready to behave like a human being, let me know and I'll feed you like a human being." When she answers the phone, I hear her telling her friend about how crazy I am because I bit myself.

"Here, Geli," Bribee whispers. She pushes a fork full of mashed potatoes toward me just as Mrs. Dorsey comes back into the kitchen.

"Well since the two of you like to share so much, you can share your food with your sister," Mrs. Dorsey tells me. When I see her take Bribee's plate and throw her food in the trash, I don't feel like crying anymore, I feel like stomping on her until her face is bloody.

"You can't do that!" I yell. "You're supposed to feed us real food, especially Bribee, she's just a little kid!"

"You will get real food when you decide to behave!" she yells back. "And now, because of you, your sister has to suffer!"

Bribee always gets nervous when people argued, so I'm not surprised when she covers her ears, but I do get surprised when she picks up her juice and throws it on the floor.

"You did that on purpose!" Mrs. Dorsey yells and then she slaps Bribee in the face. When I hear my sister cry because of that lady, my heart starts beating super-fast and I feel like I'm on fire. She doesn't say sorry for making her cry, or anything. She just gets a towel and starts wiping up the juice on the floor.

She thinks she can just starve little kids and hit them whenever she wants to! That's not right, and she's not gonna get away with it. When she leans over to pick up the dirty towel, I jump on her back and pull her hair as hard as I can. She screams and we both fall on the floor. I don't hear Bribee crying anymore. All I hear is Mrs. Dorsey yelling and cursing while she tries to knock me off of her. I don't even know how long we fight. All I know is that I kick, and I punch, and I bite, and I pull, as hard as I can.

All of a sudden, she screams really loud and shoves me away. When she stands up, I see that her face is red and her hair is all over the place. At first, I didn't know what happened, but then she starts patting her hair with a crazy look on her face. That's when I look down at my hands and I see that I'm holding blonde pieces. I didn't even know she wore a weave.

"Don't you come near me again, you little bitch!" she screams, and then she runs into the living room. I hear her on the phone saying that she's been attacked by a foster child and asking for the police to come, but I don't even care. I just go over and put my arm around my sister. I think she calls the social worker too, because I hear her yelling that she wants us out of her house in an hour. "This is what happens when a junkie and a convict make babies," she yells. "That child is an animal and she's gonna end up just like them!"

She stays in the living room when she gets off the phone, but I see her peek in and spy on us a few times. The police come and ask us a bunch of questions, and then a social worker comes and asks us a bunch of questions. We tell them what Mrs. Dorsey did, but I don't think they believe us because they don't arrest her or anything. I don't even care though, I'm just happy we get to leave.

I look around the conference room to see if any of these people are telling on themselves. Sometimes, all you have to do is look at their faces and you can tell what kind of foster parents they are behind closed doors. Like the lady who rolled her eyes when I talked about my mom being sick. Yes, my mom was, and probably still is an addict, but did she even hear the part about my mom being bipolar? She's probably one of those people who thinks mental illness is fake. She'll probably slack on taking the kids to their therapy appointments and then wonder why they won't just "get over" what happened to them.

When I talked about Bribee getting slapped for throwing her juice on the floor, everybody was shocked, even that grandma-looking lady, but her husband wasn't. He almost smiled. I can already tell he's old-school. He's the type of foster parent who goes through all the trainings and agrees not to hit the kids, but then ignores everything once they're in his home. As a matter of fact, he probably has a belt and an extension cord for when the kids act up. You can look at him and tell that he has ass-beating tendencies.

Most of them surprised me though. They were tracking with me like they knew what was up. Like when I talked about my dad, I saw a lady hold her husband's hand. I looked him dead in his eyes, and I swear he was about to break down. He's the type of foster parent that'll try his best, because he's been through some stuff and he knows what it's like. I wish all foster parents could be like that.

"We didn't need a new family when we went into foster care, and we definitely didn't need strangers bad-mouthing our parents," I tell them. "We needed people who understood that we were grieving. That no matter how bad they thought our mom and dad were, they were still our mom and dad. But no, we ended up with foster parents who piled their personal problems on top of ours."

7

"I think she threw our clothes away," I tell the social worker as she buckles Bribee into a car seat.

"Honey, I had her get everything out of the drawers and the closet," she says. "It's all in the trunk."

"That's the stuff she bought us." I feel my eyes getting watery so I look out the window. "I was talking about the stuff my mom and Daddy got for us."

"Look at me," she says. When I do, she's frowning. "You and your sister did not deserve to be treated like that. Do you hear me?" I nod my head, but I don't know why she's mad at me. "We try to find grown-ups who are nice to kids and make them feel safe, but sometimes they trick us."

Oh, she's mad at Mrs. Dorsey! "Yeah, you guys got tricked really good, but Mr. Dorsey was nice though. You did a good job with him."

"Well, thank you," she smiles and I almost do, too—a little bit. "Can you read yet?" I guess she doesn't know that I'm about to go to third grade so I nod my head. "Well since you're old enough to read, I'm going to give you something." She pulls a little card off of her clip board and gives it to me. "This is my name right here, Gina Wright," she says as she points it out. "If a foster parent, or a teacher, or any other grown-up is ever mean to you like that, I want you to call me. Have you ever used the phone to call someone?"

The phone at our house never worked so I shake my head.

"Well, when we get to my office, we're going to practice using the phone and leaving messages, okay?"

"Okay." I guess she believed us after all.

By the time we get to Miss Gina's job, it's kinda dark and the parking lot is practically empty. The streetlights have turned everything into a creepy yellow and the only sound is a weird buzzing, like maybe there's a monster-sized bug waiting for us in the bushes. All the lights are on in the office, but it's still really quiet and really empty. When we get off the elevator, another lady comes over to meet us.

"This is Nadia," Miss Gina tells us. "She's going to help me find a better place for you to stay, but before we do anything, how about some dinner?"

They take us to a really big room that looks like a kitchen. It has two refrigerators, a bunch of tables, and candy machines with snacks and drinks and sandwiches. They let us pick whatever kinda sandwiches and chips we want. We even get to put the money in and push the buttons— only we can't have sweets or drinks because there's bottles of water in the refrigerator. I don't even care though, 'cause Mom says that stuff makes kids hyper and stumps us from growing anyway.

After we eat, Nadia leaves to go find some nice people, and Miss Gina takes us over to a desk so we can learn how to use the phone. She tells us that an emergency is really serious—like when somebody's hurt really bad or there's a fire or something. "If there's an emergency," she says, "you push 9-1-1 so the police, or the ambulance, or fire department can come and help you. If it's not an emergency, dial the numbers on my card and leave me a message." Dialing is easy, but leaving messages makes me feel kind of nervous. After I practice a little bit, I know how to do it though. Miss Gina lets Bribee leave a message, too. When we're done, she takes us over to where she sits and we get to listen to our messages on a speaker phone. Bribee cracks up when she hears herself, and she asks Miss Gina to play her message over and over again.

I guess Nadia has a hard time finding nice people for us to stay with because we finish learning how to use the phone, but she's still not back.

"Would you like to see our playroom?" Miss Gina asks. "You can watch a video while we wait." She takes us down a long hallway to a room with a giant window in the wall. I can see all the kids' stuff and the TV

*even before we get inside. All of their videos are boring, but Bribee doesn't
mind because she gets to pick a cartoon she likes. I don't feel like watching
anything though. I don't feel like staying with nice people either. I just
wanna go home.*

*Nadia comes in before the video is done playing. "Ok, we're all set,"
she says. She and Miss Gina start talking kinda quiet to each other and
my stomach starts to feel weird.*

*"Alright girls," Miss Gina says. "I think we hit the jackpot this time
..."*

*By the time we pull up to the house, it's really dark. There's a porch
light on, so Bribee won't be too scared, but I'll have to hold her hand tight
just in case. I can already tell that this place is gonna be different from the
Dorsey's. It doesn't have a really big yard or that green carpet grass, but I
can see a slide and a kid's playhouse on the other side of their fence. Mrs.
Dorsey would've never had play-stuff in her yard.*

*The van in the driveway has writing on it. "Za-rate Fa-mi-ly Day
Care," I say out loud so Miss Gina can hear me read.*

"Very good," she smiles. "But, they pronounce it Za-RAW-tay."

"We're going to daycare?"

*"You don't remember me telling you about Mrs. Zarate before we left
the office?" I shake my head and look down at the stupid shoes that Mrs.
Dorsey bought for me. "It's okay, I think we're all tired," she says. "Mrs.
Zarate is a foster mother, but she also runs a daycare out of her home.
She's really nice."*

*Miss Gina rings the doorbell and a chunky lady with short curly hair
opens the door. She has a nice smile. She reminds me of the pictures Daddy
used to show me of my abuelita before she died.*

*"Comb in, comb in," she says with an accent. We walk into a big
living room and all I see is a whole bunch of kids stuff—kid tables and
chairs, kid couches, kid books and three big baskets of toys. There's a
baby sleeping in a playpen by the corner and I can hear another baby crying
upstairs. Two kids Bribee's age are sitting on the floor staring at the TV.
There's cartoons on, but they're not even laughing. They don't even look
at us either. I bet they came from foster homes where they couldn't watch
cartoons either. They probably can't believe how lucky they are to be here.*

Miss Gina tells her our names, but instead of saying Angelique and Bribee, she calls us On-hell-leek and Bay-bee.

"You speak Spanish?" Mrs. Zarate asks. I shake my head no and for some reason, I feel tears in my eyes. "It's okay, Mija," she tells me. "If you want, I teach you, okay?"

I nod and wipe my eyes with the back of my hand. My chest feels heavy.

Mrs. Zarate has four TV's at her house. The one in the living room is for the kids. It has cartoons playing on it all day, and sometimes even at night for when the daycare kids stay late. Plus, there's a TV in Mrs. Zarate's bedroom for when she needs a break. Her daughter, Graciella, has a TV in her room because she's a college student and she has to watch the news a lot. And then there's the TV in the den—that's the one that Mrs. Zarate watches the most because she can keep an eye on all the kids and watch her novellas, too.

"I'm bored," I tell her one day when I get tired of watching cartoons with Bribee and the other kids. At first she doesn't say anything. She just sits there folding clothes and watching TV. "Mrs. Zarate ..."

"Con tantos juguetes. How are you bored?" She shakes her head and looks at me. "You have dolls, you have puzzles, you have colores ..."

"That stuff's for little kids."

"Fine, you want something to do?" She raises her eyebrows and hands me a towel. "Here you go. I teach you to fold the laundry."

She shows me how to match the corners up and fold it just like they do in the stores. After that, she shows me how to fold shorts and pants. Pretty soon, I even know how to do shirts.

"Can we fold something else?" I ask when the whole basket is done, but all she does is laugh and pat me on the shoulder.

"You say that now Mija, but one day, this laundry gonna make you crazy. Come." I follow her into the kitchen and watch her pull paper plates, bread, and a large bag of chips from the cabinet. After she sits them on the table, she gets some baloney out of the refrigerator. "We make the lunch."

She starts to make a sandwich, but before she can even finish, one of the babies starts crying.

"You want me to go check on the baby?" I ask her.

"No, no, you wait here," she says with a frown. She wipes her hands on a dishtowel and leaves me in the kitchen, so I decide to finish making the other sandwiches. By the time she comes back, I'm done with all of them. I even put some chips on one side of the plate just like she does.

"Gracias, Mija," she says as she pats the screaming baby on the back. She's so happy that she comes over and gives me a hug. It feels really nice.

I get to make lunch all the time now. Mrs. Zarate likes it because she can focus on taking care of the babies, and I like it because I can use as much mayonnaise as I want. The little kids don't really care because all they do is take a few bites of sandwich and then eat up all the chips.

Since I'm the oldest, I get to do a lot of stuff that the little kids aren't allowed to do. Mrs. Zarate showed me how to work the washing machine and the clothes dryer. She showed me how to vacuum all the floors and how to load the dishwasher, too. After a while, I don't even have to ask her if I can help. Sometimes she even puts me in charge. When Graciella's not home, I get to take care of the little kids whenever Mrs. Zarate takes a nap, or sometimes when she's watching TV.

Every now and then I take care of them when she has to run to the store, too. She never does that when the babies are here though. She says it's not safe for me to take care of the babies, 'cause something bad could happen and I might not know what to do. I wanna tell her that I took care of Bribee just fine when she was a baby, but I know she has to do what the social workers say.

The doorbell is ringing, but Mrs. Zarate is gone and Graciella's at school. I already know that I'm not supposed to answer it, but whoever it is keeps on ringing it and ringing it. When I peek out the window, I see Miss Gina standing there with two police officers and another lady that I never met before.

"Angelique," Miss Gina says after a while. "Honey, I need you to open the door for us."

My stomach starts to feel sick. I know that if I open the door, something bad is gonna happen, so I just stand there.

"Are you sure they're here?" one of the policemen asks.

"According to the neighbor," Miss Gina tells him.

Why does everybody always have nosey-ass neighbors? I already know that once they tell on you, you can't hide anything, so I unlock the door and let them in. The next thing I know, Miss Gina is packing our clothes and all the daycare kids have to go home early.

I try to tell all of them that I know how to take care of little kids, and that I make our food, and I even clean up, but they just look really mad. They keep using words like irresponsible and negligent. I don't know what it means, but I know she's not bad. Mrs. Zarate feeds us, she gives us toys and stuff to play with, she lets us watch TV anytime we want, and she lets me take care of my sister. She's way nicer to me than Mrs. Dorsey ever was. I tell Miss Gina—over and over again—that I don't want to go, but she won't listen to me. I don't even care when I start crying so hard that it makes Bribee and some of the other kids cry, too. I don't wanna leave, but they don't listen to what I say. They never do.

8

I hate sitting in the back seat. That's something else I tell Miss Gina, but she doesn't listen to me about anything. She tells me that if I sit in the front I'm breaking the law and she'll get a ticket, but I know she's lying. Daddy always let me and Bribee sit in the front seat of his car and he never got a ticket. Miss Gina tells lies about everything.

"Angelique, I know you're upset about leaving Mrs. Zarate's house and I'm sorry about that," she says. "It's not fair that you guys have to move again, but I want you to know that we're doing our best to keep you and your sister safe."

I don't say anything to her. I just kick the back of her seat over and over again, and she can't stop me because we're on the freeway. All she can do is sigh. As a matter of fact, I'm not gonna talk to anybody at this new place she's taking us to. I don't care how nice they are. And I'm gonna make sure that Bribee doesn't talk to anybody either.

Miss Gina drives for a long time, just like that other social worker did when she took us to Mr. and Mrs. Dorsey's house. When she gets off the freeway, I don't see a whole lot of houses. It's just dirt and rocks and dirty-looking hills with itchy-looking plants. They don't even have sidewalks. I wish she would just take us home, but every time I ask her, she just tells me that Mom is still in the hospital, and Daddy can't have visitors right now. She's probably lying about that too.

"Look, Geli!" Bribee says pointing out the window.

At first, when I try to see what she's pointing at, all I see is a dirt field behind a long white fence. It looks like somebody stuck a whole bunch of equal signs together and then pushed a big X inside every single one of 'em. But then I see what she's all excited about. A real-life horse starts following us along the inside of the fence—and there's a girl in a helmet riding it! It looks like she's around my age, but even if she's not, it's really cool to see a kid riding a horse. The only time we ever got to see real-life horses at all was when they were in a parade, and the only people who ever rode them were grown-ups. The girl doesn't smile, but she waves and then they jog off ahead of us.

The house has a porch like Daddy and Emiliana, but it's not just in the front, it looks like it's on the side, too. A lady and a man stand in front waiting for us. Both of them have on jeans and cowboy boots—and they're holding hands.

"Angelique, Bribee, I'd like you to meet Mr. and Mrs. Gavilan," Miss Gina says when we get out of the car.

"Well, hello girls, welcome ..."

"I saw a girl riding a horse. Is she in foster care, too?" I ignore the lady and talk to the man instead.

"No, that's our daughter, Kimi," he says. "But if Miss Gina's okay with it, maybe we can teach you how to ride, too."

He takes our stuff out of Miss Gina's car and the lady takes us inside. I grab Bribee's hand so they all know that I'm the one who takes care of her, and that's when their daughter comes over.

"How old are you?" I ask her.

"Eight."

"I'm gonna be eight on September third."

When Mr. Gavilan hears me say that, he stops walking and turns around with a big smile on his face. "It looks like we were planning for your birthday party and we didn't even know it."

"We always have a Labor Day party before the kids go back to school," Mrs. Gavilan says. "And this year, Labor Day is on your birthday."

I don't say anything, but when Bribee starts dancing around and singing happy birthday songs, I tell her to be quiet.

Mr. and Mrs. Gavilan seem okay, but I don't care. I'm still not gonna talk to them. And when they show me pictures on the wall of them and their other daughter, Paige, I decide that I'm not gonna talk to her, either.

71

"Paige is in college in San Francisco so she doesn't live here anymore," Kimi says. She seems sad. I guess I'd be sad if my sister was gone, too.

They take us upstairs to a bedroom that's a hundred times better than the one at Mr. and Mrs. Dorsey's house. Almost everything is pink and black and white, but it's not that stupid baby-pink. It's cool checkered patterns and squiggly shapes like teenagers on TV have. Bribee lets go of my hand so she can check out a fuzzy chair that reminds me of a giant pink bowl. That's when I notice the poster hanging on the wall. WELCOME Angelique and Bribee! is written in colorful sparkly letters.

"How'd you know our names?" I ask.

"Miss Gina told us," Kimi's mom says, but I don't say anything back because I don't want her to think that I was talking to her. "Kimi and Paige decorated this room before she left for college. And we made the poster as soon as we found out you were coming. I hope you guys like it."

I still don't say anything back, but it feels nice knowing that Paige and Kimi did all of this for us.

The grown-ups go downstairs to fill out paperwork and Kimi gets permission to show us her room. It's right next to where me and Bribee will be sleeping. She has cool checkers and squiggly shapes, too, but her colors are purple, black and white. She only has one bed in her room, but there's enough books and stuffed animals to fill two book cases.

"My grandma and grandpa got that for me," she says when Bribee walks over to a dollhouse in the corner. "I don't really play with it anymore, but you guys can. It has a family and furniture and everything."

"My sister likes dollhouses," I tell her. "They had one at our other foster home, but the lady there was really mean. She slapped my sister in the face, and tried to make me eat cat food."

Kimi looks at me for a while and then she frowns. "My mom and dad never hit us—even when we do something wrong. And they always feed us normal stuff, so you don't have to worry about that at our house."

Miss Gina comes back upstairs to tell us bye before she leaves. I wave to her a little, but I still don't say anything. Once she leaves, Kimi's mom and dad give us a tour of the whole house. In the kitchen, she shows us three drawers.

"This is where you can keep your own personal snacks," she says, and then she tears three pieces of tape off of a big blue roll. "If you write your *names on the tape, we can all remember which drawer belongs to you." Me and Kimi use markers to make name tags and then we pick a drawer to stick them on. Bribee can't write yet, but she makes lines and circles on a piece of tape. When she's done, Kimi's mom writes her name on top of it so she can have her own drawer, too. "At our house, we have breakfast, and then a snack, lunch, and then a snack, and then dinner. And if you want, you can get the snack from your drawer. Okay?" I nod and then Bribee nods, too. But I still don't say anything. I never had my own snack drawer before.*

Kimi's mom and dad sleep downstairs. They show us their bedroom and bathroom, but none of us are allowed to go inside unless we knock on the door and they give us permission to come in. Upstairs past our bedrooms is an open room that doesn't have a door. They call it the kid's loft. It has a bin filled with toys, a TV, a bunch of videos and a radio just for us. There's even a little desk just for Bribee to use.

"What's that?" I ask pointing to a door on the other side of the kid's loft.

"That's Paige's room," Kimi's mom says. She goes over and opens the door so we can go inside and look. Paige's colors are pink and gray and white, and she has a lot of books, just like Kimi does. You can tell she likes fairies because there's posters and fairy dolls all over the place.

"We wanted you to see the whole house," her mom says. "But, Paige's room is also off limits, unless you have permission."

Kimi rolls her eyes. "I can't even come in here, unless Mom or Dad says it's ok."

"That's right," her dad says. "It's important to respect people's privacy, and that doesn't change just because Paige is away at college."

"Do you guys respect people's privacy?" I ask. I know I'm being a smart-mouth, but I'm sick and tired of grownups who just tell lies all the time.

"Well, it's a little different for us because it's our job to help you and look out for you," he says. "But yes, we'll respect some of your privacy, too. For example, we'll knock on your bedroom door before we come in, just in case you're getting dressed. And you'll have privacy when you use the bathroom, unless you need help."

"I already know how to wipe," Bribee says, and I'm glad she does, because he must think we're babies or something.

When it's time for bed, me, Bribee, and Kimi brush our teeth in a really cool bathroom with two sinks and a separate area where the tub and toilet are. It's almost like a secret bathroom, because the only way people can get to it is by going through one of our bedrooms.

"Does it bother you that me and my sister are staying here?" I ask Kimi when I'm done.

"No, I learned all about what foster care is when a social worker came to my school. I'm the one who told Mom and Dad that we should be a foster family." She shrugs her shoulders. "It's boring around here now that Paige is gone. Plus, I've always wanted little sisters."

It makes me feel really good when she says that.

9

Me, Bribee, and Kimi sit around the dining room table making something that Mrs. Gavilan calls party favors. My job is to pull out a little baggie and open it for Bribee. Her job is to count out five pieces of chocolate and put them inside, but I have to help her because she doesn't always count so good. Plus, I have to make sure she doesn't eat 'em all. Kimi's job is to get the baggie from Bribee and put a key chain with Mr. Gavilan's business information inside.

"Angelique, Bribee ... you have a phone call," Mrs. Gavilan says from the kitchen. I didn't hear the phone ring, but I already know that it's Miss Gina 'cause she said she was gonna call and wish me a happy birthday today. "Make sure you stay here in the den, okay?"

I nod and she hands me the phone with a smile on her face, but she doesn't really look all that happy. After we sit on the couch, she goes back to getting stuff ready for the party.

"Hello?"

"Hey, Babygirl."

My heart starts beating really fast, and it feels like somebody is choking my throat. "Mom? Where are you? Are you coming to get us?"

"Is that Mom?" Bribee asks. When I nod, she starts to cry."

"Mom, we wanna come home," I whisper so Mrs. Gavilan can't hear me. "Please!"

"I know, Babygirl, but the judge and the social workers said you can't come home for a while ..." I don't hear what she says after that. All I

know is she's not coming to get us. My chest aches and I cry and cry. "Babygirl, are you listening to me?"

I nod my head. "Yeah."

"I just wanted to call and wish you happy birthday," she says. "They may not let me see you, but they can't keep me from calling you on your birthday."

"When can we come home?" I whisper.

"You'll be home soon, but I want you to behave—and stop all that cryin'." I wipe my eyes. "Are those people treating you right?"

"Yeah. They're having a barbeque and a party for me later on today."

"Don't let those people fool you, okay? You only have one mother."

"Okay." I don't really know what she means, but I'm gonna watch them just in case. "Bribee wants to talk, too," I say, and then I give Bribee the phone.

"Mom?" Her voice sounds so little and sad that it makes me cry all over again. I hate judges and social workers. They make us see therapists and doctors and dentists and a million other people, but they never let us see Mom and Daddy.

"Are you being good?" I hear Mom ask.

"Uh huh. Can you come get us?" she cries. "We wanna come home."

"Not right now, but I want you to be good, okay?" Bribee doesn't answer, she just cries. "Give the phone back to Geli," Mom tells her. Bribee hands me the phone and leans back into the couch with her thumb in her mouth.

"Hello?"

"Alright, Babygirl, I need to go, but I want you to know that I love you, okay?

"Okay, love you, too."

After we hang up, Mrs. Gavilan sits on the couch next to us.

"I'm sorry you guys can't go home right now," she says. "Maybe we can take pictures and make a special book so your mom can see how much you love her and miss her." I nod and wipe the tears out of my eyes. "Is it okay if I give you a hug?" She opens her arms and Bribee lets her hug her for a long time, but I don't let her hug me. I go to the table and throw her stupid party favors on the floor. She's not gonna fool me, I only have one mother.

I didn't know there were so many different ways to have a party. At our house, Mom would get our cake and candles and stuff from the grocery store. Me, her, and Bribee would sing happy birthday and eat cake while we watched our favorite cartoons. Birthdays with Daddy meant giant parties with a DJ, and friends, and cousins that I didn't even know I had. I would eat carne asada and tres leches cake until I felt sick—but it was okay as long as I didn't throw up. If I did, Daddy would make me go in the house and lay down. But the best part was after we ate. That's when the colored lights would be spinning around and everybody would start dancing and acting crazy. Sometimes, we would laugh so hard that our cheeks hurt.

I already know that this party is gonna be a whole lot different from all the other parties that I've seen. While we were in the house making party favors, somebody had put up a giant tent in the backyard. Inside the tent, I count out eight round tables and one super long table near the front. All of them are covered in white table cloths with smaller red and white checkered tablecloths on top. I don't feel like counting all the chairs, but Kimi says there's enough for a hundred people.

"Look it!" Bribee says when we go back in the house. She runs over to a box on the floor and starts pulling out party hats, balloons, and decorations and stuff.

"We got a pretty nice birthday cake, too," Mrs. Gavilan whispers. "Would you like to see it?" When I nod, she goes over to the refrigerator and pulls out a really big box. She sits it down on the counter and we all crowd around it.

"I can't see!" Bribee whines and Kimi picks her up so fast that I don't even need to.

"What do you think?" Mrs. Gavilan asks as she pulls the lid up. Inside is one of the biggest cakes that I've ever seen. It says "Happy Birthday Angelique" in cursive, but that's not the only thing. On top of the white frosting is red, yellow, and blue balloons with colorful squiggly lines and sprinkles to match. The sugary-sweet smell makes my mouth water. And for a while, all I can do is stare.

"That's for me?"

"Well, you can't eat the whole thing by yourself," Kimi says. I know she's joking, but I still feel kinda silly.

"We're having quite a few people over today and I want to make sure that everyone has a chance to celebrate with us," Mrs. Gavilan says as she covers the cake back up.

I really wish we could eat it right now, but just knowing that it'll be in the refrigerator makes me feel really good—and really bad, too. I wish I hadn't thrown those party favors on the floor.

The guests start to arrive right before three o'clock, just like Mrs. Gavilan said they would. Car after car starts coming up the driveway and pretty soon there's a bunch of people sitting at the tables and standing around talking. There's a lot of kids, too, some older and some younger. Mr. and Mrs. Gavilan take us all around to say hi to everybody.

"These are our new house guests, Angelique and Bribee," they say every time we meet somebody new. Almost everybody seems really nice, but I can tell that some people don't want us here. Those are the ones with the fake smiles like Miss Dorsey.

When it's time to eat, me, Bribee, and Kimi sit at the long table with all the other kids. Mrs. Gavilan calls it the birthday table, because it's the only one that has party hats and noisemakers and confetti in the middle.

"Where's your mom and dad?" One of the older girls asks me. All of a sudden my chest feels heavy and the burger in my mouth feels dry. When I don't say anything, she shrugs. "My dad left us and started another family, and my mom had to go back to school. Now I stay with my grandma and grandpa." And then just like that, she turns to the girl next to her and starts talking about her horse.

After we eat, Mr. Gavilan carries out the cake and puts it on the table in front of me, only now there's a number eight candle right above my name. He lights it with a cigarette lighter and Mrs. Gavlian takes pictures for Mom, just like she promised. When I look around, it seems like everybody is staring at me. My stomach flip-flops and I wish I could hide. Mrs. Gavilan starts the happy birthday song and everybody starts singing with her. It's not so bad after a while, especially when Bribee starts clapping and giggling like crazy. Hearing her laugh makes me feel better.

When they're done singing, I wish to God that we can go home, but that Kimi and her family can visit us. I don't know if it'll come true with only one candle instead of eight, but I open my eyes and blow it out anyway. When I look over, Kimi is smiling at me. Maybe she read my mind and could tell what I wished for.

"Rachel, Jeff, you guys made it!" Mrs. Gavilan says with a big smile, but when Kimi looks over, her smile disappears.

Mrs. Gavilan hands the cake knife to an older lady and then goes over and gives the new people a hug. Mr. Gavilan goes with her. I can tell they're family members because the lady looks kinda like Paige—only her hair is blonde. The man is a little taller than Mr. Gavilan and he has a poochy stomach. There's three boys with them. Two of them look like they're around Bribee's age, but the other one is a lot older. I'm pretty sure he's a teenager.

"It's so good to see you guys," Mrs. Gavilan says as she hugs the kids. "I want you to meet Angelique and Bribee, our new houseguests." The five of them walk over to where me and Bribee are sitting. "Girls, this is my sister Rachel and her husband Jeff. These are my nephews Wyatt and Noah; and the young man growing like a weed over there is Craig."

All the boys have light brown hair and blue eyes like their dad. Mrs. Gavilan's sister and her husband shake our hands and give Kimi a hug. The two younger boys wave, but Craig just tosses his head back trying to be cool. I turn to Kimi and roll my eyes like we usually do with annoying people, but she's not looking.

"What's wrong?"

"My stomach hurts," she says, and then she leaves the table and walks back to the house. That happens to me a lot, but I always feel better after I go poo.

We eat and play and eat some more. Pretty soon the sun starts to set and the sky looks like it's on fire with orange and yellow flames.

"Alright kids, are you ready for a movie?" Mr. Gavilan asks after most of the guests leave. Bribee, Wyatt, and Noah run inside and grab a video that me and Kimi have already seen a million times. We don't wanna see it so we start complaining. "How about you and Angelique pick out something else and watch it upstairs in the loft?" I think it's a good idea, but I can tell that Kimi doesn't really want to.

"Come on Kimi, you can pick whatever you want," I tell her. She finally picks one of Paige's old movies about kids who go looking for a pirate's treasure while being chased by some bad guys. The movie is a little scary sometimes, but I like it; plus, it's really cool having our own space to hang out in while the adults are outside talking. At least it was cool until

Craig comes in and grabs the remote. He turns the movie off like we're not even there.

"Hey, we were watching that!" I yell, but he ignores me and flicks through the channels.

"That's better," he says after he finds a video with a half-naked hoochie-mama. The volume is down so low that we can't hear it, but Craig nods like he can hear the music in his head.

"Come on, Angelique." Kimi grabs my hand and pulls me up from the couch. We try to leave, but he stands in our way.

"Move!" I yell with my hands on my hips, but instead of bossing me around, he just smiles and touches my hair. I hit his hand away and we walk around him.

"What's his problem?" I ask Kimi once we get downstairs.

"He's a jerk and he's really mean," she whispers. "Whenever the adults aren't around, he turns to nasty videos. One time he even turned to a nasty movie where people were doing it." My eyes get big when she says that. "I tried to tell Mom and Dad, but he just lied and said it was an accident."

"Did they believe him?"

Kimi shrugs. "They already know he's bad. He punches his little brothers and makes them cry all the time. He doesn't even listen to his parents. He's supposed to take medication, but his mom and dad are in denial." I don't really know what that means but I nod anyway. "He used to punch me, too. But one time, Paige saw and slapped him right in his face!" When she tells me that, I start cracking up. Kimi laughs a little, but then she looks kinda sad. "But now that Paige is gone, he's even worse."

"Don't worry, I can look out for you," I tell her.

"Thanks, I'll look out for you, too."

10

Bribee fidgets and takes wide steps over the cracks and cement bumpers in the parking lot. "Walk right," I tell her and hold her hand even tighter. She listens for a little while, but then jumps from one foot to the other and almost lets go of my hand altogether. I grab her wrist and walk faster, but instead of complaining, she just starts singing one of her made-up songs about nothing, over and over again. She's getting on my nerves just like everybody else.

Everybody keeps telling me that I can talk to them about my feelings anytime I want to, but sometimes it's too much. Like when I talked to the therapist. I told her that I wanted to see Mom, but then my chest started to hurt so bad … Sometimes it's better to just keep your mouth shut.

Mrs. Gavilan opens the door for us and we step into an empty waiting room that smells like pine cleaner and cigarettes. She walks over to the lady at the front desk while I look around at the posters—a sunset, a sad-looking lady, and kids playing. They have stuff written on them about taking steps and recovering and stuff, but none of it really makes sense. I see shiny blue chairs that remind me of the dentist's office, and I see stacks of magazines on the coffee table, but I don't see Mom.

"We're scheduled for a one o'clock visit with Angela Bailey," she tells the lady.

"Go ahead and sign in. You'll be in room three down this hall to your right."

Mrs. Gavilan writes some stuff down on the clipboard in front of her and then motions for us to follow her. Room three has a brown couch, a coffee table, two chairs, some kids books, and a couple of bins filled with toys. Bribee walks right over and starts digging through one of them, but I sit in the chair next to Mrs. Gavilan and wait.

"When will it be one o'clock?" I ask. I look at the clock on the wall, but I can't figure it out.

"Do you see the little arrow?" she asks. "When the little arrow is pointing to the number one, and the big arrow is pointing straight up to the number twelve, it will be one o'clock."

My stomach feels queasy when I see how close it is, but it seems like it takes forever for the arrows to move. Pretty soon, I get up and start helping Bribee dig through the toy bin, just so I'll have something to do. I help her pull out all the Barbies, and then I pull out some blocks so I can try to spell out some words.

I look at the clock again. The big hand is way past the twelve and is almost on the two! My eyes start to sting, but I don't cry. "Did they tell her we're here?"

Before Mrs. Gavilan can answer, the door opens and a lady in baggy sweats and flip-flops walks in carrying a grocery bag. When Bribee sees her, she cries and runs to her, but I can't move. Her hair's a lot shorter now—not even to her shoulders, and she's not as skinny as she was when we last saw her. Seeing her look so different makes me sad because I missed it. And I missed her. She hugs us and we sit on the couch hugging and crying for a long time.

"You guys bein' good?" We both nod.

"When can we go home?" Bribee asks. Mom sighs and looks like she's about to start crying again.

"Whenever the judge says you can, but first, I have to get better. When I'm done here, I'm gonna get a better place for us—maybe a house with a nice backyard so you guys have a lot of space to play in." She kisses me on the top of my head and pulls me closer. "Babygirl, why are you bein' so quiet? You okay?"

I nod because I know she wants me to be okay, but how can I be when we have to live with strangers? And what about Daddy? I didn't always see him when we were at home, but at least I knew where he was. At least I could go see him, even if I did get in trouble.

"I'm sorry I missed your birthday," Mom whispers. "Did you have fun at that party?"

82

"They had the biggest party ever!" Bribee says before I can even open my mouth. "We had burgers, and a giant cake, and some presents and so many people…"

Bribee gets more and more excited, but Mom's face freezes into the same smile she gave Miss King when she complained about our house being dirty. That was right before she stopped letting Miss King come over.

"But it would've been better if you were there," I say hugging Mom as hard as I can. I don't wanna see the stupid playroom, or the dumb toys, or even Mrs. Gavilan, so I close my eyes and pretend that it's just me, Mom, and Bribee.

Mom tells us that this place is kinda like a hospital, but it's for people who are sick because of what chemicals make them do. "That's why I couldn't take care of you guys like I wanted to," she says. "But I'm learning how to live different so we can all go home."

I smile when I think about how nice everything's gonna be. I bet we'll have Captain Crunch all the time. We won't ever have to worry about roaches or poisoned pizza again. Plus, the kids at school won't tease us because we'll have clean clothes all the time. Maybe we can even have friends come over after school. But then my stomach feels sick.

"Mom, school is gonna start soon!" My heart beats really fast and I start to feel dizzy. "We have to go home so we can go to school!"

"Did they tell you when the next hearing is?" Mom asks Mrs. Gavilan.

"Our Notice says December tenth and we were told to enroll them in a school closer…"

I don't hear what they're saying anymore. But it doesn't matter. Everything is always gonna be, "No," and "I can't," and "The social worker says," or "The judge says." If I had magic powers, I would make everything different. Or maybe I'd just go to sleep until December. That way, when I wake up, the judge would let us go home.

"I brought you something," Mom says. She reaches down into the bag that I forgot she had and pulls out two packs of powdered donuts. She has apple juice, too. "I can't get a lot of stuff here, but they have some pretty good snacks."

She spreads out a napkin and then makes three stacks of donuts— one for me, one for Bribee, and one for her. Mrs. Gavilan doesn't get any *though. Mom talks about getting healthy, and making good life choices, and some other stuff, but after a while, I don't really hear what she says.*

"Did they tell you where Daddy is?" I ask.

"Locked up again, and he's probably not gettin' out for a while." She shrugs and goes back to talking about how good everything's gonna be when we go home in December. Bribee's excited to hear all about how wonderful Christmas is gonna be, but I just listen.

"I know I'm supposed to have an hour, but I need to go take care of some things," Mom says after a while.

I grab her and hug her as tight as I can. "No, don't leave." I hate crying like a baby, especially when I know it's gonna make Bribee cry, too, but I can't help it. We haven't seen her in a really long time, and kids need to be with their moms.

"You guys need to stop all that. I'm gonna see you in a few days, but I need you to behave, okay?"

I nod and wipe my eyes, but it doesn't feel like it's gonna be okay. It feels like nothing is ever gonna be okay again.

11

We get to the women's recovery center at 12:50. I know what time it is because Kimi and her mom and dad have been helping me learn how to tell time for weeks. Mrs. Gavilan signs in, and we go to playroom number three just like we always do. Bribee goes straight for the toys, but I pull out some of the Dr. Seuss books that they have. My favorite one is about a kid who doesn't want to get out of bed. I used to feel that way all the time because of the terrorists.

For a while, all everybody did was talk about the planes crashing into all the buildings. They talked about it on TV, and at church, and even when we went shopping. I got really scared and sometimes I didn't want to get up or go outside anymore—not even to ride the new horse that they let me name Shalooby. When I started having bad dreams about planes crashing into our school and everybody dying, Mrs. Gavilan had the principal put me and Kimi in the same class. I can't wait to tell Mom that the nightmares went away. I'm gonna tell her about me, Bribee, and Kimi dressing up like the Powerpuff Girls for Halloween, too.

The clock says 1:22 now. Mrs. Gavilan's been looking at it off and on for a while, but I'm not worried because Mom's always a little late. Last time she didn't come in until the clock said 1:33. I was sad that our visit was so short, but it wasn't her fault that she had an upset stomach. She felt so bad about bein' late, that she brought us a ton of snacks. We even took some back for Kimi.

A little while later, we hear the doorknob. Bribee jumps up, and I move the books to the table so Mom has a place to sit, but when I look up, it's not her. It's the lady from the front desk. She smiles at us, but for some reason, my stomach feels queasy.

"Carrie needs to speak with you for minute," she tells Mrs. Gavilan. "I can hang out with the girls while you do."

Mrs. Gavilan leaves and closes the door behind her.

"How about I read you guys a story?" the lady says. She picks a book up from the table and sits in the middle of the couch.

"Who's Carrie?"

She tries to smile at me, but I can tell it's fake. "Miss Carrie is the boss of this whole place."

I go over to the giant widow and pull some of the blinds to the side; Bribee does too. Every now and then, Mrs. Gavilan looks over at us and I can tell something bad happened. Maybe Mom's back in the other hospital. When Miss Carrie leaves, Mrs. Gavilan comes back into the playroom and the lady from the front desk leaves.

"Come sit with me," Mrs. Gavilan says as she sits on the couch. Bribee goes over and sits on her lap, but I just stand there.

"Where's my mom?" My eyes sting and something is pounding inside my head.

"Miss Carrie sent someone to your mom's room to check on her, but when they got there, they couldn't find her."

"Did they check the bathroom and the kitchen?" My head starts to hurt even worse and it gets hard to breathe. "She probably just went to get us snacks."

"They looked for her all around the property. They even checked other people's rooms," she sighs. "I'm sorry, Honey, but they don't know where she is."

"It's not a big deal," I say louder than I mean to. "She probably just forgot, she does that sometimes. One time when I was in kindergarten, she got so busy that she forgot to pick me up from school, but that didn't mean anything. She just forgot. Moms do that sometimes." I wipe away the tears and try my best to catch my breath, but it feels like somebody is pushing a fast forward button inside of me. "She just forgot!" I yell when she looks at me with sad eyes. "She just forgot!" I yell at Bribee when she starts to cry.

Mrs. Gavilan puts her arms around us and hugs us tight. I feel like pushing her away, but I don't.

12

"Why?" Bribee asks for the millionth time, but I don't know what to tell her. I don't know why she kept leaving rehab. I don't know why we couldn't just visit her somewhere else, and I don't know why it's okay for a judge to decide who can and can't be our mom and dad.

"Does that mean we're gonna have two moms now?"

"Why do you keep asking me?" I snap. "I don't know!"

She knows I'm lying, but I'm sick of talking about it. And I hate that new social worker. He never tells us anything, and anytime Mom and Dad try to explain stuff to us, it's like he gets mad or something.

"There's no reason to worry them unnecessarily," I heard him say one time. "In my experience, it's the best way to prevent maladaptive behavior."

I can't stand it when workers act like I'm an idiot—I'm about to start middle school. I mean, I can understand them not wanting to worry Bribee, but she's not stupid. If they let us know what's happening, we'll know what to expect. It's the not-knowing that makes us freak out. The funny thing is, I already know how to find stuff out.

Sometimes, after Bribee's asleep, I sit at the top of the stairs, or stand outside their bedroom door so I can hear what they're talking about. I almost got caught once, but I just told them I couldn't sleep 'cause of a bad dream, and they didn't think anything of it. That's how I found out about Bribee's dad. He's such an asshole, he didn't even wanna see her. He just offered to sign away his rights so he wouldn't have to pay child support. That's how I found out about Daddy, too. I knew he was locked-up

87

somewhere up north, but I didn't know he was filing petitions to keep them from adopting me—Bribee too, if they'll let him. Hearing that made my heart feel like I was flying higher than the clouds. I wanted to laugh and scream and say "I told you so" to anybody who thought he was a loser. But then I felt bad because I know the Gavilans really want to adopt us. I just wish they could understand that I love them, but I love my real family, too.

I'm pretty sure we'll never go back to living with Mom, and from what the social worker says, the judge probably won't let us live with Daddy either—even if his sentence is overturned. All I know is, it feels nice knowing that he wants us. I know everybody here wants us, too, although I wasn't sure about Paige in the beginning. It used to feel weird when she'd come home from college because everybody was always making a fuss over her. "Let's see what Paige wants to do."… "Paige and I are spending time together."… "We need to go shopping for Paige." I got so sick of it. But then she started hanging out with me and Bribee and things got better. Every now and then, she tries to boss me around, but most of the time she's really cool. She takes us places, she listens to music with us, and we go out for frozen yogurt at least twice whenever she's home.

I hate that her college starts in August, because she always misses the Labor Day party. That means she always misses my birthday, too, because for the last three years, we've been celebrating them together. I like it better that way though. I don't think I'd get as much stuff if we didn't.

Me and Kimi are out grooming the horses when Dad comes over.

"Hey guys, Uncle Jeff and Aunt Rachel are coming by with the boys," he tells us. "They'll be staying overnight and helping out with the party."

"Seriously?" Kimi complains.

"Honey, I know the boys are not the easiest to get along with, but you have to admit, they've been a lot better the last few times they've been here. That's the only reason we're letting them stay over. And because Craig's meds are finally working." He says that last part under his breath, but I heard him and I can't help but laugh. "It's just a couple of nights."

"Where are they gonna sleep? We don't even have room!"

She's grasping with that one. Paige left weeks ago, so they can use her room, plus the loft.

"We have plenty of room," Dad says sounding a little annoyed.

And then I get a brilliant idea. "Ooh, Kimi, you can sleep in our room! Like a sleepover for my birthday. We can stay up late and watch movies and stuff."

"It sounds good to me," Dad says, but Kimi just glares at me, like I stabbed her in the back or something.

13

You can always tell when we have visitors. Between the barking dogs and the sound of tires rolling over the gravel in the driveway, people couldn't sneak up on us if they tried. When they get here, Bribee follows Mom and Dad out to the porch, but Kimi goes upstairs. I guess she's still mad at me, oh well. When I peek out the window, I see their car making its way up the driveway, only it's not Aunt Rachel or Uncle Jeff driving—it's Craig. Man, they let him do whatever he wants.

The minute they get out of the car, Wyatt and Noah start running around like wild animals, and, of course, Bribee has to join them. It's a good thing though. She doesn't always get a chance to play with kids her own age, and I get tired of her always following me and Kimi around. I can't believe how different Craig looks. He's almost as tall as Dad and he's not scrawny anymore. He'd actually be kinda cute if he wasn't such an asshole all the time.

"Angelique! You're getting so big," Aunt Rachel says as she hugs me.

I'm not really sure what to say because it sounds like she's calling me fat, so I just smile and hug her back, Uncle Jeff, too. There's no way I'd ever hug Craig though. I wave at him just to be polite, but I almost wish I hadn't when he stares at me like a weirdo.

"Alright, let's get you guys settled in so we can get to work," Mom says. "Rachel, you and Jeff can have Paige's room. She has a queen-sized bed. Kimi will be bunking with the girls, so the boys can use her room. There's a trundle under her bed."

I guess it makes sense for the boys to sleep in Kimi's room, but I already know she's not happy about it. I hope they don't break all her stuff. That's probably why she's mad at me.

After they get settled in, they start talking about a bunch of boring stuff like jobs and houses and cars and stuff. Mom shows us what she wants in all the gift bags, and we start an assembly line so we can finish a lot faster.

"Hey Uncle Rob, check it out," Craig says when we take a break. He reaches into his back pocket and pulls out an iPod. The same kind Kimi and I've been begging for all year but can't have, because Mom and Dad say it's too expensive. "I just got the newest one, it holds over seven-thousand songs."

Man, he gets on my nerves.

"Do you even know seven-thousand songs?" Dad asks shaking his head. "I swear you kids are becoming obsessed with these gadgets. But I guess I can't blame you. We had our vinyl, and now everybody's using CD's—but I'm never getting rid of my cassettes."

"Uncle Rob, nobody uses cassettes anymore," Craig says, as if Dad's a moron. "Everything's digital now. You just download the songs you want for ninety-nine cents."

"That reminds me," he says, "I brought something for Kimi and Angelique."

Kimi and I stare at each other and then look at him to see if he's joking. In the entire three years that I've known him, he's never done anything nice for anybody—especially us. As a matter of fact, he's always been a bully. Whatever he's giving us is probably gonna be falling apart, or poisoned. He goes out to their car and comes back in carrying two big boxes that he sits on the floor by Kimi.

"I downloaded all of my music onto my iPod, so I don't need these anymore," he says. "And since you guys are starting junior high, you're gonna need a good music library."

Kimi stares down at the boxes like she's expecting something to jump out, but I'm pretty sure he's not gonna do anything mean with the adults around. I go over and take a look inside, figuring it has to be something broken or weird, but inside are a bunch of CD's.

"Are you serious?" I shake my head and pull out a couple. It's actually good music. "These are practically brand new."

Kimi frowns. "You're giving these to us?"

"If you want 'em," he shrugs. "You guys are growing up and I want you to have something cool. Plus, I know it's Angelique's birthday."

I can't help but smile when he says that.

"Awww, my nephew is maturing," Mom says as she puts her arm around Craig's shoulders. "Girls, what do you say to your cousin?"

"Thank you," Kimi says in a small voice. She doesn't even bother looking up, but it's okay because I'm grateful enough for both of us.

"Yeah, this is so cool. Thanks!" Maybe his meds really are working.

"Alright, let's clear up this mess," Mom says when we're done.

We made one hundred bags. All of them have a keychain, a magnet, a pen, and lots of candy inside. They also have Gavilan Realty printed on them. Dad tells everybody that the party is the best way to hang out with friends, show off his barbequing skills and advertise all at the same time.

Dad and Uncle Jeff head outside with slabs of meat for the smoker. "Kimi, honey, can you bring us a couple of waters?" Dad asks on their way out the door.

Kimi pulls two big bottles of water out of the fridge and takes them outside. When she leaves, Craig grabs one of the boxes of CD's and heads toward the stairs.

"Angelique, can you grab the other box and show me where to put these?" he asks.

"Sure." I pick up the other box and start to follow him but he steps to the side.

"Ladies first."

He follows me up the stairs and down the hall into the loft. I already know that Kimi will wanna help me organize everything, so it doesn't make sense to even take them out of the box. "Just put them here for now," I say as I sit my box on the floor. "We can put 'em away later." I turn around and bump right into Craig. "Oh, sorry," I mumble, and take a step back, but I don't know why he's so close in the first place.

"No, I need to apologize to you." He takes hold of my arms and looks at me really serious. He's not squeezing or giving me an Indian burn, but it still feels uncomfortable. "I know I wasn't nice to you before, and I just *wanna say, I'm really sorry." he smiles at me. "Aunt Darcy's right, you know. I've matured, especially since I started driving and playing football. You believe me, don't you?"*

I don't really know what he's talking about, but I nod. I also pull my arms back. I don't like him touching me, and I don't like him being so close. He never cared what I thought before, why does it matter now?

"Good." He reaches out and touches my shoulder like he's giving me some advice. "You know, now that you're in junior high, I can tell you things and I know you're old enough to understand."

A prickly feeling runs through me, and I can feel the hair rise on the back of my neck. "We should go back downstairs and help out. They're waiting for us." I step around him to leave, but he grabs me by the hand.

"Wait. I need to tell you something." I snatch my hand away and brace myself for the shove or the mean words, but nothing happens. He just stands there looking at me. "Angelique, I really care about you." He frowns and shakes his head like he can't believe what he's saying. "And now that we're both more mature ... I want ... I want you to listen to something."

Part of me feels like I should run downstairs and stay as far away from him as I can, but I don't. I stand there and watch him pull his iPod out of his back pocket instead. He slides his thumb around the wheel and I know he's looking for songs. He's been really nice to everybody since he got here, and I haven't seen him hit his brothers once. He hasn't even been talking back to his mom and dad—and he did just give me and Kimi all these CD's. Maybe he is different.

"Here." He puts his iPod in my hand and holds it there. "I want you to keep this until tonight. You can listen to anything you want—on two conditions." I don't know what to say, all I can do is nod. "I want you to listen to the two songs on this playlist, and I want you to make sure no one knows that I'm letting you use it."

"Why?" I pull my hand away because now I know he's up to something. I've seen all kinds of movies where jerky kids say that somebody can use their stuff, but then they run and say it was stolen. Or maybe he stole it himself and doesn't wanna get caught. He's just trying to get me in trouble.

"I want you to listen to the songs so you'll know exactly how I feel about you," he says. "And I don't want Kimi or the other kids to find

93

out because I don't trust them like I trust you. They'll probably break it just to get back at me."

I can't help but smile when he says that. Everybody knows his brothers break his stuff on purpose—but that's what he gets for being so mean all the time. I'm pretty sure Kimi would never do that, but then again, sometimes she acts like she hates him. I slip his iPod into my pocket.

"Ok, I'll give it back tonight."

"Are you okay?" Kimi asks when I get downstairs.

I guess everybody else is already outside cleaning and organizing stuff for the party, because she's the only one around.

"Yeah, why wouldn't I be?" I feel kinda bad for keeping stuff from her, but it's not like it's a big deal.

"Because you know how he is and you were up there a long time," she frowns.

"Lighten up, we were just putting the CD's in the loft." If I don't make a big deal out of it, she probably won't either, so I just walk past her and make my way toward the garage. "Are you coming?"

She follows me out, but her attitude and slowpoke walk tell me that she's upset. I don't care though, just because she can't stand Craig doesn't mean I have to hate him, too.

The minute we step outside, Mom hands us both a damp rag and puts us to work cleaning off two giant ice chest coolers. They're so big that Noah and Wyatt decide to use one as a hiding place from Bribee. Mom and Aunt Rachel are so busy laughing and talking that they don't even say anything.

"Ready or not, here I come," I hear Bribee yell from somewhere in the front.

A few seconds later she's running into the garage and asking us if we've seen the boys. We don't say anything, but then again we don't have to, their giggles give them away. Like all games of hide and seek, there's suddenly screams and laughs and little kids running all around us. They're annoying, but it's not a big deal—at least I didn't think it was.

"Get the hell out of my way!" Kimi screams at the top of her lungs.

She's never been the most cheerful person, but for her to scream at the kids that way is so strange that we all stop and stare. A few seconds later, Dad shows up in his grilling apron. Craig's right behind him.

"Kimi ..." Dad says in his calm voice. "Is there a reason you're screaming at the kids?"

Instead of answering, she just stands there with her chest heaving. I notice her eyes are watery, too. She's probably embarrassed because she got in trouble in front of everybody.

"I think you need a little break," he tells her. She doesn't even bother saying anything, she just throws her rag into the ice chest and stomps back into the house.

"Thank goodness I had boys," Aunt Rachel mumbles and sips from a glass of wine that I hadn't even noticed. Dad shakes his head and goes back to whatever he and Uncle Jeff were doing, and the kids pick right back up with their laughing, screaming, and running. Craig smiles and shrugs his shoulders. I expect him to go back to hanging out with Dad and Uncle Jeff, but he comes into the garage instead.

"Here, let me help," Craig says. He walks over and picks up Kimi's rag and then kneels down next to me to clean. I feel butterflies in my stomach. It's kinda weird being close to him, but it feels kinda nice, too. "So, did you listen to the songs yet?" he whispers when Mom and Aunt Rachel go back to gossiping. I shake my head because I haven't had a chance to. "Why don't you go take a bathroom break," he suggests.

I make sure the bathroom door is locked before I pull the iPod out of my pocket. I still can't believe he's actually letting me use it. Once the headphones are unraveled, I stick the earbuds in and press the center button but nothing happens. I slide my thumb around the wheel a couple of times, but again, nothing happens. My stomach drops. "Please don't be broken," I whisper, and panic starts to set in—but then I remember that I have to take it out of hold mode.

The first song has been playing on the radio a lot. It's a guy apologizing to a girl for all the bad stuff he's done this year. When he sings that he's sorry from the bottom of his heart, I can't stop myself from smiling, and by the end of the song, the muscles in my cheeks are aching.

"Wow, he really has changed," I whisper.

The second song seems kinda familiar, like something Daddy used to listen to back in the day. It's one of those mellow songs that reminds me of being back home. And for a while, I'm lovin' it. But then I remember that Craig said he wanted me to listen to it because it's how he feels about me. My stomach drops again, but this time I'm not sure what to do. The computer-like voice is saying stuff that doesn't make sense—things like, "I can't live my life without you," and "I wanna be your man." They're even talking about kissing and a wedding ring! This has to be a joke. The minute he sees me, he's gonna laugh and tell me that he was just playin' around. He has to be. Why else would a cute high school guy wanna be my boyfriend?

I feel stupid for listening to him, so I don't go back into the garage, and I don't look at him when he tries to get my attention. Why should I? It doesn't make sense to talk to somebody who just wants to make fun of you, so I stay close to Mom and Aunt Rachel. It's obvious that they wanna talk about grown-up stuff, because they start talking about people without using names, and saying stuff without actually saying what happened. When they get tired of trying to speak in codes, they send me to go check on Dad and Uncle Jeff. That's when Craig comes over. He acts like he's joining their conversation about college football, but I know better because I can feel him staring at me.

"Hey, are you mad at me?" Craig asks when I eventually go inside to find Kimi. I'm not really sure of what to say, so I don't even bother answering. I'm pretty sure Kimi's upstairs, so I just keep walking. "Look, I know this is scary for you," he says a little louder than a whisper. He reaches out and takes hold of my hand to stop me. "This is scary for me, too." When he says that, I turn around and look at him. He's not laughing or smiling or anything. The look on his face is so serious that I start to feel bad that I didn't believe him.

"I'm sorry." He lets go of my hand and shakes his head. "I should've known you wouldn't understand—nobody does." When he looks at me, I see tears in his eyes. "I can't help the way I feel about you," he says, and my heart melts. "Angelique, I'm in love with you. Will you be my girlfriend?"

The butterflies in my stomach go crazy, but I nod to tell him yes. He doesn't have to tell me to keep our relationship a secret, but he does anyway. He says I have to be especially careful about telling girls my age, because they'll all be jealous that I'm dating a guy in high school. I think he's right about people not understanding though. Mom and Dad told us that we're not supposed to date until we're sixteen, but that's five whole years away! We can't help it if we fall in love before then.

14

The sun goes down a lot later than normal during the summer, and once it gets dark, we usually start winding down to get ready for bed. Luckily, having company changes all that. Tonight, the grown-ups light up the fire pit and lounge around with eighties music and glasses of wine. And even though it's late, Bribee and the boys still run around like a bunch of wild animals. Eventually, everybody gets tired of them, but instead of having to shower and go to bed, they get to take their pillows and blankets into the den for a Disney movie marathon.

I don't want Craig thinking I'm a baby, but Bribee keeps nagging me to sit inside with her. On top of that, Kimi's her old self again, and if I stay outside with Craig and the grown-ups instead of watching the movie, she's gonna get suspicious.

"Watch out Bribee," I say during a boring part of the movie. When she sits up, I move away from her and step over one of the boys so I can make my way upstairs to our bathroom. When I'm done, I wash my hands and open my bedroom door to something I definitely wasn't expecting. Craig. He's kicking back on my bed with his fingers laced behind his head.

"I was wondering when we'd have a chance to be alone," he smiles, and the butterflies in my stomach start going crazy again. I'm not really sure what to do when he gets up and walks over to me, so I just stand there feeling like an idiot.

"Are you sure you're okay with being my girlfriend?" He holds my hands and I feel like jumping up and down inside. "It would break my heart, but I'd understand if you changed your mind."

I nod, because for some reason, my voice won't work. He kisses my hands like I'm a princess, and then stares at me for so long that I feel weird and have to look away. And then just like in the movies, he takes my chin and lifts it towards him. I close my eyes, and he kisses me on the lips. It's the softest, sweetest, and most wonderful thing ever. When I open my eyes, he smiles at me and I feel like my insides are melting. I wish I could tell Kimi that we're together.

"You're so pretty," he whispers. I feel his hand on the back of my head and we kiss again. It's not as soft as the first time, but it's still really nice—until I start gagging.

"Ugh, what are you doing?!" I pull away from him and his slimy tongue.

"It's okay, you're my girlfriend now." He sighs as if he's annoyed or something. "Just open your mouth and move your tongue around."

It's gross, but I see couples tongue-kissing all the time, so I just do it. These kisses aren't soft, and after a while, it gets hard to breathe. I try to pull away, but he just holds me tighter. And then his hand is inside of my shorts.

"Stop!" I push away from him and he glares at me.

"What the hell is your problem?" he snaps. "I just asked you and you said yes!"

My stomach drops and goosebumps spread across my arms. "I don't think I wanna be your girlfriend after all." I try to leave, but he stands in my way.

"Oh, so now you wanna change your mind? What the hell did you think boyfriends and girlfriends did?" A million mixed-up thoughts go through my mind and I can't think of the right words to say. "Oh, I get it," he says. "You're a tease." He frowns and shakes his head like he can't believe that I tricked him. "Just a slut who gets guys worked up, so what—you can laugh with your friends?!"

I shake my head no, but before I know what's happening, he grabs my hand and shoves it inside the front of his shorts. He's not wearing underwear. I try to pull my hand away from his privates but he won't let me go.

"You caused this and you're gonna take care of it." A crooked smile spreads across his face, and that's when I realize that he's the same old Craig that he's always been. "Tell you what," he whispers and then he grabs me by my hair. "If you don't wanna take care of it, I can always get your little sister to do it for me."

My stomach turns and a prickly feeling creeps through me. "I'm gonna tell," finally comes out of my mouth, but it doesn't sound like my voice.

"No you're not, because eleven-year-old sluts get sent away. And if that happens, your little sister's gonna be all by herself."

Why does everybody lie? Some of the girls on our street are always talking about how much fun they have hooking up with boys. In the movies, women always have those dreamy smiles on their faces, and the girls in the videos are always showing off their stuff like they can't wait to do this. I wanted it to be like that. But now I know they're all lying. What he's doing isn't fun, and it doesn't make me feel good or sexy. What he's doing makes me turn my head and close my eyes. It makes me cry.

"Just relax," he tells me, but it's hard to breathe with him on top of me.

How could you let this happen? I ask myself.

"Shut up!" he snaps when I can't stay quiet, but then he moans in my ear.

Why would he even think about doing this to Bribee? She's just a little kid.

"I love you," he groans. His fingernails scrape against my scalp and he pulls my hair.

If this is what it's like to have a boyfriend ...

And then he's off of me. When I open my eyes, he's pulling up his shorts.

"It'll feel better next time," he smiles. And then he's gone.

Next time.

Those words float around in my head while I put my panties and shorts back on. I feel sore and sick to my stomach and I can't stop shaking. And then I hear him outside my door. I can't understand what he's saying, but I can tell he's mad. My stomach drops. Somebody must've heard us. I wait for the door to fly open. Any minute now, Mom or Dad, or somebody else is gonna be giving me nasty looks that tell me exactly how nasty I am. I stand there waiting, but nothing happens. I force myself to go over and crack open the door. When I look in the hallway, Craig has Kimi pinned against the wall. I can't hear what he's saying to her, but I don't need to. He pushes himself against her and touches her in places that should be private.

"Now I have two girlfriends," he says, then he lets go of her and walks downstairs.

Kimi stares into space for a while, but then she looks up and sees me. Neither of us say anything. We don't have to.

15

"Mom's waving for us to come down," Kimi says as she looks out my window, but I don't say anything. She sighs after a while. "Angelique, we have to tell."

"No!" I pull my knees up to my chest and lean back against the wall.

"She's on her way up." Kimi steps away from the window and sits on the floor across from me. A few minutes later, there's a knock on the door and Mom comes in.

"Ok you two, what's going on?"

"Nothing, I just have a bad stomachache," I mumble. I can tell she doesn't believe me.

"Honey, can you bring Angelique a ginger ale?"

Kimi looks at me. She's probably hoping that I'll change my mind, but I can't because it's different for her. I mean, Craig's her cousin, and she was just a little kid when he started doing stuff to her. Plus, everybody knows she hates him. I'm the one who wanted a boyfriend. I'm the one who used his iPod, and I'm the one who let him ... If we tell, they're gonna find out that this whole thing is my fault. My eyes sting but I try my hardest not to cry.

After Kimi leaves, Mom sits down on the floor next to me. "You know, Sweetie, you can tell me anything."

A queasy feeling hits my stomach and my heart starts pounding in my ears. How did she find out? Kimi's been with me this whole time. Craig must've told on me!

"Sweetie, you don't have anything to be embarrassed about," she says. And that's when the tears come. "It's okay." She puts her arm around me and pulls me close, but it feels like a weight is being pulled off my chest. She doesn't think I'm nasty after all. "We talked about this, remember? It's just your body's way of preparing you to be a woman."

When I look up at her, she has a smile on her face, and then it hits me—she thinks I got my period.

"I saw some things in the laundry last night," she says as if she read my mind—or at least part of my mind anyway. "Pretty crummy way to start your birthday, huh?" My head is pounding, but I nod because I don't know what else to do. Luckily there's a knock on my door. "Come on in," Mom says. Kimi comes in with a can of ginger ale. She stares at me for a little while and then puts it on my night stand.

"I have some ibuprofen if you need some," Mom says, and then kisses me on the forehead. "But you should come down soon, I'm sure your guests are wondering where you are." She hugs me again and stands up to leave. "Ten minutes?" I nod and she leaves.

Outside, everybody is talking and laughing and eating and having fun like it's a normal day. But I don't feel normal. I don't think I'll ever feel normal again. Me and Kimi make our way toward the tent and that's when I see Craig staring at us, at me. My stomach drops and I freeze because I'm not sure what to do. Kimi just avoids him, and if she can do it, I know I can, too. It'll be fine, we'll just watch out for each other just like we promised. I almost start to feel better, at least I do until Craig walks over and whispers something to Bribee. My heart starts pounding, and all of a sudden, I can't catch my breath. He kneels down and she climbs on his back because she doesn't know that he'll hurt her.

And then I'm running as fast as I can. "Stay away from her!" I scream. "You don't touch her!"

Craig's eyes get big and he looks around to see who's watching, but I don't care. I'm not gonna let him hurt Bribee. I slam my fists into his stomach and scream like a crazy person.

"Geli, stop! What are you doing?" Bribee yells.

He tries to grab my arms and push me away, but feeling his hands makes me fight even harder. Bribee falls to the ground. I hear the shock in people's voices and the yells for Mom and Dad, but I don't stop, not *even when the tears make it hard for me to see. Somebody grabs me from behind and pulls me back, but I don't stop kicking and screaming at him.*

"Let her go!" Mom says to whoever's holding me. She kneels down in front of me and puts her arms around me. I grab her and hold onto her as tight as I can. I wanna tell her about what Craig is doing, but I can't catch my breath and I can't stop shaking. I close my eyes and try my best to breathe again.

"It's okay, it's okay ..." Her voice is calm as she rubs my back and I can feel my mind start to settle. "Tell me what happened," she whispers. What's wrong?"

"She's crazy—that's what's wrong!" Craig yells behind her. "She attacked me for no reason! I wasn't anywhere near her!"

I hear mumbling and whispering. When I look up, everybody's staring at me with frowns and twisted faces. They all think I'm a monster or some throw-away kid that nobody wants. My head spins and all I wanna do is hide.

"Aunt Darcy, I'm sorry, but some of these foster kids are psycho!" Craig yells. He leans in and looks right at me. "She needs to be locked up."

Maybe I am psycho, because all of a sudden, I'm back on my bed and he's on top of me. "I can always get your little sister to do it for me," he whispers. When he smiles, a cold feeling creeps down my back and I know he's about to hurt us.

I pull away from Mom and grab a grilling fork off the table next to him. The wood handle feels heavy in my hand, but I hold it tight and use every ounce of strength I have to shove it into his stomach. I wish I was strong enough to make it come out of his back, but I can tell I'm not even close. When I let go, it dangles from his shirt like some weird magic trick. For a little while, the whole world is quiet. When I look up, Craig's eyes are so big that he looks like a cartoon character. Like any minute a loud horn's gonna blow and his mouth is gonna hit the ground. Just thinking about it is so funny that I almost start laughing. A dark stain spreads across the bottom of his shirt. He looks at me like he's scared and it makes me smile, because now I know he's not gonna mess with us anymore. And then the sounds come back. I hear screams and yells, and Bribee's crying, but I can't see her and I can't move because somebody's holding me down.

And then I'm being taken away.

103

People talk to me at the hospital, but I don't talk to them. They give me medicine and tell me that I have to stay for a while.

I have a new social worker now. She tells me that Kimi told Mom and Dad about Craig. She tells me that we can't live there anymore because they didn't protect us. She tells me that Bribee is with another family and I can visit her when I'm better.

I guess Craig was right. She's all by herself now.

16

WHEN I'M DONE TALKING, the only thing I hear is the fan from Aaron's laptop. I notice that a couple of people are teary-eyed, but most of them won't even look at me. *How could they?* I think. *Not only did I embarrass myself, I just stood here and made myself look like a psycho. I should've kept my mouth shut. Maybe then I wouldn't be feeling like I'm standing here in shit-stained underwear.* When I feel the tightness pull at my chest, I know I need to get it together. *A full-scale anxiety attack is not gonna help your case, Angelique. Just breathe and keep going.* I take a deep breath and exhale slowly through my mouth. *They need to hear this kind of stuff, and if they wanna look at me crazy, that's on them.*

"Here's what I've learned since working at a group home," I tell them. "All kids are vulnerable, but kids in foster care are even more at-risk. Yes, our families didn't take care of us like they should have. But what about *your* family? Are there family members that you need to be wary of? If so, don't bring those people around the kids in your home. Just because there's no case, doesn't mean they're safe.

"In the end, social services decided that me and my sister were in an 'unsafe environment.' And even though the Gavilans pressed charges against Craig, even though they were trying to adopt us, and even though we had lived there for three years …" I shake my head… "They didn't just move us, they split us up." I take some time to swallow the lump forming in my throat. "My sister was placed with a family who ended up adopting her pretty quick, but my situation was a lot more complicated."

I feel kinda stupid when I laugh, but it's all so ridiculous, sometimes that's all I can do. "Think about it," I tell them. "What if Aaron called you and asked you to open your home up to an 11-year-old girl. You'd wanna know what was wrong with her, right?" Almost everybody nods their head. "What if she had a bad attitude and mouthed-off all the time? What if her mom was a heroin addict and her dad was locked up for murder? What if she was not only on psych meds, but had also been in a mental facility for stabbing a 16-year-old boy who may or may not have been her boyfriend?" I look at the dude with ass-beating tendencies. "Would you let a kid like that into your home?" And just like I thought, he looks me dead in the eye and shakes his head no.

"Well guess what, the case managers don't always have that much information. That's the kind of stuff you might not find out until later." I notice a couple of people are looking around and acting nervous. *Looks like somebody's changed their mind.* "I swear I'm not tryna scare you guys. I just want you to know the reality of some of the kids who may end up in your homes. Their experience might be a lot better than mine, but it might be a lot worse, too." My voice cracks and I can feel my eyes start to water. "If you don't hear anything else I'm saying, please hear this." I take my time and look around the room. "The fact that these kids are in foster care means that they've gone through something traumatic. That's what makes them angry or depressed or sneaky or whatever."

I take a deep breath and shake my head. "Listen, I don't have time to go into detail about every home I got sent to after I got separated from my sister, but I can tell you that things didn't get better. I've been in sixteen different placements, and every time I moved, I was the one who had to adjust." I know I shouldn't be raising my voice, but I can't help it. "Think about that! All those different rules, different foods, different schools, different ways of talking, different ways of cleaning, and definitely different ways of getting punished whether I did something wrong or not! But I can tell you one thing they all had in common: almost all of them expected me to be *grateful* and *obedient*. How does a kid do that when their whole life has been turned upside down?!"

I calm myself and look at Mr. Ass-beater. "These kids need help. So instead of demanding gratitude and obedience, how about you try to be patient and understanding. They shouldn't have to worry about your ego on top of everything else they're dealing with." Something tells me that I've said too much. Did I take some stuff out on them? Probably. But I'm not sorry about it. If somebody decides not to be a foster parent because of what I said, then they weren't ready to have foster kids in the first place. Strangely enough, that makes me feel pretty good. So much so that I give them my fakest smile and clap my hands together.

"So, now that I've thoroughly stressed and depressed you, do you have any questions?" There's some awkward laughter, but nobody says anything, so I take a sip from my bottle of water. "Don't be shy…I'm not. And you might not get this opportunity again." There's a smirk on my face, but I'm not playing. I don't think I could stand up here again.

The grandma-looking lady raises her hand and I point to her.

"First of all, thank you for sharing your story." She shakes her head with a frown. "I can't imagine having to deal with all of that as an adult, let alone as a child." Almost everybody in the room agrees and I force a tight-lipped smile. "I have two questions," she says. "First, you talked about the family that almost adopted you, but I was wondering if you had any other positive experiences with foster parents. And second, what was it like for you after you left foster care?"

I pause and think about her questions for a little while before I answer. "There were some decent people," I finally admit. "Unfortunately, it's the bad ones that tend to stand out more in my mind. Plus, almost everybody started out cool, but it always got heated after I'd been there for a while. And as far as aging-out goes, my situation was a little different because I didn't emancipate on my eighteenth birthday like a lot of other people. I ended up falling behind in school because I got moved so much. Luckily, my worker fought to keep my case open until I got my diploma in January."

Aaron and his staff catch me off guard with their applause, and everybody else follows their lead. "Congratulations!" he says. He's all serious and clapping so hard that I have to stop myself from laughing. "That's a huge accomplishment when you understand what's going on behind the scenes," he says when the room quiets down. "We have programs and services and even legislation to help our kids with school, but it's a constant struggle. They still have the highest dropout rate and the lowest graduation rate, so anytime we hear success stories, we celebrate!" His staff members start raisin' the roof and doing these stupid little dances in their seats. They're so damn corny that I can't help but laugh.

"Well, in that case," I say with my best bashful grin, "I'm also taking classes at River Beach Community College." They give me an even bigger round of applause, and of course, I gotta put extras on it. I thank them like I'm getting an Academy Award or something. Pretty soon, my cheeks start hurting from smiling so much.

"After my case was finally closed, I went to stay with one of my friends and her mom, but that didn't work out. I didn't mind helping them out with the bills, but when I started working, her mom expected me to give her my whole paycheck!" Melinda frowns and shakes her head just like she did the first time I told her that story. "I wanted to keep some of my money, so I started crashing with different people. That's the first time I heard about Perdido's Transitional Housing Program. I went in and applied but they had a three-month wait list. I didn't care though, I called them every week just to make sure they knew I was serious." A few people laugh and I can't help but do the same. "Two and a half months later, they called me to tell me that I could move in. It was like winning the lottery. So now, not only am I taking classes at

108

RBCC, I'm working part-time at a group home, *and* living in my own apartment."

When the applause dies down, Melinda's friend Brenda raises her hand and I point to her. "Angelique, do you have contact with anyone in your family?"

"Yes, and no." Most of them look just as confused as I do. "Every year since I was thirteen, my mom gets herself together and tracks me down in September, right around my birthday. Sometimes, I have no idea how she finds me." I notice a few people have a horrified look on their faces, but I just smile and shake my head. *They don't know my mom.* "At first I used to get mad 'cause I thought it was proof that she could get her life together if she wanted to, but then I realized that she can only handle real life for a few weeks at a time. My dad is still locked-up. I tried to see him a couple of times, but he says he doesn't want me to see him behind bars.

"What about your sister?" someone asks.

A dull ache forms in my chest and I take a deep breath. "After we got separated we had visits for a while, but we lost touch after she got adopted. I think they live somewhere out in the Valley. I worry about her a lot 'cause I know kids who got adopted and then ended up in foster care—or on the streets." My voice cracks again and I blink away tears. "My sister's not going through that, which is why I'm gettin' my life together. I'm gonna make sure she's taken care of." I take another deep breath and wipe away the tears that managed to sneak out.

Once again there's dead silence. "Any other questions?" Aaron asks softly, but I'm pretty sure they all know I've reached my limit. "Angelique, thank you so much for sharing your story with us," Aaron says. He initiates a more subdued round of applause and I make my way to the back of the room. People offer me sympathetic smiles, and I realize that I'm not as annoyed with them as I was when I first started.

When I take a seat next to Melinda, she gives my shoulder a slight squeeze and I feel the corners of my mouth move into a smile. That's when I notice the brochures. There are three stacks grouped together by a band of paper, like the strips they wrap around new stacks of cash from the bank. She has them piled one on top of the other, but I know they're different because I can see slightly different colors on the sides. I recognize the top brochure because it's the same one I got when I first applied to THP. It has a bunch of information about the program, like how it's supposed to help us become self-sufficient and stuff. It also talks about the type of services we get while we're in the program.

"Before we wrap up for the evening," Aaron says, "I'd like to invite Melinda Brooks up to discuss some of the transitional housing programs for the youth in our county. This will be especially helpful for those of you who are fostering teens."

Melinda hands a stack of brochures to a couple of Aaron's staff members and they pass them out one row at a time. "Good evening everyone," Melinda says as she makes her way to the front. "I won't take up much of your time. I just want to let you know about the state-sponsored housing programs for current and former foster youth."

Current foster youth? That can't be right. She must be talking about group homes.

"I'm curious," she says, "by a show of hands, how many of you are planning to foster kids ages three and under?" I already know that everybody wants babies, so I'm not surprised when more than half the people here raise their hands. Melinda scans the room and asks, "What about ages four to seven?" Quite a few hands go down, but some go up, too. Overall, you can tell it's less though. "Alright, how about ages eight to twelve?" Her tone makes me think she already knows the answer. When I count six people, my heart sinks because I know what that means for the teens. "Ages thirteen and up?" she asks. Brenda and the guy next to her raise their hands—and I'm pretty sure he's her husband.

Dang, nobody ever wants to help teens.

Another lady raises her hand, but then it's like she reconsiders and lowers it again. "I definitely want a younger child," she says, "but I'd be open to a younger child and their teenage sibling."

I cut my eyes at her. Switch out the words and you'd think she was talking about fashion or something. *I definitely want a plain skirt in light blue, but I'd be open to one that came with a brown belt.*

"There's nothing wrong with having preferences," Melinda says with a smile. She's talking to everybody, but I know she sees the crazy look on my face. "If that's what leads to a successful placement, then we're all for it. And you never know, people change their minds all the time."

I shrug and give her a little nod because I know she's right. I guess if they can keep kids stable when they're young, maybe things won't be so jacked-up by the time they're teens.

"Regardless of how old they are when they go into foster care," Melinda continues, "most of our kids face the same issues when they emancipate. They don't have the life skills they need to be successful after foster care, and they don't have stable housing." She picks up the three brochures and lifts them for everyone to see. "These are making their way around, but if you know of anyone who qualifies, please take more and pass them along."

I didn't even know they had two other transitional housing programs, so when the staff members come back my way, I motion to them so I can get some brochures, too. Maybe I can find a better placement for Max.

"The first program is called the Transitional Housing Placement Program, or THPP," Melinda says holding up the brochure. "This is a program for current foster youth between the ages of sixteen and eighteen. Instead of a foster home or a group home, the kids in this program are placed in an apartment with another teen in the program."

I'm sure I look stupid with my mouth hanging open, but I can't believe what I'm hearing. THPP sounds just like the program I'm in, only it's for younger people!

"In our county," Melinda continues, "adults do not live in the apartments; however, a mentor and case manager live on the premises to make sure the kids are supervised. They also teach life skills so the kids can live more independently once they emancipate from foster care."

A queasy feeling washes over me and my mouth goes dry. "Melinda, how long has THPP been around?" I ask, trying to keep my voice steady.

"If I'm not mistaken," she says with a slight frown, "THPP became a permanent program in 1998, but not all counties participated, and that's still the case today."

I shake my head and try to swallow the lump in my throat. I've had at least a half dozen social workers since I turned sixteen, and not one of them ever said anything about this program. *All that time I was bouncing around foster homes and group homes and I could've had my own apartment when I was sixteen?*

"... Because everything we've seen tells us that kids do better in a positive family environment. That's why a lot of counties opt-out of this program in favor of foster homes," she says as if she's reading my mind. "Unfortunately, there aren't enough good foster homes out there. THPP is an amazing program, but the reality is, most sixteen and seventeen-year-olds aren't ready to live on their own. They tend to struggle with ..."

That may be true for some people, I think. *Hell, some of the residents in my building aren't ready to live on their own and they're grown. I could've handled it though. If they would've just given me a chance, I would've taken it seriously and handled my business from day one.*

"... So our county has only approved funding for *ten* youth to participate in this program."

Ten teens in the whole county? Hell, no wonder nobody knows about it! The workers are probably keeping it secret and holding spots for the kids that don't ever give them any problems. That's alright though, I'ma start telling kids like Max to bring it up in court, that way the judge will force their workers to let them in. Some people think they're slick, but I know how this system works, too.

"The second program is called the Transitional Housing Program Plus, or THP-Plus, which is the program that Angelique is doing so well in." She smiles at me and I put extras on it by getting all cheesy and giving everybody a Miss America wave. They laugh just like I knew they would.

"THP-Plus is a two-year program similar to THPP, but it's specifically for former foster youth between the ages of eighteen and twenty-four. The program covers all expenses—rent, utilities, food, clothing and transportation—so residents can focus on going to school and getting a job. Once they're employed, we help them with a budget and they gradually assume responsibility for some of their own living expenses."

The whole room starts to buzz with excitement and I know just how they feel. I did the same thing when I first found out about the program. Once I got in, though, I realized that there were a whole bunch of problems. It's still amazing and I know I'm lucky to be in it, but it all depends on who's running it.

"We also set up a special savings account for each participant," she continues. "Each month that they're in the program, we match the amount of money that they save—up to $100 a month. So, if a participant puts $50 into their program savings account, the program matches it by placing an additional $50 into their account. Once they leave the program, they're able to access those funds to get their own apartment or a car, or whatever else they choose."

"How many spaces does that program have?" a lady asks.

"Right now, our county has funding for forty-five young adults," Melinda answers with a grin. "And we're in the process of increasing that number to an even fifty by the end of the year."

Aaron initiates another round of applause, but I can't help thinking about how five more people are gonna change things in our building. I do a mental check of the folks who don't have roommates right now. *Thank goodness I'm in a studio 'cause I don't have to worry about that.*

Melinda sighs and smiles, but somehow it doesn't make it to her eyes. "The last program officially started on January 1st of this year, but there are a lot of kinks that still need to be worked out. It's called THP-Plus Foster Care, but you may hear it referred to as AB-12 or Extended Foster Care." The

Creekside staff and a couple of foster parents nod, but the majority of us have no idea of what it is. "This is a voluntary program that allows emancipated foster youth to remain in foster care until their twenty-first birthday. If an eligible young adult has left foster care, AB-12 also allows them to return to care. "

I'm speechless. I remember seeing something about AB-12 at work and I know that there's an upcoming training on it, but I had no idea that they were tryna get kids to stay in foster care.

"As long as they're in school, working, or in a job readiness program, the young adults in THP-Plus Foster Care will get funds for housing and living expenses. Like foster care, they will be dependents of the court. That means they'll also have a social worker assigned to them."

"Why would anybody choose to go back into foster care?" I blurt out without thinking.

Melinda seems caught off guard by my question. "Well ... not everyone has friends or family members that they can turn to when they leave foster care, and as you know, THP-Plus has a long waiting list. If a young adult is broke and homeless, and no one else is offering help, the system doesn't seem so bad anymore."

I know she's right, but there's no way in hell I'd ever be desperate enough to go back into foster care.

17

THE KNOCK ON MY NEIGHBOR'S DOOR breaks my concentration, but I don't mind because it's a good time to rest my eyes. I stretch across my futon with a yawn and put my book face-down on my chest so I don't lose my page. I hate that I have to waste a Saturday reading about a bunch of prideful and prejudiced, proper-talking people. *Why does the reading for this class have to be so boring? Nobody cares about a bunch of old-school chicks and their search for a husband with deep pockets.* Although, that's exactly the kind of stuff that Reality TV is made of. It's taking me forever to finish this book and I'm not even halfway through—plus, I still have to write the paper! Granted, it took me a while to finish those Lovecraft stories, but that's because I had to use a dictionary for practically every other sentence. His stuff was old-school, too; but it was creepy, so at least it was interesting.

There's another knock, but this time it's louder. *Oh, that's my door!* I'm so happy for the distraction that I don't even care if it's Liz doing a pop-up inspection. When I open the door, Dani's standing there with a guilty grin and a box of Captain Crunch.

"Whaaat, Miss OCD neat-freak? Don't tell me your apartment is jacked-up!"

"Yeah, yeah," she rolls her eyes. "I've been busy and I let my place go a little bit. You want this or not?"

"Yes, I do." I take the box from her and open my door wide. "I'll even share."

Dani steps inside and glances around my apartment, which is basically a mirror image of hers. Both of us had even decided to keep the program's furniture instead of dishing out money for new stuff. The only real difference is how we decorated.

"You got more pictures," she almost whispers as she walks over to my wall. All of a sudden, she looks back at me like I did something special and it catches me off guard; but then I remember—it's not as easy for her.

She could probably guess who everybody is because she's heard me talk about them enough times, but it feels good to be able to share this kind of stuff with somebody. "That's me, that's my little sister Bribee, and that's my mom ..." As I point out all of my friends and family members, I notice that she's smiling, but she has a faraway look in her eyes. I can't imagine losing everything from my childhood. Maybe that's why she and Luis can relate to each other so well. " ... And you've already seen the picture of me and my dad."

"Uh huh, with his fine self," she laughs. I shake my head, put the cereal on the table and make my way to the kitchen.

"That's really cool," she says. "I don't have any pictures of my family, not from when we were little."

"I feel you. I had to beg and plead just to get those."

I don't talk to my aunts and uncles that much, and God knows Emiliana has never been the easiest person to deal with, but at least I can kiss up to them or guilt them into giving me pictures. Dani can't even do that. Most of her family's still alive, but they might as well be dead since they don't want anything to do with her. That shit blows me away, because it's not even her fault.

I rinse off a couple of bowls and spoons, dry them with a clean dishtowel, and hand them to Dani so she can put them on the table.

"So whatchu been up to, aside from work and school?" I ask.

"Not much. I don't really have time for anything else. Although ... one of the girls from work did invite me to her church tomorrow," she says, plopping into a chair.

I put the milk on the table and sit across from her without saying a word.

"She's cool," Dani says. "But I'm not sure if I should go, 'cause church people are strange, and it could be a cult or something."

"Yeah, well you know I don't do the church thing."

All of a sudden, she gets quiet and starts mixing her cereal around all slow, as if it needed to be stirred. "I wanna go ... but I don't wanna go by myself." I roll my eyes, because I already know what's coming next. "Will you come with me?" she asks. I tilt my head and stare at her like she's crazy. "Come on Angelique, just this one time. I need you there in case it gets weird." Three hours of some slick dude telling me that I'm going to hell is *not* how I imagined spending my Sunday, but then I think about all the times she's had my back and I soften up a little. "Candace said there's gonna be food, and you know church people can cook!"

That makes me laugh because she definitely ain't lying about that! All of a sudden, it hits me and I glare at her.

"What? I got something on my face?" She wipes her mouth a couple of times.

"You set me up."

"What are you talking about?" she asks looking around.

"All this time I've known you, I have never once seen your apartment dirty. You bribed me with some cereal so I would go to church with you!" I put extras on it and shake my head real slow, like I'm offended.

"What?" She laughs because she knows she's busted, but she still tries to play innocent. "I don't know what you're talking about. As a matter of fact, I gotta go finish cleaning my apartment right now." She shovels the rest of her cereal into her mouth and makes her way to the door with chipmunk cheeks.

"You're a mess!" I can't help but crack up at her 'cause she's not even a good liar.

"Candace said their service starts at noon," she says as she opens my door. "So I'll be here tomorrow morning at eleven-fifteen."

"You owe me big-time," I tell her, with my finger in her face. But she knows I'm playin' around. If it was anybody else, I wouldn't have bothered, but Dani's my girl. I know how hard it is for her to step inside of a church.

She turns to leave but then stops dead in her tracks. When I follow her gaze, I see a plastic bag that somebody must've put on my step while we were eating. We both bust up laughing this time, because inside the bag is another box of Captain Crunch cereal. I look around to see who the real slob is, but all I see are the newbies, Orlando and Ernesto, bringing in boxes with this month's moving crew. I knew Chris was scheduled to help out because he's not working and he needs the volunteer hours. But I'm surprised to see Omar pushing a dolly stacked with boxes, 'cause he has a full-time job.

"What's up with that?" I ask Dani, but I get my answer as soon as I see Ashley leaving the apartment that Monet used to have all to herself. She's wearing too much makeup again, but her long weave is cute. It's light brown and parted down the middle with blonde highlights on both sides. Unfortunately, her clothes are gonna clash with the dress code. She's wearing a white tank top, with no bra, and *very* short cutoff jeans. Omar slows down and stares at her like she's a t-bone steak, but she's the one eating it up.

"That is badness waiting to happen," Dani sighs.

Suddenly, Monet storms out of the apartment with her usual can of strawberry soda. She plops into one of the patio chairs near my door and glares across the courtyard in the direction of the moving crew. Her knees bounce up and down, which is a good thing. It means she's taking her meds again.

"What's up, Money?" Dani asks.

"That new chick they have me rooming with … she's working my nerves!"

"She hasn't even moved in yet," Dani laughs.

"I know, but she's already pissing me off. First, she walked up in here actin' like she owns the place. She's tryna move everything around and telling me where I should be putting *my* stuff. What the hell is 'fung shway' anyway?"

Me and Dani can't help but laugh. We figured Ashley was bougie, but that's doing too much. She must be putting on a show for Omar.

"And she's already scheming!" Monet says in a lowered voice. Me and Dani look at each other and then scramble for chairs so we can get in on all the gossip. "She's tryna sneak some dude up in here—tonight! I told her that they're doing pop-up inspections, and I'm not tryna get in trouble." She shakes her head and sips some of her soda. I can't help but cringe every time I hear her swish it around. In my mind, dry-mouth is better than rotten teeth, but I guess everybody handles meds differently.

"She was in group when they announced it, so if something happens, she can't say she didn't know," I remind her. "You can't be a snitch, but if they ask … hell, I'd squeal like a pig."

The three of us look over and watch Ashley shamelessly flirt with Omar whenever the case managers are out of sight.

"Just try not to get caught-up in her mess," Dani warns. "At this rate, she's either gonna get kicked out, or she's gonna end up pregnant. Either way, you're probably gonna get a new roommate."

We all nod because we've seen it before. Suddenly, Chris looks over in our direction and throws his hands up.

"Aye, we gettin' a game a bones goin' in a couple hours. Y'all down?" he yells from across the courtyard.

"Did he just say 'bones'?" Monet frowns and shakes her head. "Why does he talk like that?

"Chris is a little different, but he's cool," I tell her. "He's one of the few dudes I don't mind dealin' with." She looks at me with a raised eyebrow and I can already tell, she thinks we have something going on. "It's not like that. We were in the same foster home for a while. He's like my brother."

119

I can't stand when people assume that just because you're friends with a guy, you gotta be sleeping together or something. Maybe that's how other chicks are, but that's not my thing.

She thinks about it and then tosses her head back the way my dad used to do. "Aye, you puttin' some food in?" she yells back at him.

"Of course!" Chris grins.

Dani raises both of her thumbs to let them know she's in, too. But all I can do is sit there mad because I still have homework.

Playing dominoes and cards has become a serious event around here, which is something else we have Melinda to thank for. She was always getting on us about isolating ourselves and not reaching out to our neighbors, so when somebody donated sets of patio furniture, we started hanging out in the courtyard. The cool thing was that we could hang out all night, as long as we didn't get too loud and the furniture didn't get damaged. And then there was the food. Residents didn't always have money, but we almost always had food, especially the folks with EBT cards. When we got hungry, we didn't stop playing and go inside, we just brought the food out.

At first, people like Amanda and Dani (and sometimes me) would end up feeding everybody, because folks weren't tryna contribute, but we shut that down real quick. Now, everybody who wants to eat has to contribute something. One dude tried to be funny by bringing out some plain saltines, but we weren't playin'. Amanda brought out a block of cheese and a butter knife and we ate them crackers right along with everything else. Or that time India boiled enough Ramen Noodles to fill a crockpot. After we clowned her, we got our bowls and forks, and ate like we were having a gourmet meal. Chris took it to a whole new level when he started making wings though. We have some serious food now, and if enough people put in, we can eat off the leftovers for days.

"Text me when the food is out," I tell Dani.

"Alright, what are you bringing?"

I know my choices are limited because I haven't been grocery shopping in a while, but then it hits me, I have more than enough of the perfect appetizer. "Hors d'oeuvres de la Captain Crunch and leche del moo cow."

She and Monet both stare at me like I'm crazy.

"You know you're gonna get clowned, right?" Dani warns me.

"Yep, but I'm gonna eat good tonight, and you guys are gonna have a nice breakfast tomorrow."

18

AN ANNOYING BUZZ WAKES ME up from the best sleep I've had in months. I slide my cell out from under my pillow and see two texts from Dani.

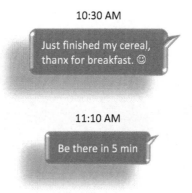

10:30 AM

Just finished my cereal, thanx for breakfast. ☺

11:10 AM

Be there in 5 min

Dang! I lay there for a minute trying to figure out how I can get out of going to church with her and her holy-rollin' coworker. I'm not feelin' this in any way, shape, or form—but I know she needs my support. I remember when she first told me about getting caught-up in the life, and how scared she was that if she ever stepped foot in a church, she'd be struck down by lightning. She wasn't playin' either. I told her that I didn't know much about religion, but I knew that if God struck her down for something that wasn't her fault, he wasn't much of a God.

My AC is giving off the perfect chill and my bed is more comfortable than it's ever felt, but I force myself to get up. Of course the minute I do, there's a knock on my door. *Dang!* I take a deep breath and answer it without even checking to see who it is.

"Seriously Angelique?" Dani says the minute she sees me. "Candace and her sister are supposed to be here in like, fifteen minutes, and you're not even dressed!"

I can't help but roll my eyes. "It's not even gonna take me that long." I close the door behind her, grab some clothes out of my dresser, and head into the bathroom to get ready. "By the way, you look nice all dressed up in your skirt and heels, but I'm wearing jeans and flip-flops," I announce after I brush my teeth. "And I ain't playin', if somebody says something or looks at me crazy ..."

"What are you gonna do, start a fight in the sanctuary?"

All of a sudden, she starts cracking up, which makes me laugh, too. I know it's twisted, but I can't help thinking about all the YouTube videos of people coming to blows at church. We're both still chuckling about it when I step out of the bathroom, but then I see that Dani is practically delirious. Her face is red, tears are streaming down her face, and she's struggling to take a breath. It was funny, but it wasn't *that* funny. Then it hits me, *this is nerves!* She's talked about having anxiety and nervous laughter in group before, but this is the first time that I've actually witnessed it.

"Ahh, you need to breathe," I joke, trying to hide how worried I am.

She takes a deep breath, but then something changes and all of a sudden she's sobbing. I've never seen Dani lose it before, and for a split second, I have no idea what to do. As I stand there watching, I start to feel an ache in my chest and it's almost more than I can handle. It's like being at a funeral and listening to somebody who's bawling. Their grief hits your heart in a way that makes you break down, too. But I know I

123

have to put my feelings aside, so I ignore the tightness in my throat and blink away my tears. When I put my arm around her, I wanna tell her that she doesn't have to go, and she doesn't have to be scared of a building, or the people in that building. I wanna say something that's gonna make her feel empowered so she stops feeling ashamed about what happened to her. Most of all, I wanna tell her that everything's gonna be okay, but the best I can do is let her cry on my shoulder—and then it happens. In the middle of taking a breath, she snorts and starts laughing again.

"Should I go get somebody?" I know she's lost it now, and this is way beyond my capabilities. Apparently, my expression shows how scared I am because she looks at me and starts cracking up even more.

"No, I'm okay, seriously," she finally says. She takes a deep breath and wipes her tears away with the palms of her hands. "I didn't mean to freak you out. Sorry," she laughs, and suddenly, she's her old self again.

"As long as you're okay," I tell her, but I'm not buying it. I've never seen anybody flip the switch like that. I don't even know if that's normal.

Dani walks into the kitchen, pulls a paper towel off the roll, and uses it to blow her nose. After she throws it in the trash, she pulls a compact from her purse and checks her makeup. It looks fine to me, but she dabs on powder and mascara anyway. When her phone chimes, she glances at the screen.

"They're here," she says.

I'm still tryna process what just happened, but I grab my backpack and follow her out the door. As we walk across the courtyard, she speaks to people in her usual upbeat voice, like she's perfectly fine. Nobody would've guessed that she was having a full-on breakdown five minutes ago.

"Check it out," Dani says.

Omar's baby-mama is dropping off their little girl, and the three of them look like a perfectly happy little family. Especially all hugged up like that. He's a player and I wouldn't touch him with somebody else's ten-foot pole, but I have to admit, he's a really good father. I can't help but smile whenever I see him and his daughter together. She's a daddy's girl, just like I was.

"I wonder if the new girl knows about this situation," I mumble. When we walk past Monet's place, I see Ashley looking out the window and she does not look happy. "I guess she does now."

19

"YOUR CHURCH ISN'T A CULT, is it?" That's the first thing I ask after Dani makes all the introductions. She looks at me like I have a third head, but I know she was wondering the same thing. "What? I wanna know what I'm getting into."

"I hear you," Candace laughs. "And no, we're not a cult. We sing, somebody talks, we study the Bible, and we eat. That's basically it. In and out in about an hour and a half."

An hour and a half? That's good to know.

Less than ten minutes later, we pull into the parking lot of a couple of buildings that I pass by on my way to campus. "I never even realized this was a church," I tell them. "I thought these were medical offices or something."

"Yeah, we've been coming here for a few years now," Candace says. She waves to a couple of guys directing traffic and that's when I notice how packed their lot is.

After we park, we make our way over to the main area and I notice that Candace's sister is dressed in jeans and flip-flops like I am. As a matter of fact, almost everybody I see is dressed casual. Some of them are even tatted up and pierced, but that doesn't stop me from feeling nervous. *I hope they don't try to embarrass us.*

"If somebody gets the Holy Ghost and starts falling on the floor, I'm leavin'," I blurt out. "That shit's creepy as hell!"

"Angelique!"

"What? Dani, you know most churches are about two things—Holy Ghost seizures and makin' money!"

She shakes her head without even looking in my direction. I know I need to stop acting up and embarrassing her, but I wanna make sure they know that I'm not the one. Other people may fall for some smooth-talkin' shyster, but that's not me.

"Honestly, I used to feel the same way," Candace admits. "I didn't grow up in the church, and I was skeptical the first time I attended. Every church is different, and yes, some of them are creepy. But let me try to put your fears to rest," she says as we step inside. "Here, only church members are expected to tithe, so you can keep your money. And I haven't seen anybody have a seizure yet—unless you count Mr. Whitaker, but he has a medical condition. If you see that, don't leave, call 9-1-1."

Oh, she got jokes. Maybe this won't be so bad.

Candace introduces us to some of the people hanging out in the foyer. They seem friendly enough, but I'm glad they're not tryna hug up on us like they do each other. *I wonder how many of these smiles are fake.* We pass through another set of doors into a high-school sized auditorium with tinted blue mood lighting and elevator music playing in the background. Candace's sister leads us to a row of empty seats and I take in the scene around me. A small wooden podium with a cross is planted in the middle of the stage, but staggered behind that is a set of drums, a keyboard, guitars, and mics. They even have a sax.

I lean forward and look past Dani so I can get Candace's attention. "Is this a concert?" I ask, pointing towards the front.

"No, our church has a worship team instead of a choir."

As if on cue, a group of people walk up on the stage and start situating themselves. They're not dressed up in robes or even suits and choir dresses. As a matter of fact, they look just like everybody else does. All five of the guys are in jeans and shirts with collars, and all three girls are wearing regular stuff that you'd see at the mall. They're not hoochified, but they're definitely not dressed like nuns either. As a matter of fact, I hate showing my legs, but I'd consider wearing a blue jeans dress and black leggings like the chick on the keyboard.

"Good morning and welcome," the guy in front says into a mic, but his voice is drowned out by the buzz of everybody talking. He motions toward the back of the room and taps the mic with his hand. "Let's try this again," he says after a pause. This time his voice blares from every speaker in the building and he gives a thumbs-up to whoever fixed the problem. "Good morning and welcome. Let's stand up and go to the Lord in prayer."

I force myself to my feet and watch almost everybody, including Dani, close their eyes. He prays about gratitude and stuff, but for the most part, I just think about my empty stomach. I was so busy focusing on Dani's mini breakdown that I forgot to eat breakfast. Surprisingly, their sound isn't bad for Christian music. If I had heard their stuff on the radio, I would've thought it was just another love song about somebody struggling to stay faithful. It's definitely not the holier-than-thou organ music that I was expecting. After a couple of songs, the lead singer tells us that we can sit down and another older guy walks onto the stage.

"Good morning. My name is Bob McClure. I'm the Senior Pastor here at Calvary Hill River Beach. I want to welcome you and thank you for coming. Let's open in prayer."

Dang, they just prayed! I look around and watch everybody bow their heads—again. While they do, the band steps off the stage and takes up seats in the front row.

"As many of you know, we use different types of spiritual gifts and ministries to glorify God and to help each other," he says after the prayer. "For example, some of us teach and some of us sing. Some of us travel around the world sharing the love of Christ while others stay at home and live it out in their daily lives. Some have been given such amazing powers that they're able to work miracles ... in the children's ministry." Even I laugh when he says that, because I know how bad Christian kids act. "Well, we have a guest this morning. He has a unique ministry that glorifies God using the very special gift of butt-kicking—but it's all in love." A grin spreads across Pastor Bob's face. "I can see that some of you are concerned, but it's okay." He holds up both hands as if he's calming people down. "Trust me, when I tell you that you will be blessed. Please help me welcome Vincent Marks."

Most of us give a polite round of applause, but a few people sound off like a celebrity just entered the building. A distinguished-looking dude with a Tony Stark beard makes his way to the podium carrying a big backpack and a pool stick case. He's wearing jeans and a collared shirt like a lot of the other guys here, but I can tell that he's not from River Beach, because he's wearing dress shoes. They might even be cowboy boots.

"How y'all doin'?" he asks with a slow Southern drawl and a warm smile. "Now for y'all who don't know, I'm kinda into martial arts." A few people laugh but I have no idea what the joke is. I watch as he puts his stuff on the floor and opens up his case, but instead of pulling out a pool stick, he pulls out a Samurai sword!

What the hell?

"I'ma try to get Pastor Miguel up here to volunteer for a demonstration. Y'all wanna see that?" He twirls his sword making it blur like a windmill out of control, and the whole auditorium goes crazy. Meanwhile, a nervous-looking dude walks up on stage like it's the last place he wants to be. A couple of guys from the audience each bring up a chair and Vincent arranges them kinda close together.

This may not be a cult, but these people are definitely crazy.

"Pastor Miguel, I'ma have you lay down across these two chairs and I'ma put a towel over your shirt so it don't get too messed up—or so you can wipe up the blood," he chuckles. Pastor Miguel's eyes get huge and he turns to walk off the stage. "I'm just kiddin' ... I'm just kiddin'," Vincent laughs. Suddenly he has a dead-serious look on his face. "But make sure you hold still." You can tell he ain't playin' now, but we all crack up laughing anyway.

Vincent puts down his sword and helps Pastor Miguel lay back on the chairs. His head, neck and shoulders end up on one seat and the back of his thighs end up on the other. Then he pulls a towel out of his backpack and lays it across Pastor Miguel's stomach and chest. I have no idea what he's about to do, but I know from stories about my granddaddy that if you put a Southerner and a big knife together, something crazy's about to go down—and that's when it happens. Vincent pulls a watermelon out of his backpack and puts it on top of the towel—on Pastor Miguel's stomach! The entire church goes crazy with applause and laughter, but I just sit there with my mouth hanging open.

"Is this what churches do now?" I whisper to Dani. She shrugs and shakes her head, but I can tell she's into it by the way she's smiling. To be honest, I'm kind of into it, too. It's definitely different than what I expected.

"Now, don't laugh," Vincent warns Pastor Miguel after the audience quiets down. "Believe me, when I cut, you wanna hold still." Of course the minute he says that, Pastor Miguel breaks out in nervous laughter and his abdominal muscles make the watermelon bounce up and down. Vincent leans his head back and starts cracking up right along with the rest of us.

"Alright, here we go," he says, picking up his sword again. He twirls it around a couple of times and stands over the Pastor with a determined look on his face. When he raises his sword, my heart starts pounding and I realize that I'm holding my breath. He brings it down slowly a few times to calculate his movements, and I am literally on the edge of my seat. Suddenly he sweeps the sword down quick—with a yell, and the watermelon splits in two on Pastor Miguel's stomach! As the pieces hit the floor, Vincent yanks the towel off of him to show us that he's not hurt, and then he uses the towel to clean his blade like it's the most normal thing in the world.

"Thank you, Jesus," Pastor Miguel whispers with his eyes closed tight. I'm sure he's putting extras on it, but it doesn't stop me and everybody else from cracking up. Vincent helps him to his feet, they embrace, and the Pastor steps off the stage—real quick.

"Lemme tell you why I became a Marine, an expert competitive shooter, and a martial arts expert," Vincent says. "As a kid, I was abused by people who were s'posed to take care of me, and when I got old enough, I swore that I would always be able to defend myself."

Vincent proceeds to tell us about his childhood, and I'm absolutely floored. His dad was a drug-dealing pimp who didn't want anything to do with him. He was molested on more than one occasion, and he was left for dead by a pedophile. Besides that, he had a stepfather who routinely tortured and tried to drown him. His mom's husband was so abusive that she had to sneak her kids out of a window in the middle of the night so they wouldn't be murdered. I know that kind of stuff can jack with people's head, so I'm not surprised when he talks about having PTSD. He said it was so bad that he had to go to counseling, because it started messing up the relationship between him and his own family.

His whole story is surreal, but I already know that kind of stuff happens. As a matter of fact, some of my neighbors had talked about similar things happening to them during group. I'm not gonna lie though, I've never heard a grown man stand up and talk about being abused, and I definitely never thought folks would be talking about this kind of stuff in church.

All the church people that I've ever known were always putting up a front and acting like they were perfect, but this dude didn't come across like that. He basically said that he was grimy before he started going to church, and still struggles with the grime now. Of course, then he started in with the whole Jesus thing. About how his biological father eventually "got saved" and how that changed his life around. After his dad got churched, Vincent ended up going, too. He said Jesus had changed his life so much that his feelings about his stepfather had even changed. Now he has a ministry where he goes around talking to abused kids who are locked up in juvie.

"I want kids to know that what happened to them wasn't fair, just like what happened to me wasn't fair," he says. "I want them to know that God can take all that mess and turn it around when they're livin' for Him. That's what Romans 8:28 is all about."

Dang, I should've known this was coming.

"... And we know that all things work together for good to those who love God, to those who are called according to His purpose. That means that when we choose to love and follow God, He'll take whatever happened to us and use it for His good plan.

Or God could've just stopped it all from happening in the first place! I feel myself getting heated and pretty soon I'm struggling to stay in my seat. *I'm so sick of hearing about how powerful and loving God is. If he's so damn wonderful, why the hell would he stand by and allow nasty-ass people to hurt kids? Why would he let anybody suffer when he has the power to stop it? And if he's real, why can't he just show up and say something? If people knew he was real, maybe they wouldn't turn to drugs and maybe they wouldn't abandon their families.* I feel like an invisible hand is squeezing my throat. *Maybe God's choking the life out of me right now*, I think as I blink away tears.

"I want young people to know that God loves us all so much that He gave us free will. He gave all of us the ability to choose or reject Him. That's how *real* love works." Vincent glances around the room and his eyes settle in our area. "Real love don't hold you hostage and it definitely don't force itself on you."

I look over and see tears streaming down Dani's face. I should've known that comment would make her feel some kinda way.

"... Since the beginning of time, He's showed up. He's showed miracles, He's sent prophets, and He gave us His Holy Scriptures. But we're all such hard-headed sinners that we refuse to listen! Now, maybe we haven't been murderers and abusers, but if we're really bein' honest, we know we've broken God's laws." Vincent raises his hand. "I know I've lied, I've stolen things, I've taken his name in vain ... I've practiced idolatry and a whole bunch of other things. It's part of our nature. We've all committed crimes against God, and when we commit a crime, we gotta pay. That's why we were all on a fast-track to hell."

Ahh, there's the obligatory hell reference that I was waiting for.

"But that's not what He wants for us!" Vincent scans the audience and shakes his head. "I want these kids to know that hell wasn't created for them. The Bible says it was created for the devil and his fallen angels, but when we choose to reject God, we choose hell by default."

Here we go with this shit again!

"... The Word of God came to the earth as a human so we could all reconnect with our Creator. That's what the cross is all about. Jesus took the punishment and died for the sins that *we* all committed, but He didn't stay dead. God's Word is greater than death, so He rose up from that grave and went back to His rightful place in heaven. God knows our nature and He knew that we could never reconnect with Him on our own. The Bible says that even when we think we're good, the best we have to offer Him is like filthy rags. There's nothing we could ever do to save ourselves, but God made it real easy for us. All we have to do is admit that we're sinners, believe that Jesus died for us, turn towards God, and ask Him to guide us. As a matter of fact, let's pray right now. If there's anybody in here who wants to accept God's gift of salvation, I want you to repeat after me."

I bow my head 'cause I don't want anybody tryna call me out, but I watch Dani out of the corner of my eyes. *Don't do it ... don't do it ...*

"Lord Jesus, I admit that I'm a sinner," Vincent says. "Today, I turn from my sins and turn toward You. I believe You died for my sins. I ask that You come into my heart and be my personal Savior. Thank you for saving me ..."

My heart drops when I see Dani's lips moving. *Dang!* I don't want her ending up like one of these crazy-ass church people.

"If you prayed that prayer out loud or silently, I'ma ask you to do one bold thing," Vincent says. "We're all gonna stand up right now, and I want you to make your way up here to the stage so I can welcome you to the family."

I didn't even realize the band was on stage again, but they start playing as everybody stands. About a dozen people start walking toward the stage and folks start clapping like crazy. Luckily, I can breathe easy because Dani's not one of them.

20

WHEN THE SERVICE ENDS, we walk over to a picnic area and stand in line for street tacos. The smell of grilled meat calls my name and I have to swallow a couple times to keep from drooling. I watch people start off with empty plates, but by the time they inch their way to the end of the line, those bad-boys are filled! The closer we get, the more my stomach starts talking to me. Aproned servers in hair nets and plastic gloves have formed an assembly line of heavenly deliciousness. I'm not really feelin' chorizo or carnitas, but they have carne asada *and* pollo asada—which is my absolute favorite. They also have refried beans, rice, tortillas and a whole separate table with stuff like salsa, cilantro, jalapenos, and diced onions.

Man, church folks know how to throw down when it comes to food!

"So, what did you guys think?" Candace asks, pulling my attention away from the food.

"It was a little crazy at first," Dani says, "but I really liked it."

"Yeah, that didn't even seem like church," I admit. "Everything was cool—except for the whole Jesus speech."

"That was kinda the whole point," Candace smiles. "Otherwise, it would've just been a motivational talk with a samurai sword. Jesus was the reason he was able to change his life."

I nod, but I don't say anything because I don't feel like getting preached at again. "I liked when he was talking about his life," I eventually admit.

"It's the same thing you did at that foster parent training—except you're a heathen," Dani laughs. I put my hand on her shoulder and slowly extend my arm to push her away and she laughs even harder. "Angelique, get me a couple of chicken tacos and some rice. I'm gonna go stand in line for something sweet." She tosses her head toward the dessert table. "You guys want anything?"

"Just, bring me something good," I tell her.

Candace and her sister shake their heads, and Dani walks across the courtyard to a slightly shorter line. They talk about buying Vincent's video and his book, but I don't say anything because I purposely left all my money at home. Plus, all I wanna do is focus on filling the empty plates in my hand.

"Hey Candace... Hey Teri," a voice behind me says. I recognize it instantly and turn around with a Cheshire grin on my face. "Angelique?" Brenda tilts her head in one of those frowning smiles and catches me off-guard with a hug. Strangely enough, I'm not really that annoyed. "I didn't know you went to church here!"

"I don't. I'm just visiting," I tell her as the servers start piling food on my plate. "Candace invited my neighbor and I came with her." I know they're wondering, so I explain the connection. "Brenda was one of the people at the foster parent training that I spoke at on Friday."

"God is about to do something here," Brenda announces as her plates are filled.

I look at her crazy and all three of them start laughing.

"Brenda doesn't believe in coincidences," Candace explains. "So when stuff like this happens, she's convinced that God is working something out."

"Alrighty then ..." *Dang, even normal people start acting weird at church.* I scan the crowd for Dani 'cause I'm about ready to go now. She's still working her way through the dessert line, so I head over to the condiment table. Of course the three of them follow me. Nobody says anything while we add stuff to our tacos, but I already know it's coming.

"When was the last time you went to church?" Brenda asks as we sit at an empty table. I notice that she's not eating with the rest of us. Her plates are covered with napkins.

"I don't know. Probably the last time somebody died? I don't do church."

"Exactly! But it just so happens that you get invited here, on the day Vincent Marks is speaking?" She puts extras on it by frowning like she's thinking hard. "Hmm, let's see. He's an amazing speaker; he had a very rough childhood; he's engaging, and he uses his experiences to help young people." Her eyes get wide as she looks at me. "That sounds like somebody else I know."

I roll my eyes and we all laugh.

"Well, I gotta go find my husband and kids," Brenda says as she stands to her feet. "He's probably talking somebody's ear off while my babies are starving." She walks around and gives us all side hugs. "Think about what I said Angelique, because God is definitely working something out with you." She slides her plates off the table and makes her way back to toward the main building with a smile on her face.

"Sorry, I took so long," Dani says when she finally joins us. She puts two plates in the middle of the table. They're filled with different types of cupcakes, cookies and mini pies. "I couldn't decide what I wanted, so they basically gave me a sample platter."

"Yeah, in case you haven't noticed, we like to eat around here," Teri laughs. "They don't call us Calorie Hill for nothing. Speaking of food, our church barbeque is coming up. If you guys don't have plans, you should come. All you need to bring is an empty stomach, and maybe some running shoes. They'll have a bunch of different games, but dodgeball is always the main event."

"It sounds like fun," Dani says, and for some reason, I'm nodding my head and agreeing.

21

I'M TIRED and Tuesdays are the worst. Having to stay on point with school is a struggle in and of itself, but then I gotta go straight from there to dealin' with a bunch of girls who are struggling just to be normal. On top of all that, I gotta go to group and spend an hour and a half listening to drama … It's too much!

At least I'll get to eat some bomb-ass burritos and cookies.

I get to the common room with ten minutes to spare. As always, everybody's either on their phone or standing around socializing. I don't have time for that right now because I'm on a mission. I head straight over to the food table for the slice of chicken burrito that I've been dreaming about all day, but when I get there … *Oh hell no!* Instead of burritos, the staff picked today of all days to get some damn sandwiches. *Dang!* My chest tightens up and I swear to God, I feel like flippin' the damn table over.

Week after week they had us up in here eating burritos and now that we're hooked, they just take 'em away and give us some janky-ass sandwiches? Hell, I got bread and sandwich meat in my refrigerator! If I wanted a damn sandwich, I would've made a damn sandwich.

I put eight of the biggest, juiciest strawberries I can find on my plate and then grab five chocolate chip cookies from the dessert platter. Do I feel bad about it? Not at all. When I take my seat, a couple of folks look at my plate and then cut their eyes at me with their mouths all twisted.

"Good evening everyone," Melinda says as soon as she walks through the door. Everybody moves into their seats and the buzzing starts to die down. She goes through the usual routine of checking in and getting praise reports, but I'm honestly not feeling it today. I'm sick of having to sit through lame-ass group meetings where people just bitch and complain the entire time. *What the hell is the point of doing all of this anyway? It's not like anything's gonna change.*

" ... Anyone else?" she asks after folks stop their whining, but of course nobody says anything. Nobody ever really talks about anything anyway. We just sit here wasting time because those are the rules. "Is there anything specific that needs to be addressed before we move on?" She glances around the room. "Well then, I have a question for the group. How do you handle special days, like Christmas or birthdays, when it brings up painful memories?"

I get a queasy feeling in my stomach and I'm suddenly blinking away tears.

"I used to hate Christmas," India laughs, suddenly breaking the silence. "In foster care, it's more like Halloween. You goin' door-to-door, never knowin' whatchu gettin' at the house you're at." A few people nod and laugh. "Seriously, sometimes you hit the jackpot and sometimes you don't get shi– ... nothin'."

"Thank you," Melinda says, probably for speaking up and for watching her language.

"Rod, you remember the Hutchinsons?" Amanda asks. He rolls his eyes and folds his arms across his chest. "They did Christmas real big," she tells us. "They decorated everything, they cooked, they even had Christmas music playing. I remember we got presents from our social worker, but they wouldn't put them under the tree. That should've been our first clue, but we didn't think about stuff like that because we were just kids. We were just excited, 'cause we never saw Christmas like that before. But when their family came, they made us stay

139

in our room, and we had to eat and open presents by ourselves." Amanda shrugs it off, but Rodrick looks like he wants to kill somebody.

"Hell, Christmas was crazy for me before foster care. My pops didn't stop beatin' my ass just 'cause it was a holiday. Seemed like that made it worse." We all look over and stare at Ernesto because dude never says anything. "When I turned thirteen, my dad came over and tried to take my new Playstation so he could get high. I got in his face—he broke my jaw."

Some people stare at him like they can't believe what he's saying. I don't know why though. We've been hearing these same crazy-ass stories for years.

"So how do you get through those days when everybody expects you to be happy, but the memories and the stress take you somewhere else?" Melinda looks around the room like we're all supposed to have the answer.

"Sleep," Ernesto tells her.

"Yeah, but sometimes you can't just go to sleep," Amanda says. "Plus, that stuff can give you nightmares." Him and a few other people nod like they've been through it.

"I don't want stuff from my past messing up what I'm trying to do now, so I just try to have a good time," Dani blurts out. "We may have had some crazy holidays back then, but I'm goin' all out now. That's why I'm the one who decorates, I'm the one who cooks, and I'm the one who dresses up. I'm gonna celebrate the way it should've been done back then."

"That's right—getchu some empowerment girl!" Rodrick shouts and they all bust up laughing. I almost crack a smile myself.

"I like that," Melinda says. "So what about birthdays?" She may be asking the entire group, but she's looking at me. I have to fight the urge to walk out.

It's the same thing," Monet says staring out into space, but then she looks at Melinda and shrugs. "Celebrate."

"That's right," Orlando says. "Cause I'ma always party on my birfday. Matter a fact … I'ma be up in the club like …" His

140

silly-ass throws up his hands and starts dancing in his seat. It's so random that almost everybody starts cracking up. I don't. I just get more annoyed and, surprisingly, it has nothing to do with his poor hygiene—this time.

"All I know is, I'ma take care of business so my daughter don't have to go through all that," Monet says. "I want her to have good memories."

The minute it's out of her mouth, Ashley whips her head around and drops her jaw. "You have a daughter?" Monet nods with a smile on her face. It's the first real smile that I've seen on her in a long time. Ashley frowns and shakes her head. "I thought you were gay?"

Monet shrugs. "And ...?"

"Wait, how old is she—and where does she live?" All of a sudden, Ashley looks offended. "And how did I not know this? I'm your roommate!"

"Why don't you two discuss that later?" Melinda says and then turns back to the group. "Do we have any other ideas about getting through the holidays?" She looks around, but nobody says anything. "Do any of you feel like you're just bearing through it until the day is over?" Almost everybody raises their hand, myself included. "So it sounds like a few strategies are being used. Some people try to avoid those days altogether, some people make new memories, and some people just bear through it. Sometimes you might even go back and forth. The important thing to remember is that when you're not feeling excited about the holidays, there are people who can relate. And if you come across someone who's struggling, try reaching out to them. Sometimes simple human contact can make all the difference.

22

I SHOULD GET UP and get ready for work, but I pull the covers up to my chin instead. The Fall Semester just started last week, but I couldn't even make it to class this morning. *I don't even know why I keep trying, everything's just gonna fall apart in the end anyway.*

I slide my phone from under my pillow and text Zoila at work.

12:17 PM

Zoila, I've been throwing up and having chills all day. I think I'm coming down with the flu. Can you let everybody know I'll be out sick the rest of the week? I'll bring in a Dr's note.

I hate lying, but it's not like I have anything to offer them anyway. I don't even know why they hired me. *How am I gonna mentor and advocate for these kids when I'm barely keeping my own head above water?* How am I supposed to tell them that the emptiness never really goes away because they'll always want their mom and dad?

I swear, God has a sick sense of humor. It's like our lives are just a game for him—jigsaw puzzles that he made—only we have to put ourselves together. Most people got their pieces in a box with the picture on the outside. They know where things are supposed to go. Somehow my shit ended up in a plastic bag with a hole in the bottom.

7:05 PM

Angelique, ur late for group!

7:15 PM

You ok?

7:42 PM

I'm coming by when group is over.

For a split second, I think about answering the door when she knocks. I just can't. I know she'll give me some space tonight, but if she doesn't hear from me by tomorrow, she'll go to Liz. I guess it's not a bad thing considering what they said happened last year. I wonder how long it would've taken them to find me if I would've slit my wrists.

23

WHY DO I DO DUMB THINGS? I wasted a whole morning waiting to see a doctor so I could get a note for an illness I never even had, only to have him prescribe me medicine that I don't even need. I didn't miss much in any of my classes, but missing four days of work means my paycheck is gonna be short. I completely forgot that I don't even qualify for sick time off until my probation period is up—next month. *Dang!*

As I walk down the hall toward the staff offices, I hear Max at the front desk going on and on about something. Whatever it is has her so amped that she's bouncing up and down while she talks to Zoila. *I hope they didn't jack her meds up.*

"Guess what, Angelique!" she says with a huge grin. "I found two of my brothers online!"

For some reason, I had never even considered tryna find family members that way. I guess I just assumed that everybody would be all secretive about where they were and what they were doing. "Really?"

"Uh huh, we went to the library, and I got on the computer, and I looked up some of my family, and I found one of my brothers, and he was friends with my oldest brother!" Max rattles off.

"Dang, slow down," I laugh. She looks a little embarrassed, but I know she's waiting for me to say something supportive. "That's cool. Look at you, Miss Detective!"

"And Zoila said that if my worker approves it, we might even be able to have visits!" I offer her my fist and she bumps it with her own. "Oh, I almost forgot, I made this for you." She reaches into the back pocket of her skinny jeans and pulls out a plastic string keychain that she probably made during rec. "Happy birthday!"

"This is really cute. Thank you," I smile. "Shoot, you could sell these at the swap meet and make you some money," I say inspecting it on all sides. I give her a one-armed hug and her face lights up. But then I remember ... "Wait! Shouldn't you be in rec?" She gives me a guilty smile and starts inching away.

"I'm on my way right now."

Sometimes that girl is such a trip that all I can do is shake my head. When I get to my desk, I can't believe my eyes. The whole thing is covered in balloons, streamers, party hats and candy—plus, my dry erase board is filled with happy birthday wishes from the staff!

"Happy birthday, Chica," Zoila smiles.

I'm so caught off guard that all I can do is stand there with a goofy grin on my face. *How did they even know it was my birthday? Oh yeah, human resources has it on file just like everybody else's.* I know they like to decorate for people's birthdays, but for some reason, I didn't think they would do it for me. Or maybe I was just hoping that everybody would forget. The funny thing is, now that I'm actually standing here looking at it, I'm glad they're celebrating. "I can't believe you guys did this! Thank you."

"You're very welcome," she says. "Are you feeling better?" The concern in her eyes makes me feel bad and my smile starts to fade.

"At first, I couldn't even get out of bed," I tell her, which is technically true. "But I feel a lot better now." I know I said the right thing when she nods and turns back to her computer. "So what do you think about Max finding her brothers online?" I ask.

"I don't know yet," Zoila sighs. "What I *do* know, is that most of her brothers are adults and yet none of them have ever made an effort to contact her before. I also know that if she found them online, they could've just as easily found her—but they didn't."

Zoila's right, Max shouldn't have had to do all the work; she's just a kid. If her older brothers really wanted to connect with her, they would've done it a long time ago. I can't stand how family will talk a good game about sticking together, but the minute it's time to take action, everybody disappears.

"You know what else is crazy?" Zoila says all of a sudden. "You can find just about anybody on the internet these days. She found the eleven-year old first—*eleven*! That's a little scary."

"Yeah, that's crazy."

24

AFTER WORK, THE FIRST THING I do is make my way to the common room so I can get on the computer. Of course they're all taken, but I add my name to the sign-up sheet and hover around so folks know I'm serious. After the longest twenty-three minutes of my life, I sign onto one of the most popular networking sites around. It feels like an electrical current is running through my whole body as I type letters into the search box.

Brianna Bailey, California

About a dozen faces pop up, but none of them are my sister. I do the same thing on four other sites with the same luck. *Dang!* I rub my aching eyes and stretch so far back in the chair that my spine cracks a couple of times. For some reason, that's when it hits me. *I'm so stupid.* I shake my head and laugh so loud that the folks around me catch attitude. I know I'm in the wrong, but I can't help throwing back a little attitude of my own. "Sorry," I say as I roll my eyes. I am not about to let these folks mess up my mood right now. I go back to that first website and type in a new search with a smile so big that my cheeks ache.

Brianna Marshall, California

How could I forget that her name had changed? This time, quite a few profiles pop up. Most of them seem to be my age or older, but toward the end of the list is a picture of dirty soccer cleats. When I see that the page is associated with a city in the Valley, I get goosebumps and my heart starts beating like crazy. *Don't tell me it's that simple.* I click on the page. My heart sinks when I see that it's restricted, but I click on one of the profile folders anyway. After a couple of seconds, a picture pops up. The hairstyles are different and the faces look a little older than the last time I saw them, but there's no doubt about it—it's Bribee's adoptive parents. Now I see why Max was so amped when she talked about finding her brothers. I feel like bouncing up and down myself!

I take a deep breath and do a search for Bribee's parents. Nothing pops up for her dad, but her adoptive mom's page appears almost instantly. It's restricted too, but one of her profile pictures is a family portrait that she posted about a year ago. It shows her and her husband, a Dennis-the-Menace look-a-like, and a teenage version of my mom with braces. *Bribee!*

I sit back and stare at the screen, just trying to take in as much as I can. *Six years. I haven't seen my sister in six years, but here she is in front of me, like it's nothing. Like this is the most normal thing in the world.* There's a dull ache in my chest as I look around the common room. Everybody in here is acting like this is just a regular day, too. *Pictures of my baby sister are online with some other family, like the family we had didn't even exist. She went from a little girl to this beautiful young lady, and I wasn't even allowed to be a part of it.*

I save a copy of the picture onto the computer's hard drive and then open it in an editing program so I can make changes. Once it's cropped down to a picture of my sister by herself, I save it again and then email it to myself. I already know that I can print it out in color at work. Once I do that, I'll add it to the collage on my wall where it belongs.

My heart is pounding like crazy, but I open another program so I can write a letter.

Marshall.ltr

Save 🖫

Sherry,

It's been a long time, so I'm pretty sure you won't remember me. My name is Angelique Lopez. I'm Brianna's sister. I'm pretty sure you're surprised to hear from me after all these years. I'm kind of surprised myself, because it's been a long time since I've seen my sister. I pray that she's doing well and that she's happy, but I don't know how she is because I haven't been allowed to see her. I don't understand why visits were stopped without any explanation, but I do know that I have never stopped thinking about her.

I've spent a lot of time wondering why you guys just up and moved without telling me. Maybe you thought I was a bad influence, or maybe you thought I was dangerous or something, I don't know. What I do know is that there were a lot of other ways you could have handled things. Brianna and I are family. That may not mean much to you, but family means everything to me. We're not just puppies that can be separated just because one of us is cute and cuddly. If you really cared about Brianna, then you should have been willing to care about me too.

I know she had a hard time with me not being there because she always had a hard time when I wasn't around. From the day she was born, I was always there. I'm the one who fed her. I'm the one who changed her diapers, and I was the one who made sure she was safe. When we didn't have anybody else, we had each other. At least we did until you and your husband decided to keep us apart. I want to see my sister and I don't want to wait until she's 18 to do it.

The heaviness on my chest gets so bad that I have to stop and give myself a minute to breathe. I feel somebody giving me the side-eye, and when I turn my head to see what their problem is, I feel moisture on my cheeks. I wipe my eyes really quick and turn back to the screen so I can re-read everything that I wanna say to Bribee's adoptive mom. I want these people to know that what they did was wrong. But then my mind goes back to something from my communications class about the acronym *T.H.I.N.K.* It's supposed to be a guideline that people use to check themselves before they say something that might cause drama in their lives.

*Okay, is what I'm saying **T**rue?* I think to myself. *Absolutely, every single word of it. Is what I'm saying **H**elpful? Hell yeah, it's helpin' me speak my mind! Is it **I**nspiring? Maybe not. Is it **N**ecessary? Well, I think it's necessary for people to know that they're triflin'. Is it **K**ind? As if I care. Those people don't deserve kindness. They deserve to have somebody get in their face for a change. But then again … is my goal to tell this lady off, or is it to see my sister? 'Cause I probably won't be able to do both. If I send this message, I already know she's gonna catch attitude.*

I take a deep breath, select the entire document and hit the delete key so I can start over.

Marshall.ltr

Save 🔒

Mr. and Mrs. Marshall,

I don't know if you'll remember me or not. My name is Angelique Lopez. I'm Brianna's sister. I know it's strange to hear from me after all these years (it's definitely awkward for me). I wanted to get in touch with you guys a lot sooner, but after you moved, I didn't have a way to reach you. My social workers always said they would help, but it never happened, so I just assumed that you guys wanted a fresh start or something.

I just wanted you to know that I appreciate you for giving my sister a forever family, but I can't even begin to describe how much I miss her. I hope she's happy and healthy and that you're all living a good life. At some point, maybe you can tell her about me. That I'm working as a Youth Partner at the River Beach Residential Youth Academy, and that I have my own apartment in the THP+ program. I'm also taking classes at River Beach Community College so that I can get a degree in Communications.

Please tell her that I'm doing good, but I miss her a lot. I don't know if I'll hear back from you, but I'm hoping that I will. I'm also praying that I don't have to wait four years to see my sister.

Sincerely,

Angelique Lopez

After re-reading the letter a couple of times, I copy and paste it into a private message. I let the arrow hover over the send key for a few seconds, but then I take a deep breath, and click on it. I don't know what's gonna happen, but I guess I'll see soon enough.

25

THERE'S A SMILE PLASTERED to my face as I walk across the courtyard. *I can't wait for group so I can tell everybody that I found my sister.* When I get back to my apartment, I slide my backpack to the floor and head straight for the closet so I can change into my pajamas. Once I'm comfortable, I make my way to the kitchen for a celebratory bowl of Captain Crunch. Apparently there were a lot more nasty people living here than I thought, because in addition to Dani's set-up cereal, I ended up with a total of five boxes.

I put in one of my favorite DVD's and settle onto my futon with a blanket covering my legs. Halfway through my bowl of cereal, there's a knock at my door.

Must be Dani.

I put my bowl on the table and throw my blanket aside. I can't wait to tell her about the Marshalls. Unfortunately, Dani's not the one standing there when I open the door. The chick in the Chucks, skinny jeans, and black hoodie is my mom.

"Happy birthday, Babygirl!" she yells. She's holding one of those jumbo-sized designer cupcakes that you have to get at a special bakery. I can tell it's red velvet, which is my favorite. The frosting looks like it's cream cheese, but somebody took it to the next level by adding shavings of white chocolate. It would've been perfect if it wasn't for the candle, which in this case was a blazed joint.

153

"Mom, you cannot bring weed up in here!" I say as I pull her inside. I scan the courtyard to make sure nobody else is mindin' my business, and then I shut the door with a quickness. When I turn around, she hugs me. The whole thing is so awkward and strange that I have to break away. I pull the joint from the cupcake and go into the bathroom to flush it down the toilet.

"Well, hello to you, too!" she says with an attitude. "And don't be so uptight. I got my medical marijuana card." She puts the cupcake on the table, slides off her backpack and makes herself comfortable on my futon.

"They don't care about that card. Just *having* drugs in here can get me kicked out!"

"Babygirl, marijuana's not drugs, it's natural. The poison they give you at those clinics ... those are drugs." As she talks, she pulls two plastic forks from her backpack and hands one of 'em to me. This whole thing is so surreal, all I can do is stare at her.

"You surprised to see me?" She grins.

"I'm more surprised you found me." I sit next to her and try to wrap my head around the fact that she's here in my apartment. I don't understand, addicts are supposed to be ugly and worn-out looking with bad teeth and skin. They're not supposed to be in flawless makeup, and they definitely shouldn't be sportin' light-brown highlights with a few cornrows on the side. "How'd you even get in?"

"I just walked in. The secret to getting into any place is dressing the part and acting like you belong." She gestures to her outfit and then takes off her hoodie. Underneath, she's wearing a low-cut tank top that's giving off way too much cleavage. "Remember those people who crashed that White House party to poison Obama?"

I can't help but roll my eyes. "Mom, they were not tryna poison the President." The minute it's out, I realize that I should've kept my mouth. Now I'll probably have to spend the next hour hearing about crazy-ass conspiracy theories. I shake my head and dig into the cupcake.

"You can believe what you want, but I know better. The point is, nobody asked questions because they looked like they were supposed to be there. If they can get past the Secret Service, I can get past a little security gate for my Babygirl's birthday."

She puts her arms around me and kisses me on my forehead. It's been a while since we've been this close. It's been even longer since she's held me. I close my eyes and take in all I can, but a knock at the door pulls me out of my feelings. When I open it, Chris and Orlando are standing there with goofy-ass grins plastered to their faces.

"Wuz up Angelique?" Chris asks.

"Nothin'." I'm not tryna give him attitude, but I don't feel like playing games either. He tilts his head back and sniffs. "It don't smell like *'nothin'*."

"Yeah, whatchu doin' up in there?" Orlando asks and then has the nerve to try and look inside my apartment!

"I'm mindin' my own business, the same thing y'all should be doin'." I pull the door closer to me to block their view even more.

All of a sudden, Mom is behind me. "Don't be so anti-social," she says as she pulls the door wide open. I should've known that having dudes around was gonna peak her interest. Orlando and Chris gape at her, and of course she eats it up. "Hi, I'm Angela," she says as she pushes her hand, and her boobs, out toward them. They shake hands with her, but they can't hide the fact that they're mesmerized by her cleavage.

"I'm in love," Orlando says as he scans her from head to toe.

Now I'm heated. "Seriously? Dude, that's my mom!"

They both stand there looking dumb and for some reason, Beavis and Butt-head pop into my mind.

"Damn!" Orlando says practically drooling.

"And that would be a goodbye." I slam the door in their faces without even tryna hide the fact that I'm annoyed.

"I still got it," Mom says as she rolls her hips.

I'm not tryna see her hoochie-dance, so I ignore her and make my way into the kitchen. "You want something to drink?" I ask. "I got grape juice, tea, water, and milk."

"Just water."

I don't hear anything while I pour her water, and for some reason, I have an image in my mind of her sneaking out the front door without saying goodbye. *Don't be dumb, Angelique, you would've heard the door open.*

"You know, I'm proud of you for getting into this program," she finally says. It's kinda crazy, but I actually breathe a sigh of relief when I hear her voice.

"How'd you even know I was here?" I ask.

"See, you young people don't understand." I hear her unzip her backpack, and when I walk back into the living room, she's lighting a cigarette. "Y'all go online just because it's somethin' to do, but whatchu really doin' is leavin' yourself open to being traced." I take the cigarette from her and make a beeline to the bathroom to flush it down the toilet. "Anytime you pay a bill, send a text, check the bus schedule, register for a class … anything you do online, you're being watched."

"Mom …"

"I'm serious! Especially now that they have all these smart phones with GPS. Y'all put way too much information out there." She pauses and stares at me. "You really wanna know how I found you?" I nod with some attitude, because I wouldn't have asked if I didn't really wanna know. "Your webpage." She leans back with a smug look on her face.

"Whatchu know about webpages?" I don't even try to hide the fact that I'm skeptical.

"Babygirl, I was high, not dead," she sucks her teeth. "Why do you think so many homeless people hang out at the library, for a roof over their head? Please. There's empty houses all over this county, thanks to all these Illuminati-run, multi-national corporations."

I roll my eyes. *Every time I see her, I gotta hear this mess.*

"Homeless people go to the library for the free internet. But I don't use my real name because I'm not tryna be tracked."

156

"Whatever. Anyway, my page is private." When I say that, she laughs at me and I feel myself getting heated.

"Are you serious? Privacy on the *internet?* Babygirl, that's an oxymoron—it's not possible!" She pulls a pack of gum out of her backpack and offers me a piece. "Your page was private, but most of your friends' wasn't. Plus, you had this program flagged. I checked it out, put two and two together, and here I am. Oh, I got you something else," she says as she reaches into her backpack. She pulls out an Alice in Wonderland DVD and a warm feeling spreads through my entire body. "You used to watch this all the time when you were little."

"Thanks, Mom." She puts her arms around me and hugs me tight. I close my eyes and breathe in the familiar hint of cocoa butter. *If it could just stay like this, everything would be perfect.* "Visitors need to be out by ten."

"Okay."

We still have a couple of hours until she has to leave, so I put the DVD in and we snuggle up together on the futon. *She seems to be doing good; maybe she'll stay clean this time. Maybe she'll visit more often now that we don't have foster parents and social workers tryna control everything. Now that I have my own place, things can be the way they should've been from the beginning. All we're missing is Bribee.*

I close my eyes and imagine what it would be like if we were all together again. Pretty soon, a peace settles over me and I can actually see it in my mind. Me, Mom, and Bribee sitting around the table eating breakfast and laughing. Mom dressed up for work and happy for the first time in years. When I open my eyes, the DVD symbol is bouncing around the TV screen and the clock says 1:07. *Dang!* I look over and see Mom curled up on the other side of the futon. She looks so peaceful. I don't wanna disturb her, so I cover her with my blanket and let her sleep. It's been twelve years since we slept under the same roof.

I pull an extra blanket and some toss pillows out of my storage chest so I can make a pallet for myself on the floor. *This was just an accident. We didn't mean to break curfew. I know residents who are doing a lot worse—on purpose. Staff better not start trippin'.*

26

THE CLANGING OF POTS AND PANS jolts me out of a deep sleep. I pull my blanket up past my ear and huddle into a ball on my side, but it doesn't do much to block the noise. When I open my eyes, the lights in the kitchen are on and the clock says 3:48. I can't take a breath without inhaling the sickening smell of overcooked eggs and burnt toast.

"Mom. It's almost four in the morning," I say, trying my best to control my temper. "What are you doing?"

"You have five boxes of Captain Crunch, but no organic turkey bacon or sausage? Babygirl, you need to watch all that sugar. It's just FDA-approved poison. That's why there's so much diabetes in this country. And every country that starts eating like us gets diabetes, too..."

Dang, why can't she just take her meds? I pull the covers over my head and try to block out her crazy rants.

" ... And we didn't have to deal with all that mess when I was growing up, but now all the wheat, all the corn, almost all the food they sell at the store is genetically modified, and the corn is the worst thing. That's why so many kids have autism and ADHD ..."

I roll onto my back and stare at the ceiling while she rambles on about how psych meds are part of some conspiracy to pacify and kill the masses.

"I made breakfast. You gettin' up?" She puts two plates on the table and then sits down to eat. "Babygirl, I was thinking about getting a portfolio together so I can start modeling, or acting or something. You know a lot of women my age start to let themselves go, but I still got it. Hell, I look better than most thirty-seven year old women out there. And if Kimora can do it, I know I can, too. You know we're the same age, right? Ooh, Babygirl, we should get a place together! With both of us working, we could get something ten times bigger than this little box they have you living in, and then we could work on buying a house."

"Mom, STOP!" I sit up and look at her, irritated beyond words. "Where are you staying? Or maybe I should ask, who are you staying with?"

"With a friend," she shrugs with a guilty smile. "He's really nice, and he loves the fact that I have so much energy."

"Oh, is that what we're calling it now, energy?"

Her smile fades and her eyes narrow into a glare.

"Let me tell you something," she hisses. "Everybody wanted to fuck me, or be me because I was the party-girl and I was beautiful. But the minute I hit thirty, suddenly I'm 'bipolar' and people wanna poison me? I'm so sick of this shit!" She pushes herself away from the table and walks over to me. "I didn't change. I still like to party, and I'm still fine as hell."

My heart pounds when she picks up her backpack and starts to collect her stuff. "Mom ... what are you doing?" I make sure my tone is gentle so she doesn't get upset. "If somebody sees you leaving now, I'ma get in trouble."

She pauses and looks at me and then rolls her eyes. "I'm not leaving," she lies. "I'm just gettin' my stuff together." She shoves something else into her backpack and sits on the futon with her arms crossed. There's an awkward silence, but I already know how to fix it—I always do.

"You were right," I tell her. "All that stuff you were saying about the internet? I found Bribee the other day."

Her eyes get wide, and for a split second, I see them dart around like she's nervous or something.

159

"You talk to her yet?" she asks. I shake my head. "I know you love your sister, Babygirl, but trust me when I tell you, you need to leave all that in the past."

I feel myself getting heated again. "What are you talking about? She's my sister—and your daughter!"

"She's not my daughter. Not anymore," and then she has the nerve to smile. "I'm not gonna lie, sometimes it felt like she never really was. I used to think that janky-ass hospital sent me home with the wrong baby, 'cause God knows, it was hard to feel anything for that child."

I can't even pretend to hide the look of disgust on my face, but it doesn't matter. It's not like she notices anyway.

"But it was different with you, Babygirl." She looks at me with so much love that I can't stay mad. She sits next to me on the floor and a lump forms in my throat. "Sometimes I would ache for you so bad that I couldn't breathe," she says as she pulls me close. I just sit there and enjoy being in her arms. "They thought I would straighten up and get my act together when they took you, but they didn't understand," her voice cracks. "When they took you ... they took away my whole reason for living."

27

11:20 AM

They're here.

11:20 AM

K, on my way

BY THE TIME I STEP OUTSIDE, Dani's already in the
courtyard waiting for me. We walk past a group of folks who I
already know are gonna be spending their Saturday playing
cards and gossiping. But I guess I'd be doing the same thing if
we hadn't gotten invited to hang with these church folks.

Candace and Teri are waiting for us in front of the complex,
but they're not in the cute little blue sedan. They're sportin'
aviator sunglasses and ponytails in a silver SUV. The sound
system is bumpin' so hard I can feel the base before we even
get inside. We do the usual hellos as we climb into the backseat,
but I'm not tryna engage in small-talk right now.

"You got a new car?"

"No, it's our mom's," Candace says as she pulls off. "She's just letting us use it because we didn't have room for everything in mine."

Hell, even if my mom did have a car, we'd probably never have that type of relationship. I got my annual birthday visit, so as far as she's concerned, her job is done 'til next year. I stare at Candace from the backseat—the way her ponytail is perfectly combed and held in place by an accessory that I've never even seen before. I stare at her perfect, pierced ear that's holding sunglasses that probably cost more than my entire paycheck. I stare at the way she nods her head to the music, clueless about how good she has it.

When we get to the park, I can't believe how big the crowd is. It seems like thousands of other perfect people are sprawled across the grass on blankets and lawn chairs. There aren't any open spaces in the parking lot, but we find a spot on the street about a block away.

What am I doing here? I don't even know these people.

"We brought some extra camping chairs if you guys don't feel like sitting on blankets," Teri says as she lifts the rear door. She starts unloading stuff and handing it to us and I feel myself getting heated.

Hell, she could've at least asked me. I fling one of the camping chair cases over my arm and stand off to the side so Dani and Candace can carry some stuff, too. *I don't care if they drove or not, I'm not some damn pack-mule.* I get even more annoyed when they struggle to lift a giant cooler. *This is probably the only reason they invited me in the first place. Hell, I'm not about to carry this big-ass cooler all the way back to that park.* I start scanning the street for a bus stop in case I need to get myself back home.

"Angelique, can you grab the handle on the other side?" Candace asks. And since she actually asks me, I bite my tongue and help her lift it.

"This is way too heavy for two people to carry," I say, sitting it on the ground.

"Yes it is." She pulls at the back of the cooler and lifts up a hidden handle. "But luckily we won't have to." Next thing I know she's rolling it around on wheels that I didn't even know were there.

As we walk down the street, Candace and Teri and even Dani speak to some of the other church folks that we pass along the way. I honestly try to be social, but the best I can manage is a crooked smile that probably makes me look crazy. *I should just take my ass home.*

The minute we get to the grassy area, I'm hit with the unmistakable smell of carne asada, and what I think is popcorn, but then we pass by a grill filled with rows and rows of corn. Some of them are bright yellow, like they've been pulled right from the husk, others have the dark brown kernels that tell you they've been roasting for a while. The folding table next to it is filled with napkins, drinks, limes, and an eight by ten picture frame with Elotes $2 written on it.

Maybe I'll stay for a little while.

We make our way past crowded picnic tables, and then walk through a maze of lawn chairs and blankets. It seems like every other family is holding a baby or dealing with toddlers who can't sit still. In a crowd this big, somebody should be coming to blows, but it doesn't look like that'll happen here—at least not anytime soon. There's nothing worse than tryna have a good time, only to have it ruined by fights—or shootings. Maybe that's one of the benefits to hanging out with church folks. Their shootings are usually behind closed doors, not at parks.

I scan the crowd to see if I can find Brenda, but it's just too many people. What I do see is a huge area marked off by orange cones and neon yellow caution tape.

"Why is that area roped-off?" After following my gaze, Candace and Teri exchange grins.

"That's where the dodgeball games are played," Teri says. "But I have to warn you, some of the people here are fanatics."

Fanatics over dodgeball. Who does that? Church folks, that's who.

We finally make our way over to a group of about fifteen people. I vaguely remember meeting most of them at the church. After introductions, and re-introductions, we help

Candace and Teri set everything up. The lawn chairs are taken out of their carrying cases and once they're unfolded, a blanket is spread out in front of them. I guess they like their snacks kept in a neat and orderly fashion, because they lay everything out on the blanket.

"So here's how it usually works," Candace says after we get situated. "We have sodas, juices, tea and water in the cooler, so help yourself to whatever you like. Now, most of the food stations are free, but if there *is* a cost, you'll see it when you go up to order. The junk-food on the other hand, is all barter."

"What exactly does that mean?" Dani asks, and I'm glad she does 'cause I don't have a clue myself.

"Ok, so you see how our stuff is laid out?" We both nod. "If you look around, you'll see that almost everybody else has stuff on display, too."

Sure enough, there's cookies, chips and candy in the middle of almost everybody's blanket. Some people even have portable tables and baby strollers filled with stuff.

"So, let's say there's something you don't like on our blanket," Candace explains. "If you want, you can take that particular item around and offer it to somebody else in exchange for something you like better."

I guess my confusion shows on my face because Teri offers to demonstrate.

"Hey Quin," she says to one of the guys nearby. "Let's show 'em how we do it." The guy grabs a six-pack of mini candy bars off his blanket and strolls over to ours like he's inspecting a car or something. When dude starts stroking his imaginary beard, we all start cracking up.

"I'll trade you these candy bars for … three fruit roll-ups," he says.

"Deal." Teri hands him the fruit roll-ups and he gives her the candy bars, but then he walks over to the people sitting in front of us.

"Hey," he says to a little kid with no front teeth. "I'll trade you three fruit roll-ups for your Ironman action figure."

The kid straight mad-dogs him and holds his toy behind his back. "That's not a good deal!" He yells and everybody starts rolling.

"Dude, you've been trying to get that kid's Ironman for two years," somebody says. "Just buy your own!"

Quin comes back looking all pathetic and defeated. Everybody knows he's putting extras on it, but that doesn't stop us from cracking up anyway.

"Hey, Brenda and her family are here," Candace says looking off toward the parking lot. When I follow her gaze, I see Brenda, her husband, and two little kids making their way towards us with chairs and a couple of beach bags.

"Hello everyone," Brenda says placing their items on the grass next to us. Once their hands are empty, she and her husband go around greeting folks with a wave, a handshake, or a hug. "Angelique, you remember my husband, Tony, from the training?" I nod and shake his hand. "This is our daughter, Jordan, and our son, Kobe." I wave to them and then introduce them to Dani.

"So who's the basketball fan in the family?" I ask, looking between Brenda and Tony.

"That would be me," he says raising his hand. "I figured it was the best way to show my respect to the legends."

Brenda shakes her head and rolls her eyes. "I didn't mind, as long as he wasn't trying to name them something too crazy. The funny thing is, there are quite a few Jordans and Kobes at their school.

"It looks like they're about to start the dodgeball game," one of the guys announces. Suddenly, Quin and a few other guys jump up and start getting rowdy. Me and Dani stare at them like they're crazy.

"Sorry, it gets a little intense sometimes," Candace says. "But don't worry, some of the little kids even play. I have to warn you though, some people are over the top." She points to a couple of guys across the lawn. They're both wearing gray sweat pants, and white t-shirts with EDP printed on them.

"Extreme Dodgeball Players," she laughs. All I can do is shake my head.

Me and Dani walk over to the dodgeball game with Tony and Jordan. *It can't be all bad, Jordan's only around six, and I'm pretty sure they won't be gunning for little kids.* The majority of the players are teens and young adults, but there's about half a dozen kids who look like they're around Jordan's age, too.

I swear they crack me up. Before we get started, one of the Pastors says a prayer about fellowship and love, and basically reminds people to act right. I guess what he says sinks in, because they decide to make the teams "fair" by letting the two youngest kids be team captains. That job falls to Jordan and a little boy with flaming red hair. They take turns picking teams, but the drama starts as soon as the little kid logic takes over. In the end, Jordan picks her dad, me, and Dani—and almost everybody else who sat near her lawn chair. The other team ends up with both EDPs, and all their friends.

This should be interesting.

They flip a coin to find out who'll be dodging first—it's the red-head's team. The rest of us spread out and form a huge circle around them. Six colorful dodgeballs are handed out to our Captain and five other random team members. When the whistle blows, we go to work gunning for the other team. The younger kids are eliminated pretty quick, and once they're gone, you can see people putting some serious muscle behind their throws. At any given moment, balls are flying around from all directions, but the circle formation is cool, because they never know where the attack is coming from.

When their team starts to thin out, I finally get a chance to see the EDPs in action. They taunt people, they show off dance moves, and they do flips, all while avoiding the balls. After a while, there's only five people left and the EDP really start showing off. One of them even does a quick handstand. A ball comes right at his partner and I know he's about to get pegged in the stomach, but all of a sudden, he does some kind of crazy ninja move and flips right over the ball! Everybody loses their mind. It was sweet as hell, but then dude gets real cocky. He starts doing backflips and pop-lockin' like he's a celebrity or something. I'm not gonna lie, I start to get heated. Luckily, the guy next to me ends up with a ball.

"Let me see that." I grab the ball out of his hands without even waiting for a response, and when cocky-dude does his next backflip, I throw it as hard as I can. It hits him dead in the face, and he hits the ground—hard. For a minute, we all freeze. But then I run over to him. "Oh my God! Are you okay? I'm so sorry!" I'm on the verge of crying when I start hearing people laugh. Pretty soon, folks are bustin' up. Cocky-dude sits straight up and shakes his head like he's a cartoon character. I'm so happy that he's okay, I don't even mind all the extra theatrics. He looks at me and tilts his head with a smirk on his face. I offer him my hand and he lets me pull him to his feet. "I really am sorry."

"That was good," he says offering me a fist-bump. Afterwards, he takes a deep bow and joins my team in a round of applause.

I'm too shaken up to keep playing, so I make my way back to our seats and watch from a distance.

"You okay?" Brenda asks.

"Yeah, it just freaked me out a little," I admit. "I'm gonna go get something to eat. You want anything?"

When she shakes her head, I step back through the maze of blankets and chairs. I can hold off on the carne asada until Dani is done with dodgeball, but that elote is calling my name. A couple of people are in line ahead of me, but that's cool 'cause it gives me a chance to see what's going on. All I can say is this corn man is on point! I watch him slather mayonnaise on an ear of corn with a little paint brush. After it's coated, he covers every inch of it with Mexican cheese, and then sprinkles chili powder on top—just like they did when I was little.

I don't even wait until I get back to eat it. I just grab a slice of lime and stand off to the side of the table so I can do my thing. That first bite is more than smoky, creamy, spiciness with a hint of lime. It's Mom before she was too sick to take us to the swap meet. It's Daddy taking us to the Mexican

Independence Day Parade and Festival. It's me and Bribee hangin' out with Miss King and her grandkids. It's all the good things from my childhood, and I make sure dude knows it.

When I'm done, I make my way back to our seats with a smile plastered to my face. That's when random people start coming up and giving me props for my dodgeball skills. I swear, you'd think I was a celebrity or something. *Church folks are crazy.*

We spend the rest of the day listening to music, eating, socializing, and bartering for snacks. As we pack up to leave, the EDPs come over to say bye. That's when I notice that Cocky-dude's bottom lip looks like a mini-sausage.

"I still can't believe you clocked that guy in the face like that," Dani says as we walk across the courtyard. She laughs and so do I, at least I do now.

"I'm gonna get on the computer real quick," I tell her as we pass by the common room.

"OK. You going to church tomorrow?"

"Church folks two days in a row ... I don't think so. But tell everybody I said hi."

We say our goodbyes and I make my way over to the common room. There's only two other people there, so I don't even have to put my name on the wait list. I sign into my home page and find a flag on my inbox. My stomach flip flops and I start to feel a little light-headed when I see that it's a message from Bribee's adopted mom.

Sherry Marshall ✕

Angelique,

Thank you for reaching out to us. Of course we remember you!

I want you to know that it was never our intention to keep you and your sister apart. Unfortunately, Garrett's job took us to Europe for three years. While we were there, we attempted to call and write a few times, but we never got a response. We eventually found out that you had been moved several times. I also got the impression that there were a number of changes to the workers overseeing your case. I'm sure that caused some of our attempts to fail as well.

We tried to get back into a routine after we returned to the States, but we were told that continued visits could cause Brianna more harm than good. There seemed to be some truth to that, so we stopped trying altogether; and for that, we do apologize.

We can't change what happened in the past, but we're open to moving forward for Brianna's sake. Garrett and I will be at a retreat near River Beach in a couple of weeks. I'd like the three of us to meet if you're available. I'll send you our availability in a few days.

Sincerely,

Sherry

Write a message ...   > >

I read it and re-read it more times than I can count. *Why would anybody think that me visiting my sister would cause her harm?* It doesn't make sense, but I guess the important thing is that they're willing to let me see her now. I'm so amped, I feel like I'm floating on air.

As I walk across the courtyard, I hear music and laughter coming from Chris and Orlando's apartment. *Sounds like I'm not the only one having a good night.* All of a sudden, the air that I'm floating on is polluted by the skunk-like smell of crazy-strong weed. *Dang!* I'm glad the two of them are getting along, but Chris should know better. This is what got him kicked out before. *Hopefully the R.A.'s don't say anything.*

When I get to my apartment, there's a note sticking out from the side of my door.

Hey Babygirl,
I came by to see you but
you weren't home. I'll be
at Orlando & Chris's
place. Swing by when you
get home.   Mom

Really? A slow burn starts growing in my chest. I march over to Chris and Orlando's place and pound on the door so they can hear me over the music. When Chris finally answers, the smell of weed hits me even harder. I don't know if I should be madder at Mom for ignoring the rules (that I had just told her about) or Chris and Orlando for risking their housing just to get high with her.

"What's up, Jelly!" he says. He's covered in sweat and there's a smug grin on his face. I swear I feel like smacking him, but he doesn't stay there long enough for me to respond. He just leaves the door open and goes back to whatever he was doing.

I step inside to find Mom teaching them old-school dance moves. For some reason, Ashley's there, too.

"We need to go on tour! Y'all can be my back-up dancers." Mom waves her hand around as if they're peasants and starts doing something they used to call the Running Man.

"That ain't old-school!" Orlando laughs. "They do that at the club. That's the Dubstep Shuffle!" As if to prove his point, he does the same dance, only faster with extra moves added.

"Hey Babygirl!" Mom says when she finally notices me.

"Mom … what are you doing here?"

"What does it look like I'm doing?" she says, as if I'm stupid, but then she smiles. "I'm showing your friends how I used to get down back in the day." All of a sudden she starts doing the Humpty Dance. Orlando and Chris follow her lead, but Ashley collapses on the couch.

"I'm done," she says, tryna catch her breath. "No wonder people were so skinny back then," she laughs. "All they did was cardio!"

"That's right, this is what Pac was doin' before all eyes was on him. Betchu didn't know he was a backup dancer back in the day, huh?" She laughs when Orlando stops and stares at her. "See, you think I'm playin'. That's hip-hop history baby! Y'all need to educate yourself."

Mom turns her attention to Ashley with a devious smile. "Here you go, girl, I got something easy for you." She makes her way to a cluttered table where an iPod is bumping Bell Biv DeVoe's *Poison* from portable speakers. After skipping past a few songs, she settles on something that I vaguely remember from when I was little.

"All you gotta do is move like you're making love to a fine-ass man," she says to Ashley, but I catch the side-look she gives Orlando. When the beat drops, she starts singing dirty lyrics and walking towards him like she's a video vixen.

I'm not surprised she's acting up, but when she spreads her legs and starts rolling and grinding her hips in front of him like a dancehall queen, I can't take it. My stomach drops and I feel like dragging her back to my apartment; unfortunately, before I get a chance to say or do anything, Ashley stands up and starts doing the same thing with Chris! I don't know what the hell is going on here, but I know I'm not staying around to watch this foolishness. I storm out of there and take my ass back home just as Mom and Orlando start tonguing each other.

A few minutes later, there's a knock on my door. I open it to find Mom frowning at me with her arms crossed. "What the hell is your problem?" she asks.

"The fact that you have to ask is really sad." I leave the door open and go sit on my futon. She follows me in and throws up her hands like *I'm* the one who's trippin'.

"You want me to leave?"

"Mom, you can't ..."

"I can't what?" she snaps. "I'm so sick of everybody telling me what I can and can't do. I'm a grown-ass woman, and I can do whatever the hell I wanna do!" She mumbles something under her breath and makes her way to the door. "I got somewhere to go," she says, slamming the door behind her.

28

THE MINUTE I STEP INSIDE of Wonderland Tea & Coffee I'm out of sorts. The first thing that catches my eye is the mismatched bistro sets and overstuffed Queen Victoria chairs. I usually hate this kinda furniture, because it's always in some old person's off-limits living room covered in plastic. But for some reason, the red and purple crushed velvet isn't so bad here— especially with all the psychedelic clocks and hookah décor. And then there's the paintings. One of them is a shirtless dude in a top hat with an evil-looking rabbit tattoo on his chest. The other one is an emaciated chick with a clown-white face and blood-red hair that fills the whole canvas. Tiny playing cards are painted above her eyebrows, and the glossy red heart on her lips make it look like she's puckering. It's like Alice in Wonderland for grown folks. I love it.

Most of the tables are filled with people on their laptops, or folks pretending to socialize when all they're really doing is messing with their phones. Nearly everybody is sipping on some kind of expensive coffee drink with whipped cream on top. I'm not about to start that kind of habit 'cause Dani already schooled me on how expensive it is.

Garrett and Sherry show up a few minutes before we're supposed to meet. It's pretty easy to recognize them, because they look just like the pictures on their homepage—that, and the fact that they're a couple of Malibu Barbies in a room full of Bratz. I'm tryna figure out why they wanted to meet here; not that it matters, this place is cool. Hell, I would've met them at a cemetery if it meant seeing my sister again.

"Angelique, it's been a long time," Sherry says as she hugs me. I fight the urge to push her away and even manage an awkward little hug back. "You remember my husband, Garrett?"

"Yeah, hi." I offer him my hand so he doesn't try to hug me, too.

"I'm gonna grab a latte," he says to Sherry. "What do you want, Babe?"

"Just a large green tea, thanks."

"Angelique, can I get you something?" he asks.

"Uh … sure." I'm surprised he offered. "I'll try a green tea, too. Thanks."

He leaves to stand in the growing line while me and Sherry sit there exchanging awkward smiles.

"Oh, I brought you something," she says all of a sudden.

She pulls a manila envelope out of her Coach bag and hands it to me with a grin. My name is written on the outside, so I pinch the metal clasp together and lift up the flap. Inside are dozens of pictures. There's school pictures, soccer pictures, pictures at the beach, pictures at Christmas, pictures of people in costumes, pictures of kids playing, pictures of people posing … and every single one of them have one thing in common— Bribee.

Some of them were taken when we were still having visits, so she looks just like I remember, but the other ones make me feel like I got robbed—only this time, they didn't take money or my phone—they took my memories. I should've been able see her get those braces, and I should've been there to help her stay away from that bright pink lipstick in seventh grade. I wanna say something to Sherry, but my throat is tight, and I know that if I open my mouth, I'm either gonna start bawling like an idiot, or say something I'm gonna regret. The best I can do is offer a fake teary-eyed smile. Luckily, Garrett comes back with our drinks and it gives me time to get my mind right.

174

"She looks happy," I finally say.

"She is, but she still struggles," Sherry says. Garrett covers her hand with his own and they exchange sad smiles.

I chew at the skin on my bottom lip instead of saying what's on my mind. *Hell, if you weren't allowed to see your family, your ass would be strugglin', too!*

"Angelique, we're really glad you reached out to us," Sherry sighs. "It answered a lot of our questions. I mean, we didn't know what to expect or what was going on with you, but it's nice to hear that you're doing so well now."

Now? What the hell's that supposed to mean?

"I hate to say it, but the visits with your mom ended up being a disaster," Garrett says. "She always said the two of you were just alike, so we just assumed ..."

"What do you mean, 'visits with my mom'?" I interrupt because he's not making any sense. They exchange looks like they're confused or something.

"We've always had an open adoption. No one told you?" Sherry asks. I shake my head and fight the sick feeling growing in my stomach. "I knew things had fallen through the cracks with all of us moving around so much, but I thought somebody would've at least told you." She shakes her head. "Once we moved back to California, your mom started having visits again. Everything seemed fine at first."

"So what happened?" I ask with a lump in my throat. *I can't believe Mom knew where Bribee was this whole time.*

"It was supposed to be four visits a year, but she started to become unreasonable." Sherry kinda laughs and shakes her head. "At one point, she even asked for overnight visits. When we made it *very* clear that wouldn't happen, she tried to pressure us into letting her pick Brianna up from school."

"She didn't even bother to show up for the fourth visit," Garrett frowns. "Brianna took it really hard. So, when Angela called a week later and told us she'd gotten the days mixed up, we decided to give her the benefit of the doubt. We rescheduled, but she showed up high as a kite with a 'friend' she'd met earlier that day. We ended it and told her to call after she got herself cleaned up. We haven't heard from her in almost two years."

I feel like I've been kicked in the stomach.

"Look, Angelique, we'd love for Brianna to have a relationship with her family," Sherry says, "But if it's harmful to her …"

"No, I get it." I shake my head and try to process everything they're telling me. "I don't know what my mom was tryna accomplish by tellin' you guys that we're just alike, but here's what I *do* know—I don't get high, I'm stable, I have goals, and I would *never* bring random people around my sister. I just wanna see her and get to know her again. If that means I have to start out with texting or phone calls, then that's what I'll do."

I can tell they're relieved when I say that, because they smile at me and then smile at each other.

29

I WALK INTO THE COMMON ROOM a few minutes after group starts, but I'm not concerned because I already texted Dani and asked her to save me a seat. I also asked her to let Melinda know that I'd be running a little late. I'm not really hungry, but I grab some grapes and make my way towards Dani.

"We have two visitors this evening," Melinda says. "Perry and Franklen, can you raise your hands?" If she hadn't said something, I probably wouldn't have even noticed them because they're sitting in the back, but neither of them are hard to miss. They both look like football players; only Perry is light-skinned with shoulder-length dreads, and Franklen is brown-skinned with a short fro and a goatee. "As you may have guessed, their presence here means that they've both passed their initial interviews."

Like always, they're thrown off when everybody claps. Honestly, that's the best part of having applicants sit in. I don't know about everybody else, but I remember what it was like when I first got here. Having people show you love after you've been through craziness makes you feel like a million dollars.

Melinda apparently says something really important, because discussions start flowin' like crazy; unfortunately, I'm only half-listening to what's going on because my mind keeps goin' back to my conversation with Garrett and Sherry.

"What else?" Melinda asks as she scans the room.

"I'm reconnecting with my family," I say when nobody else volunteers. "I saw my mom on my birthday, and I'm supposed to see my little sister pretty soon."

I get a light clap and some smiles and nods, but I'm also noticing some haters—especially India.

"Don't give 'em no money … don't sign for they phones … and don't let 'em talk you into leavin' the program," she warns, as if I'm the one who needs the advice.

"It's not like that." *Hell, just because your family's all about drama doesn't mean mine is, too.* "My sister got adopted and I haven't been able to see her in a long time. I met with her adoptive parents for coffee, and it was cool. And I already know that my mom has issues, so I'm not giving her nothing."

"You nervous about seeing your sister?" Monet asks.

"Not really … I'm more worried that something'll happen and they'll change their minds. I'm just hoping that they've been treatin' her right."

"Well, they adopted her, so they can't be that bad," Ashley says.

"Gettin' adopted don't guarantee shit'!" Chris says. "I got adopted and we see how that turned out."

Quite a few people nod in agreement.

"Did they pay for they own coffee?" India grills. When people start laughing and groaning, she gets heated. "Y'all think I'm playin'! Shoot, ever since I got in this program, my family been sweatin' me for money."

"Seriously?" Dani rolls her eyes. "Every week, you complain about your family being triflin' and wanting money, but what was the first thing you did when you got your check?"

All heads turn to India and you can tell she's heated for being called out. She crosses her arms and sulks back in her seat. "I took a picture and put it on my homepage—but I deleted it!"

"But they still saw it, so of course they're gonna call you for money! And even if they did, you didn't have to pay for their hair and nails and phones," Dani tells her. "Your nieces and nephews aren't even in school yet, but you're putting Jordans on their feet? What happened when the money ran out?"

India's eyes get glossy and she stares into space. "They didn't have time for me."

"Look, I'm not trying to make you feel bad," Dani says in a softer tone. "I think we've all been through it at one time or another."

Several people nod in agreement, but Omar shakes his head. "I never had to deal with all that," he laughs. "Y'all just gotta know when to say no."

"Or get bled dry," Ernesto adds. They nod like they're the only ones who know what's up and the rest of us are just stupid or something.

India uses the palms of her hands to wipe away her tears, and I find myself actually feeling bad for her. She's not wrong for tryna help her family.

"Let's break and meet back in ten minutes," Melinda says. After everybody scatters, she goes over and talks with India, probably checking in to make sure she's okay.

"So your meeting went okay?" Dani asks.

"I'ma need more than ten minutes, can you come over after group?"

"Of course." She smiles at what's quickly becoming a new routine. Even though we both have to wake up early for work, we stay up late after group to keep the conversation going.

A few minutes before the break ends, I head over to the snack table to see if anything good is left. India's there loading her plate with the last of the grapes. One of the new guys, Franklen, steps up to her.

"Aye, it don't matter how fine you are," he says with a voice that's nothin' but bass, "you cain't be broadcastin' ya money situation like that."

India looks at him like she's some shy-ass school girl and actually smiles! When he smiles back, the silver grill on his front teeth catches the light, and I have to stop myself from laughing. It's like the beginning of a ghetto love story or something.

Ashley's standing nearby, but she's not amused. "No fraternization," she grumbles to India and then walks away. When I look over, I see her watching Omar as he flirts with somebody else. *I don't know why she's mad. A couple of weeks ago, she was grindin' on Chris.*

30

I SIT AT A TABLE FOR FOUR in a small café near campus, with a brand new copy of *Beloved*. It's required reading for my Literature class, but I also want Bribee and her adoptive parents to see that I'm not some average hood chick. I'm not about to end up a statistic—pregnant, crazy, and on welfare just because I was in foster care. I'm cultured. I can read stuff by Pulitzer Prize winning authors just like everybody else. The problem is, I have no idea what they're talking about because I can't concentrate.

I showed up early to get us a table by the window, but some greedy-ass family was taking their sweet time, so ended up with a table in the middle instead. It's not bad, but I hate the fact that I can't see them walking up. I also can't stand people looking at me like I'm some loser who has to eat by myself. I don't have time to be worried about a bunch of haters, but I have the waitress put menus out so everybody can see that I'm expecting other people.

I see the three of them as soon as they walk in. I see them pause in front of the hostess stand and glance around the restaurant, but most of all ... I see my sister. She's thin like she always was, but there's muscle on her small frame. Her light brown hair has platinum highlights, but I can see dark roots in her French braid. It's like watching a young Nicole Ritchie in a blue tennis dress.

I catch their attention with a wave and my heart starts beating like crazy when they walk towards me. *Just breathe and keep it together Angelique.* I wanna run over and give her a hug, but I force myself to stand up and embrace Sherry and Garrett first.

"Can I give you a hug, too?" I ask my sister.

When she shrugs, I wrap my arms around her and pull her close to me. I pick up a hint of strawberries and cream, I also pick up the fact that she doesn't hug me back. She just stands there stiff like I'm some stranger. I guess I am. When I look up, Garrett and Sherry are beaming, but Bribee just looks uncomfortable. When we take our seats, Garrett gestures for her to sit next to me. She sits across from me instead.

"Were you waiting long?" Sherry asks.

"Not really, I just went ahead and got a table so we wouldn't have to wait."

"We appreciate that," Garrett says. "I know it gets really busy here. I heard their food is amazing."

Sherry grins and nods, but then there's an awkward silence. Luckily the waitress shows up and takes our drink and food orders. That's when I notice Bribee sneaking glances at me. When the waitress leaves, Bribee focuses her attention on the Mardi Gras themed walls.

She just needs time to get to know me again.

"So Bribee, you're gonna be a sophomore in high school, right?" I know there's a goofy grin on my face, but I can't help it.

"Yeah, but I go by Brianna now," she says with a little attitude.

She's probably just tired of people calling her out of her name. I can definitely understand that. Shoot, not everybody can call me Geli. And let somebody call me Ann or Angel, they're lucky if I don't pop 'em upside the head.

"Oh, okay then—Brianna." I joke with a little bit of attitude myself, but it just sounds like I'm trying too hard. "I just can't believe how grown-up you are."

She nods and turns her attention back to the walls until the waitress shows up with our drinks.

"The last time I saw you, you were into SpongeBob and The Incredibles," I tell her when the waitress leaves. Me, Garrett, and Sherry laugh, but Brianna just rolls her eyes. "So what are you into now?"

"Nothing really," she shrugs and suddenly gets really interested in her glass of water. Garrett and Sherry exchanged confused looks.

"What about soccer?" Sherry asks, but all Brianna does is shrug.

"Are you kidding me?" Garrett turns to me and leans in like he's sharing government secrets. "She's made the All-Star Team every year since she was eleven. She's been in a ton of tournaments *and* she's playing on her high school's Varsity team."

Even after he says all that, Brianna just sits there. Correction: She just sits there stirring her ice-water with a straw.

"It's alright, she probably doesn't wanna brag," I say with a nervous smile. *This visit is turning into a huge fail.*

"Angelique, why don't you tell us about what's going on with you?" Sherry suggests. I'm grateful she does.

"Well, right now I'm taking classes at River Beach Community College and working part-time at a group home for girls ..."

"Like the ones you were always in?" Brianna looks me dead in the eye like she's daring me to say something back. I'm so caught off guard that I just sit there like an idiot.

Garrett leans in toward her. "Brianna, don't be rude," he says, but it sounds more like a threat to me.

That's probably why she's acting like this. They must be threatening her!

"Yeah, just like some of the ones I was in." I sip my water to get the cotton feeling out of my mouth.

"Is it true you're living in a place for homeless kids?" She looks disgusted.

"Brianna!" Sherry stares her.

A sick feeling forms in my chest, but I suck it up, because I want her to know that I'm real. "Some of the people in the program were homeless, but most of us just didn't have a stable place to go after we got out of foster care."

The food shows up before I can go into more detail, but it doesn't matter. It's pretty obvious, Brianna's not interested in hearing about it anyway. We eat with tension hanging in the air and painful efforts to make small-talk. I mean, she answers my questions, but she doesn't even try to have a real conversation with me. And when she's finally done nibbling on her fries, she pulls out her phone and starts texting.

"Can we leave?" she asks. "I need to wake up early."

I'm glad people realize that the whole sticks and stones saying is bullshit, because the words that come out of my little sister's mouth hurt worse than getting kicked in the stomach. Garrett and Sherry's looks of pity definitely don't help either.

They leave after promises of staying in touch, but I already know it's not gonna happen.

When I get back to Perdido, Amanda and Monet are sitting in the courtyard playing cards with a bag of chips and a couple of strawberry sodas between them.

"Hey Angelique, how'd your visit go?" Amanda asks.

I sit in one of the empty chairs and take some time to collect my thoughts. "It was weird." I swallow the lump in my throat and try my hardest to keep my emotions in check. "She didn't even wanna talk to me. It was like she seriously hated me or something."

Monet sits there emotionless like she always does, but Amanda's jaw drops. "She didn't say anything about why she was mad or what was going on?"

I shake my head no, and blink away the tears.

"It's those people who adopted her," Monet says. "They might be cool with you to your face, but talking shit behind your back."

Amanda shakes her head. "That doesn't make any sense. Why would they even bother meeting up then? They could've just ignored her messages altogether."

"Maybe they're just crazy." Monet shrugs, but then she looks at me. "You need to talk to your sister when nobody else is around."

"Yeah, but I gotta go through them to get in touch with her." I wipe away the tears that manage to escape.

"You said she's into soccer right? Just show up after school. That's usually when they practice." Monet sips her strawberry soda and swishes it around in her mouth. It makes me cringe on cue.

"Just be careful," Amanda warns. "You don't want them thinking you're stalking her or something."

31

A COUPLE OF DAYS LATER, I skip my Monday classes and get on the bus that takes me downtown to the subway system. I'm not gonna lie, I'm nervous because I only know how to take the bus, but I'm on a mission, so I'ma get it done. I load the two dollars and seventy-five cents into the kiosk on the train platform and wait for the system to spit out my pass card. The whole process is a lot easier than I expected. As a matter of fact, it only takes ten minutes for the train to show up. When it does, I take a seat towards the back of the car so I can scope out everybody and make sure nothing crazy is going on behind me.

Warehouses and abandoned buildings covered in graffiti fly by, and pretty soon, we're high above the streets. It's kinda cool looking down at all the rooftops. I don't even mind the vacant lots with garbage and junked cars. After a while, the scenery changes and the grimy gray of the city turns into open fields with row after row of vegetables. It makes me think about all those times that I ended up in placements where chicks could do hair. It didn't matter what was growing from your scalp. Those chicks could take a rat-tail comb and make lines and angles straighter than a protractor. And when they started braiding, it felt like they were pinching the hell out of your scalp! But it always ended up fly and perfectly lined up, just like these rows of vegetables. *Maybe that's why they call them cornrows.*

I downloaded a guide to their bus system on my phone, but all it does is confuse me once I get there. Luckily there's people around.

"Can you tell me what bus to take to Laramie High School?" I ask the first bus driver I see. She points me toward a green bench on the other side of the street and I get there just as the bus pulls up. There's not enough change in my wallet, so I unwrap the roll of quarters I got from the bank and slide four of them into the fare box.

So this is where my sister lives. I wouldn't really call it a city… it's more of a big town. A place where people have picnics and little dogs that they dress up in sweaters and Halloween costumes. It's kinda nice knowing she got away from all the craziness of the city.

When I get there, school hasn't let out yet, but luckily there's a sandwich shop across the street. I order a bag of overpriced chips and a soda with extra ice. The guy behind the counter looks at me strange when I give him three dollars and seventy-five cents in quarters, but I ignore him and grab a seat by the window.

When the bell finally rings, a flood of students pour out of the gates, and it reminds me of how much I hated high school. I wait until the flow dies down and then make my way over to the soccer field. Thank goodness for smartphones with satellite images and earth view, otherwise I'd be wandering around this place like an idiot.

I could spot my baby sister from a mile away, but I keep my distance because I don't wanna freak her out. Plus, I wanna make sure Garrett and Sherry aren't around. I make my way to the top of the bleachers and watch her do her thing. She runs all over that field doing fancy footwork and keeping the ball away from folks. I don't know anything about soccer, but I know my baby sister got skills. I swear to God, it takes everything I have to stop myself from jumping up and down and cheering for her.

After practice, I make my way onto the field where her and her teammates are gettin' their stuff together. When she glances my way, I smile and wave, but the look on her face tells me that I'm the last person she wants to see. I can understand her being surprised, and I know that me showin' up here catches her off-guard, but when she turns around and starts to walk away ...

"Brianna!" Maybe my voice is a little harsher than I mean for it to be, but I'm startin' to get heated. It doesn't help that a couple of her teammates are lookin' at me with their faces all twisted. I cross my arms and stare at her like she's crazy—she is *not* about to ignore me.

"I'll catch up with you guys in a minute," she says and then walks over to me like she's about to get in my face. "What are you doing here?"

"I wanted to talk to you—without Garrett and Sherry."

"Okay, so talk." She crosses her arms and stares at me with so much shade that my mind goes blank. I don't even know what to say, so I take a deep breath and just speak my mind.

"Why are you acting like this?"

"Acting like what?"

"Like you're mad at me or something."

"What, am I supposed to jump up and down because my screwed-up family's coming out of the gutter to find me?" Her words are worse than a slap in the face, and all I can do is stand there. "I don't know why you guys won't just leave me alone," she says. "I finally have a family, and guess what—they actually care about what happens to me."

My heart pounds, and I honestly have to force myself to keep an even tone. "You don't think I care about you? You're my *sister!* I'm the one who took care of you. You don't remember that?"

Tears start to fall every time she blinks, but her voice is steady. "What I remember is that you had your dad *and* our mom. I also remember that we were happy, but you went crazy and tried to kill somebody just for being nice to me. Then you were gone, just like everybody else."

"Brianna, you don't know the whole story..."

188

"I don't wanna hear it!" she yells, but then she kinda laughs and shakes her head. "The only reason *Angela* came to see me was because she wanted money. Did Mom and Dad tell you that?"

A heavy feeling settles on my chest and I shake my head.

"Typical. Of course it started out small. She'd forget to bring money for food, and then she needed bus fare to get back home. Pretty soon she needed cash for utility bills—and let's not forget the thousand dollars she wanted for back-rent. When Mom and Dad finally said no, she disappeared." All of a sudden she laughs, and it reminds me of Dani's little breakdown.

"Brianna ..."

"She called me once after that though. You know what she said? She said it was too hard for *her* to see me. Too hard for *her*!" She wipes her tears and looks through me. "I'm over it, and I'm sick of everybody's excuses. If you really care about me, then leave me alone."

And just like that, she turns and walks away.

32

I'M ON THE TRAIN back to River Beach, but I honestly don't remember getting back to the station. It feels like I'm in some kind of slow-motion dream where I'm having a heart attack but nobody notices. They're all just going on with their lives like normal.

By the time I get back to the downtown station, my hands are shaking and I'm sweating like I've been running. I sit down on the bench closest to me and try to take deep breaths, but every time I do, a stabbing pain jabs me in the chest. *Maybe I am having a heart attack.* I pull out my phone to call Dani, but then I remember—she's at work. For some reason, I hit Brenda's number instead.

"I think I'm dying," I say as soon as she answers.

People start staring at me like I'm psycho when I break down, but I don't even care. I try my best to answer her questions, but I can't think straight and I'm pretty sure I'm not making any sense. I don't know what I tell her or what I expect her to do, all I know is I feel like I'm losin' my mind.

And then she's there.

"What do you think about spending the night at our place?" Brenda says as she drives. "I don't want you isolating yourself when you get home, and we all know you have a tendency to do that."

I honestly don't know what to say. She and her family are cool, but I don't know about staying overnight. Yeah, we've hung out a couple of times, but I don't really know them—and you never know what people are like behind closed doors.

"If it's strange for you," she says, "I understand, but promise me that you'll at least talk to your friend, Dani."

I know she's tryna help, but I don't feel like being around anybody. I just wanna go home, climb in bed and listen to Adele until I fall asleep. Although … it might be nice hangin' around Jordan and Kobe. They're sweet kids.

"Yeah," I tell her. "It might be good to get away for a night."

She drives into one of those newer communities with cookie-cutter houses and perfectly cut lawns. I picture them living in one of the giant two-story houses with a courtyard and a three-car garage, but nope. We pull into the driveway of a normal single-story house with one of the smallest yards in the neighborhood.

"I'm so tired," I mumble, mostly to myself.

"Tony and the kids went out to get pizza," she says, "so if you wanna take a quick nap, now is a good time."

She takes me through their modestly decorated house and shows me to their guest room. She even lays out a remote control in case I wanna watch TV. Once she closes the door, I kick off my shoes and crawl into the most comfortable queen-sized bed that ever existed.

After a few minutes, I hear the muffled sound of Brenda's voice through the walls. "Hey Melinda … Not too bad. I just wanted to let you know that Angelique is staying the night over at our place … Yeah, she saw her sister this afternoon, and it didn't go too well. OK, sounds good, I'll talk with you later."

I know it sounds crazy, but I actually forgot that she and Melinda are friends. *I need to be careful about tellin' her stuff.*

I wake up to soft voices and the faint smell of pepperoni.

"Can I tell Angelique that we have pizza?" I hear Jordan ask.

"Peek in and see if she's awake; if not, let her sleep," Brenda says.

I hear her little footsteps on the hardwood floor as she makes her way down the hall. When she cracks the door open and peeks her head in, I can't help but smile. It's the same thing I used to do when I was tryna be sneaky as a kid. I wave to her.

"Daddy got pizza if you're hungry," she says.

"Okay, thanks, J."

She walks over and looks at me with sad eyes.

"I can be your sister if you want," she says.

She's so sincere and matter-of-fact about it that I can't help but smile. I love how honest kids are. I sit up and give her a hug.

"Thank you, J. I just might take you up on that." She smiles like I just made her day and my heart melts. "Come on, let's go get some food."

My stomach starts talkin' to me the minute I step into the hallway.

"Did you get some rest?" Brenda asks when we walk into the kitchen.

"A little," I say quietly. She hands me a paper plate and motions for me to help myself. I lift the lid on the box closest to me and put two slices of pepperoni on my plate. Normally I'd start out with three or four slices, but I don't want them thinkin' I'm greedy. Jordan sits at the table watching me until I take a seat in the empty chair next to her. The minute I pick up a slice, she imitates me and starts eating, too. This kid cracks me up.

"Angelique's gonna be my sister," Jordan says, catching me completely off-guard. "Can she go to Big Daddy's house with us?" Me, Brenda, and Tony laugh because she says it like it's the most natural thing in the world.

"That's sweet, J, but Angelique has responsibilities at school and work," Brenda says. "She can't just leave."

"I forgot you guys were going on vacation—Alabama, right?"

"Yeah, my dad has a ranch near Mobile," she says.

192

"Two weeks of barbeque and southern-fried everythang."
Tony rubs his stomach, making Kobe giggle like crazy. *It's cool hearing little kids laugh again.*

"What are we gonna do, Daddy?" Kobe asks with wide eyes.

All of a sudden, Tony busts out with some kinda crazy song in a voice that reminds me of Animal from the Muppets. "We gon' put it in our belly ... We gon' put it in our belly ... We gon' put it in our belly!"

Brenda shakes her head like she's heard it a million times, but Tony and the kids crack up like it's the funniest thing in the world. I look at him like he's crazy for a minute, but after a while, I can't help but laugh, too.

33

HOMEWORK IS RIDICULOUS. In high school people just copied off each other—and those were the folks who even bothered to turn something in. I thought it would be different in college, but nope, they just give it a fancy name—plagiarism. Everybody knows about it. As a matter of fact, my Lit Professor even told us which computer programs she uses to check for it. It doesn't make sense. If they know people cheat, why assign homework in the first place? It's just a waste of time. I'm not worried about it though, I may procrastinate and wait 'til the last minute for a lot of assignments, but I stopped cheating a long time ago. If I'm gonna fail, I'ma do it because I deserve it, not because I cheated off somebody dumber than I am. Plus, it's not like the work is hard. To be honest, some of the readings are confusing, but they're a good distraction from everything that happened with my sister.

Brenda says that I should just give her some time, which I guess makes sense. I would've needed time to process everything, too, especially when I was fourteen. I just hope she's right about Brianna probably getting in touch with me in the future. The fact that she didn't tell Garrett and Sherry that I showed up at her school is a good sign.

My phone vibrates letting me know that I have a call. I know I should silence it altogether—or at least until I'm done with my reading, but I'm not that disciplined yet. It's an

194

unknown number, so I ignore it and go back to my book. *If it's important, they'll leave a message.* Of course the minute I say that to myself, it beeps letting me know that I have a message. I slide it off the table and hit the voicemail key hoping that it has nothing to do with work.

The voice of a chain smoker with asthma mumbles something in the background and then speaks into the phone with a slur. "I'm lookin' fa Angela's daughter." *Dang! Just listening to 'em makes me wanna cough.* "She axe me to call cuz she over here at Kingston Park. She ain't say what happen, but somebody beat 'er up real bad. You need ta come get 'er." There's more mumbling in the background. "Aight thin," they say right before hanging up.

Oh God, Mom's in trouble! I close my eyes and take a couple of deep breaths, trying my best to control the panic that's starting to sink in. And then it hits me, *she's always in trouble. Why should I lift a finger to help her when she's been lying to me about Bribee this whole time? If I go, there's gonna be drama and I can't risk gettin' caught up. I need to stay on track, especially with school. If I don't finish this, my entire schedule will be thrown off.*

I silence my phone completely and put it face down on the table so I can get back to my homework.

But she's my mom, I think with a heavy heart. *I can't turn my back on her. Besides, my whole schedule was set up so I could take care of Bribee. What's the point in hustlin' so hard when she doesn't even wanna have anything to do with me?*

I grab my phone and run over to Chris and Orlando's apartment. Chris answers the door in his boxers.

"Something happened to my mom. Can you take me over to Kingston Park?"

34

WE PULL UP RIGHT AFTER the sun sets, which is when the park goes from being a janky crime spot to a depressing homeless encampment. I exit on the passenger side of Chris' old-school Sentra and lift the seat up so Orlando can climb out of the back. Everything I see is infected with a jaundice-yellow glow from the streetlights—the graffiti, the shopping carts, the garbage ... even the group of sinister-looking folks scoping us out.

"We about to die!" Orlando whispers.

"Shut up, and stop actin' scared!" I snap.

"Ain't nobody actin'," he mumbles, which is crazy because I know he's spent some time on the streets. Then again, maybe that's why he's trippin'.

"I'll be right back," I tell them. A sense of dread is weighing on me, and my mind is screaming at me to leave, but I ignore it and walk over to a group with a couple of chicks sitting on top of a picnic table. The cloud of smoke surrounding them is strong enough to give me a contact high.

"Aye, y'all seen Angela around?"

Everybody shakes their head, but a chick in a tank top and pajama pants squints her eyes. "What do she look like?"

"Redbone with long hair ... got 'er ass beat for actin' up?"

One of the guys raises his eyebrows and nods slightly. "Check the playground."

We pass by collections of shopping carts, tents, and plastic blue tarps that serve as shelters for dozens of people. The smell of urine is overwhelming. If I didn't know better, I'd think we were in some third-world country instead of Southern California. All of a sudden, I catch the familiar frame of a woman on the far side of the park. She walks aimlessly, pausing every now and then to scan the drivers on the side-street next to her. A car pulls up and parks. When the driver turns the lights off, the woman opens the passenger door and slides in as if they're long-time friends. Within seconds, her head disappears from view and my stomach churns.

Lord, please don't let Chris and Orlando see her doing this.

"Is that her?" I look over to find Orlando pointing in the opposite direction. A thin figure is sitting on a swing, slowly moving back and forth with their head down. Their face is covered by a hoodie so I can't tell if it's her or not, but I breathe a sigh of relief when I see the backpack. I walk over to her with Chris and Orlando following behind me.

"Mom?" There's no answer, so I kneel down in the sand and look at her. The entire left side of her face is bruised and bloody. Her busted lip is twice its normal size and her eye is swollen shut. Orlando turns away and Chris shakes his head like it's too much for him to handle.

"Mom, what happened?" My voice cracks and I have to fight to keep from crying.

She's quiet for a while, but then the normal side of her face stretches into a pitiful smile. "Your daddy was the only man who never put his hands on me," she mumbles. "I had him sprung." When she finally looks at me, she touches my face like it's the first time she's seen me in years. "He wanted a family so bad … I just couldn't sit still," she sobs. "I messed it all up." The agony in her voice triggers something inside of me and I know what I have to do.

"Come on, Mom," I say as I help her up. "I gotchu."

35

I LOOK AROUND AS I WALK across the courtyard to my apartment, tossing a head nod to a couple of folks like always. I unlock my door and step inside to find Mom still laying on the futon. She's staring blankly at the TV, just like she was when I left this morning, and all the other mornings since she got here. The good thing is, the bruises on her face are starting to look better.

"It's just me, Mom." I slide my backpack to the floor and walk into the kitchen. "You eat yet?" When she doesn't answer, I walk back into the living room and stand in front of her with my arms crossed. "Mom!"

"No," she mumbles.

"Well there's food in there if you get hungry. I gotta go to work. I just wanted to see if you needed anything." I ignore the musty smell radiating from her and sit on the edge of the futon. "Mom, we gotta find another place for you to stay. Is there anybody you can call?" Once again, she doesn't even bother to answer. "Just think about it. We can figure it out when I get home." I grab my backpack and make my way towards the door. "I'll see you tonight," I sigh. After I lock the door, I say a silent prayer that Liz will keep slacking off on the pop-up visits that they've been threatening us with.

36

I PUNCH IN THE SECURITY CODE and scan the courtyard to make sure Vanessa and none of the other R.A. narcs are around. Luckily, there's just a few residents hanging out. I speak to the ones that I'm cool with and then head straight for my apartment. Dealing with a fight and an AWOL at work has me drained, and all I wanna do is relax; unfortunately, there's drama the minute I step inside. My papers and files are scattered all over the place and Mom is on the floor in the closet rifling through a box of my stuff. I can feel something starting to bubble up inside of me, but I know I need to keep a lid on it. I also know how thin these walls can be. I slide my backpack to the floor and speak to her as respectfully as I can.

"Mom ... what the hell are you doing?" She's so preoccupied that she doesn't even acknowledge me. "Mom!"

When I was in kindergarten, I used to walk past a house that had this little wiener dog on the porch. Everybody loved that damn dog, but it could not stand me. Every time it saw me, it would growl and bark and run after me like it was about to attack. Most of the time I could stomp my foot and it would run for cover, but one day, I stomped my foot and it stared at me like it was about to rip out my throat. When Mom finally turns and looks at me, I see that same look on her face.

"Where the fuck did you get this?" She shakes a bunch of papers at me as if I'm doing something dirty, and yet she's the one going through my shit! I'm about two seconds away from going off, but I take a deep breath and fight the urge with every ounce of strength I have.

"It's my foster care file," I say as I pick my stuff up from the floor. "I asked for it when I aged out."

"This is a bunch of shit about me!" she yells. The stack spirals towards me like a Frisbee, scatters in the air, and then drifts to the floor at my feet. For a minute, I don't know what to do. I just stand there frozen. "You believed 'em, didn't you?" She nods as if she already knows the answer, and then goes right back to digging in my box. "I knew they were watching me," she mumbles.

I'm honestly confused, until I see the way she scratches at her arms and neck. My heart sinks and a sick feeling forms in the pit of my stomach.

"I'm risking my housing to keep you off the street ... and you're getting high?"

She stops what she's doing and slowly stands to her feet. When she turns to face me, all I see is hatred in her eyes. "Did I ask for your goddam help?" Her voice sounds calm, but I can feel the rage behind it. When she makes her way towards me, I can't help thinking about something I saw on the Discovery Channel. Something about how animals make calculated moves right before they attack. A chill runs through me and I get a really bad feeling. "I'm the mother here," she says as she gets in my face. "And I don't need you to do a goddam thing for me."

I swear, I'm not tryna provoke her, and I definitely don't wanna get into it with her when she's not in her right mind, but this is out of control. "Mom, please tell me you didn't bring anything up in here."

For a split second, she looks surprised, but then her eyes narrow into slits. "I don't answer to you!" she yells.

And then I'm over it. I don't know who the hell she thinks she is, but she's not gonna talk to me any kind of way when all

I'm tryna do is help her. Hell, if we wanna be real, I may call her Mom, but she hasn't acted like a mother since I was in the first grade.

I push past her and grab her backpack off the floor, already knowing that I'm gonna find some shit that don't belong in my apartment. As soon as I unzip it, I hear a growling scream, and for a split second, I wonder if Max secretly changed my ringtone to screamo music. I don't even have time to react. I'm yanked backwards by my hair so hard that I fall onto my storage chest and then the floor. The next thing I know, she's on top of me punching and screaming like a wild woman. I try to cover my face and head as best as I can, but the metallic taste of blood is already in my mouth.

"MOM, STOP!" I scream. "GET OFF ME!"

I try to fight back, but it seems like that makes her crazier.

Somewhere in the background, I hear yelling and banging on my door. And then she's off of me. I scramble backwards as far away from her cursing and screaming as I can. Once I feel my back against the wall, I look up to see her fighting against Liz and one of the new male case managers. He's holding her back by her arms.

"CALM DOWN!" he yells, but the look in her eyes tells me that she's not even here anymore. Once she realizes she can't break free, she loses it. Her wails echo throughout the entire courtyard, and I can see a crowd of residents looking in at us through my open door. The stares, her screams, the sirens, and the feeling of getting attacked by my own mother hit me all at once. I wanna disappear, but all I can do is sit there and sob. Strangely enough, it's Vanessa who closes my door and attempts to give me some privacy.

When the police come, they ask me a bunch of questions about what happened. I already know that lying isn't gonna get me anywhere, so I tell them everything. They say they're taking Mom in for a psych eval, but I don't even care. I don't feel bad. I don't feel anything.

37

8:36 AM

Hey Shonda, haven't talked to you in awhile. Whatchu been up to? Text me when you get a minute.

8:37 AM

Hey Jasmine, this place ain't working out. I'm finally making some decent $$. You still looking for a roommate?

8:40 AM

Hey Gwen, you up for some company? I need to get away for a bit.

8:47 AM

Hey Harmony, something went down with my mom, Need to get a restraining order and file charges. U think ur mom would mind if I stayed with you guys for awhile?

NORMALLY WHEN I GO into the office, everybody's cool and all talkative and stuff—well, everybody except Vanessa. But that definitely ain't happening today. The receptionist is cordial because that's how she's supposed to act, but with the exception of the occasional phone call, she's been glued to her computer since I got here. As a matter of fact, the only time she even looked at me was when I told her that I was here for my appointment with Melinda and Liz. That's another thing; usually everybody's office doors are open and you can hear conversations going on all around you. And even when they *are* behind closed doors, the vibe is still positive. Right now, it just feels like I'm at a mortuary.

The chime from my phone is a good distraction. I slide it out of my back pocket to see who's texting me.

8:37 AM

Hey Jasmine, this place ain't working out. I'm finally making some decent $$. You still looking for a roommate?

9:04 AM

Sorry, me n Mike got a place together and I'm not into 3 ways haha. But since you making some money, you can swing by and bring us a housewarming gift.

Jasmine gets on my last nerve, I don't even know why I texted her in the first place. She's cool as long as she doesn't have a man, but the minute she's in a relationship, everybody else falls by the wayside. *I can't stand flaky-ass friends.*

My head is pounding. I close my eyes in an attempt to make the throbbing go away, it doesn't. As a matter of fact, it gets worse. I should've taken some of the Ibuprofen I got when they made me go to the ER last night. But you can't take that stuff on an empty stomach, and I haven't felt much like eating. Who knows, maybe I'll lose some weight behind all this.

Forget about Atkins and the South Beach Diet. All you need is the Momma-beat-my-ass-diet and you, too, can look like a Reality Star. Just thinking about it makes me wanna laugh, but the sharp sting from my busted lip makes me cringe the second I start to smile. *This shit is bananas.*

"Angelique, you can come on in now," Liz says. I didn't see her come in, but I do see the way she's staring at my bruised face.

I follow her into Melinda's office with a queasy feeling in my stomach.

"Have a seat," Melinda says softly. I sit in one of the chairs across from her desk and stare at the white trim on my Vans. I don't think they've ever been this dirty before. "How are you doing?" she asks.

I shrug my shoulders without even bothering to look up. Maybe she is genuinely concerned, but I'm not tryna hear a bunch of bullshit right now. *Just say what you gotta say and let's move the hell on.* I think.

"Angelique, I'm at a loss here. I honestly don't know what to say—other than I wish you would've come to Liz or me for help.

Yeah right, because Liz is such a wonderful case manager? She barely did shit for me. She wasn't about to lift a finger to help my mom. The minute I would've said something, she and Vanessa's triflin' ass would've been spreading my business all around the complex.

"Is there anything you'd like to say?" she asks. I already know it won't matter, so I just shake my head. "Okay, well as you know, you signed an agreement when you entered this program ..."

Invisible hands grab me by the throat and my lungs start to fight for air. It takes every ounce of strength I have to sit here quietly instead of screaming. *No! Please, please, please, just give me another chance!* From the corner of my eye, I see Liz slide a sheet of paper and a pen towards me. It's a three-day eviction notice.

204

This is not happening. Tears blur my vision, but I blink them away and focus on the piece of paper that's about to take away everything I have.

"The check from your emancipation fund will be a little over one-thousand, five-hundred dollars, but it'll take five to seven days to get here," Liz says. "If you can, try to stay with a friend until then. If that's not an option, you'll have to use money from your personal bank account for short-term housing. I'll give you a list of inexpensive places that we've worked with in the past. Otherwise, there are shelters ..."

That's when I stop listening. If she thinks I'm about to stay at a shelter, her ass is crazier than I thought. I pull the eviction notice towards me and sign it without even bothering to read what it says. When I'm done, I push it back towards her and wait for her to tell me something else ridiculous.

"Give me a minute to make a copy," she says as she stands. A couple of seconds later, I hear the hum of the copy machine right outside the door. The whole time this is going on, I can feel Melinda's eyes on me, but I can't make myself look at her. Liz comes back in with a folder. "Here's your copy and a list of housing resources," she says as she places the folder on the desk in front of me.

"Anything else?" I ask.

"No, I guess that's it," Melinda says. "Liz will be working with you over the next couple of days to make sure you have everything you need."

Everything I need. Really? *What I need is for somebody to have a little bit of sympathy for a change. I did everything they ever asked me to do. As a matter of fact, I did more than every other resident here. They're supposed to help people, but no, make one mistake and they're not tryna hear anything you have to say.*

The minute I step out of the office, I see a couple of nosey-ass residents gawking at me and whispering, but my phone chimes so I ignore them and check my texts.

8:36 AM

Hey Shonda, haven't talked to you in awhile. Whatchu been up to? Text me when you get a minute.

9:32 AM

Hey Angelique, I was just thinking about you! I'm packing up to leave for Atlanta TOMORROW. Me and Brian broke up but I'm leaving to go stay with one of my aunts because ...

9:33 AM

OMG, Congratulations!!!

Call me when you get moved in. We definitely need to catch up! Have a good trip. ☺

What the hell … the last thing that girl needs is a baby. Her ass can't even go to the damn grocery store without having a panic attack. I guess that's why she's going to Atlanta. Then again, if her aunt is so wonderful, why didn't she keep Shonda out of foster care in the first place?

I'm so distracted that it takes me a little while to notice the stuff by my door. While Melinda and Liz were busy throwing me out into the streets, somebody had stacked five large moving boxes next to my door. There's also a bundle of collapsed boxes leaning against the wall under my window. I clutch my fists almost wishing that somebody would mouth-off so I could have something or somebody to hit.

This shit is foul. Everybody knows I'm leaving; they didn't have to broadcast it to the whole damn complex. Whatever … I'm not about to let them get to me. I unlock my door, grab the empty boxes and throw them inside of my apartment one by one. When I'm done, I grab the collapsed boxes by the nylon cord and drag them inside. *I can't wait to get the hell up out of this place* I think as my phone chimes.

8:47 AM

Hey Harmony, something went down with my mom, need to get a restraining order and file charges. U think ur mom would mind if I stayed with you guys for awhile?

9:42 AM

Me and my mom got into it too. I'm over at Andrez now. You want me to ask him if you can stay with us for awhile?

207

No I'm cool now, but thanks for looking out. Be safe.

Always.

I am not about to get mixed up with her and Andrez's drama. How are you gonna move in with a guy who sleeps with your friends and steals money from you? That's ridiculous.

The knock at my door gives me a much-needed break from packing. When I open it, Dani is standing there looking like she's about to cry.

"Hey. Can I come in?"

I leave the door open and go back to filling a box with towels and other stuff from my bathroom. She clears a spot on my futon and takes a seat. For a while, all she does is look around and watch me.

"How are you holding up?" she finally asks.

I throw a brush into the box and take a deep breath. This is the first time anybody's even bothered to ask. "I think we need a support group for residents who are gettin' kicked out, that way we can all sit around and talk about being frustrated and pissed-off."

"Do you know where you're going?"

"I found a room for rent," I sigh. "But I need to wait until I get my emancipation check because they want me to pay for two months up front. I guess I'll just stay with friends until then."

"Angelique, you know if I could ..."

"But you can't. I appreciate you tryna have my back though." She's trying hard to not break down, so I smile to show her that I'm ok.

"Alright, I gotta get ready for work," she says as she stands to her feet. "I just wanted to stop by and check on you."

"I'm fine," I say, but we both know I'm full of shit. "Tell Candace I said hi."

I sit at the table with a spoonful of Captain Crunch in one hand and my phone in the other, scrolling through my list of contacts. So far, the only folks who even bothered to text me back are in worse situations than me. I make up my mind to contact every single female in my contacts list, whether they're crazy or not. *It's just until my check comes. After that, I can get my own place.*

12:47 PM

> Hey Yvonne, I need a place to crash for a few days. Can I come by?

Calypso music plays on my phone letting me know that I have a call coming in. Strangely enough, it's Yvonne, and that girl hardly ever talks on the phone. *It's about time things start looking up.*

"Hey girl … "

"I haven't heard from you since you gotcho own place and started thinkin' you was all that," she cuts me off. "Now all of a sudden you wanna crash at my place. You got kicked out, huh?" I open my mouth, but nothing comes out. "Yeah, that's what I thought. How 'bout you call me when you don't need somethin'," she says and then hangs up in my face.

38

ME AND ZOILA SIT at our desks filling out case notes and reports. After a while, she leans back into a long stretch and stares at her computer with tired eyes.

"I need to take a break," she says. "You want me to bring you something from the vending machine?"

"No thanks, I brought my lunch today."

"Alright, I'll be back in a few."

She grabs her wallet from her locker and makes her way out the door with a two-way radio. I already know she's gonna take her full fifteen minutes, so I pull out the list of housing resources that Liz gave me.

Lord, I know this is a sober living facility, but you know I need a place to stay. Forgive me for lying to this woman about being in recovery.

"Hi, I'm calling about the room for rent," I say to the lady who answers. "I just wanna verify. It says $100 a week, but there's a $70 move-in special?"

"Yes, we just need the completed application, proof of employment and a cashier's check," she tells me. "If you have internet access, everything you need is online."

"Perfect." Of course I still schedule an appointment to take a look at it beforehand. It's a shame how many folks are out here running housing scams. When I first got out of foster care, I remember hearing horror stories about rooms for rent. Sometimes people would pay money up front for what ended up being a bed in a garage, or an enclosed porch, and sometimes the "room for rent" was actually some old dude who just wanted sex in exchange for housing.

After I hang up, I go online and sign into my bank account; unfortunately, the $726 that should be in my savings isn't there. As a matter of fact, there's nothing there. The balance is showing zero. And to make matters worse, my checking account is overdrawn by $45! My heart feels like a jackhammer in my chest and I start to feel light-headed. *Keep it together, Angelique.* I pull up the list of recent transactions. Two large withdrawals were made last week while I was at work. Suddenly, my mind goes back to the night that Mom went crazy, the night my personal documents were scattered all over the floor. And then it hits me. She found my foster care file when she was looking for my bank account information. *Dammit!* I close my eyes and swallow the excess saliva that I always get right before I throw up.

39

MY CHEST IS TIGHT and I need to take a breath, but for some reason, I can't get enough air. And then there's the heaviness. I'm moving, but it feels like somebody tied invisible weights to my arms and legs. I feel like I'm underwater. Liz and a couple of other case managers are five feet away. They're helping me move my stuff into one of the garages in the back of the complex, but they don't even care that I'm about to drown.

Where am I gonna sleep tonight? I am not about to go to a shelter. I'll hit up every single person on my phone and online before I get that desperate. How could Mom steal from me after everything I did for her? I'm probably gonna lose my job now.

"Angelique, you need to put the heavier boxes on the bottom," one of 'em says, like I'm an idiot. "If you don't, you might break something."

I just stare at her, but I feel like cursing her ass out. *Does it really matter? It's my stuff. If I pack it and it gets broken, so the hell what! Why the hell do you care anyway? None of us wants to be here doing this, so let's just get it done and move the hell on!* I scream in my head.

My heart starts racing and every beat makes my head pound. *I need to get away from these people.* I drop what I'm doing and head to the bathroom without saying a word. Do I mean for the door to slam as hard as it does? No, but oh well, shit happens. Even with the door closed, I can hear them mumbling and

212

talking shit about me. They must think I'm stupid and deaf. *They get on my damn nerves!*

My bathroom doesn't even look like my bathroom anymore. My shower curtain, my rug, my soap dish, and everything else I bought is packed away in some box somewhere. *Liz's trifling ass probably didn't even label everything. And if a bottle of my pomegranate body wash is missing ...*

"We're finished, Angelique," Liz says after a quick knock. "Meet me at the garage when you're done."

"Alright," I mumble. I flush the empty toilet and take my time washing my hands. They may control me moving out, but they can't control how fast I go. When I finally leave the bathroom, the only evidence that I ever even lived there is the backpack and gym bag sitting in the middle of the floor. The futon has been stripped down to the bare mattress, my chest is gone, and there's a layer of dust where my TV used to be. *Every single trace of me has disappeared in less than two hours. I'm moving again, and I have no idea of where I'm going—just like in foster care.*

"This is a list of everything you have stored here," Liz says when I get to the garage. She's holding a clipboard with some forms attached to it. "The second page says that you can keep your items here for up to ninety days. If you don't move everything by then, or if we don't hear from you, your personal documents will be shredded and your personal items may be donated or sold." She flips to the last page. "I need you to sign here." I don't even bother reading it, I just sign it and hand it back to her. "We keep the keys to the garages, but if you need access to your items, just give us a call. We ask that you give us at least a two-hour notice just to make sure somebody's available to help you."

"Whatever." I don't even have the energy to argue about all that nonsense.

"I have a couple more forms for you to sign in the office and then we'll be done."

I follow Liz back to the office trying hard to ignore the stares and whispers of the residents lounging in the courtyard.

213

Everybody's familiar with the walk of shame. I just never thought I'd be one of the people taking it.

I sit in one of the chairs across from Liz's desk, secretly hoping that the final paperwork will take her a while to finish. Every now and then, I glance over at my backpack and gym bag on the floor. *At least they're not that heavy. I can take them on the bus and walk around with them. But walk around where?*

Liz pulls a form out of her desk drawer and checks off a bunch of boxes as she grills me. "Do you currently have a source of income?"

"Yes." *She knows damn well that I'm working.*

"Where are you staying tonight?"

"With a friend." *If I can get somebody to call me back.*

"Do you have a long-term housing plan?"

"Yes."

"And what is that long-term housing plan?"

"I'm renting a room." *As soon as I get some money.*

"This is an updated list of resources and shelters," she says as she hands me a brochure. "The ones with the arrows in front may have immediate openings, but everything else has a waiting list. If you ever need emergency housing, make sure you show up early because they fill up fast."

"I don't have to worry about that," I snap, but it doesn't matter because she's not listening to me anyway.

She reads through more stuff on the form and checks off more boxes. "The apartment is clean ... the furniture is in good condition ... all bills have been paid ... your personal items are stored ... and your final check has been requested," she notes. "I just need the keys to the unit and the mailbox." I slide the two keys off my key ring and push them across the desk toward her. She checks off another box and pushes the form toward me. "I need one last signature at the bottom and then we're done."

Once again, I don't even bother reading it. *What's the point?* When we're done, I shove the paperwork into my backpack and make my way to the door with my bags.

"Melinda had to go to a meeting, but she said she wanted to see you before you left, if you have time.

"I gotta go." I grab my bags and walk out the door without looking back.

40

I GET ON THE BUS to campus and swiped my 30-day pass through the fare box. At least I'll have transportation for a couple more weeks. I drop my bags into an empty seat in the back and slide in next to them as the bus pulls off. I can stay in the library until ten tonight. Maybe I'll hear back from some of the people I've been texting by then. *Yeah right, I've been hittin' up folks for the past three days. If I haven't heard from 'em by now, it's probably not gonna happen anytime soon.*

I feel sick as I open my backpack and pull out the list of resources that Liz gave me, but it's good to have a back-up plan—just in case. When I check the addresses, I notice a transitional housing program for women a few blocks away from campus. *They'll probably blow me off if I call. I'ma just show up and see what they say.*

I wanna make sure that I know exactly where the place is, so I let the bus take me past the actual address. It means I'll have to walk a couple of blocks back, but I don't mind. Maybe one of my girls will call me back by then. Plus, it gives me a chance to make sure they don't have a long line of homeless folks standing outside trying to get in. I'm not dealing with all that. I don't care how desperate I get.

Most shelters and housing programs are creepy as hell. They're in the middle of the hood, and they're usually the types

216

of places where Daniel Robitaille and Freddy Krueger are drinking forties in the parking lot. Luckily, this place is nothing like that. It's a big cream-colored building with at least two stories and a decent-sized parking lot. There's a lot of different companies listed on the sign, which tells me that people are here for different reasons. That means nobody will be staring or acting like you're a piece of trash for just showing up. It also means that the actual sleeping areas are somewhere off-site, but the most important thing is that it's clean. There's no broken glass, no graffiti, and no smells of urine making my stomach turn.

I feel weighed-down as I make my way up the wooden stairs to Suite 211. I don't know if it's from my bags or from having to be here in the first place. All I know is that my stomach is starting to hurt and I don't wanna be here. Right before I open the door, I close my eyes and take a deep breath. *God, a lot of people I know believe in you. I don't know if you're real, but if you are, I need help. I know I messed up, but if you give me another chance, I promise I'll try my best to live right from now on.*

I pull open the door and step inside of an empty waiting area with pale green walls and black and white décor. You can tell that somebody actually took the time to decorate, because everything matches. They even fanned some decent magazines across the coffee table. But did they have to have green walls? I swear, every social service agency in the world must've gotten together and decided that green would be the color of misery and broke-ass people.

A hard-looking chick with an old-school MC Lyte hairstyle slides open the glass window. "Can I help you?" I'm a little distracted by the Loyalty tattoo written from ear to ear across the front of her neck.

"How soon can people get into your housing program?" I ask.

"If we have an opening and you qualify, we can usually get people in the same day." The minute she says that, some of the weight on my chest starts to fade.

"What do I need to do?"

"First, you need to sign in," she says as she pushes a sheet of paper towards me. That's when I notice that she has crazy-long nails done in black and gold zebra print. After I write down my name and cell number, she hands me a clipboard with some forms attached. "Fill these out as best as you can. If you have a problem with reading or writing or anything, just hold onto it and the case manager will help you."

You never know what kind of people may come up in here, so I take the seat farthest away from the door and start filling out forms. The whole process is annoying, especially when they ask you a bunch of personal questions. Everybody knows they're just being nosey, but I'm not sweating it because I already know how these places work. If they didn't have the space, she wouldn't have even bothered to have me fill these forms out. As a matter of fact, they would've probably taped a sign to the door telling people not to come in.

Less than five minutes later, I'm back up at the window handing her my finished paperwork. "Alright," she says glancing over my forms. "Once I buzz you in, have a seat in the hallway and the case manager will be with you shortly. And just to let you know, you might not be called in order. It just depends on your situation."

She buzzes me in and I step into a wide hallway with folding chairs lined up against each wall. There's about a dozen women waiting to be seen and half of them have kids. *Dang! I know they don't have this many spaces.* I sit a couple of seats away from everybody else and put my bags on the floor next to me. The door at the end of the hallway opens and an anorexic looking lady with pale skin walks out with a nervous look on her face. She has a baby in her arms and a little boy, probably around three, following her. She thanks the case manager and grabs the little boy by his hand. When they passed by, I notice that her left eye looks like somebody colored on it with a violet crayon. *How can a man beat up on a woman—especially one with a baby—and still call himself a man?*

Five o'clock comes and goes, and pretty soon, everybody's gone except me and an older lady who was here before me. It's pretty easy to tell that she's just coming out of lock-up. Her natural hair is braided back into cornrows and she's wearing prison blue pants, a white t-shirt and slide-on canvas shoes. That in and of itself is a dead give-away, but the main reason I can tell is because she can't sit still. Mom told me that being locked-up made her dull. I thought she was tryna say that it made her boring, but she corrected me real quick.

"Babygirl, when you get locked up, you don't see colors like you do on the outside," she said. "Everything looks, smells, and sounds the same the entire time you're there. But when you first get out … it's like the whole world turned into a county fair. That shit is overwhelming!"

The door at the end of the hall opens and the case manager finally calls my name. I grab my bags and head to her office.

"Have a seat," she says motioning towards the two empty seats in front of her desk. I put my bags into one chair and sit in the other while she reviews my paperwork. I feel pretty confident—until I see a frown form on her face. *Aww hell!*

"So, you don't have kids …. you're not an addict … and you've never been locked up?" Her tone tells me everything I need to know and a dull ache forms in the back of my throat.

"Nope." Every cell in my body is telling me to just grab my bags and leave.

"And you're a full-time college student, with a steady job?"

"Yep." I struggle to hold back my tears. *So what if I have a job and I'm in school? Why should I be punished for having goals and tryna be successful?*

"Why are you here?" Her tone pisses me off and my heart starts pounding. I pull my bus pass out of my back pocket and slam it on the desk, and then I do the same with the change and some crumpled bills from my front pocket.

"I'm here because this is all I have right now, and I don't have anywhere to go. And if my job finds out I'm homeless, I'ma probably lose that, too."

"Look, there's a shelter downtown. You can …"

"I'm not going to a shelter!" I wipe the tears from my eyes, grab my bags, and make my way towards the door. *Whatever. I'll figure something out.*

"Hold on," she says before I get the door open. "I want you to meet somebody. She's in a meeting right now, but if you have time …"

"I don't have nowhere else to go, remember?"

She gets one of those amused looks on her face, but I don't even care. *Hell, if she's gonna hook me up with housing, she can laugh at me like I'm a damn clown.*

"Have a seat back in the hallway and I'll call you when she's available."

When I go back out, there's three more chicks waiting to be seen, but it's pretty obvious that they're different from the women who typically show up here. One of them is wearing gladiator sandals and a tennis dress. One has on a sleeveless jeans-dress and boots, and the other one is wearing a royal blue sweatsuit with a cropped top and shoes to match. Their hair and nails are done, they're wearing makeup, and they're joking around so much that even Cornrows cracks a smile.

After a while, I notice that the chick in the sweatsuit is staring at me. I'm not tryna start anything up in this place— especially if these people are about to give me a place to stay, but if this chick wants to throw down …

"Hey, you need a place to stay?" she has the same smile on her face that Omar uses when he's tryna find a chick to hook up with.

Just when I'm about to tell her that I'm cool, the chick in gladiator sandals shoves her—hard. "What the hell are you doing?" she whispers and looks around nervously.

All of a sudden, the receptionist comes back with three reusable grocery bags. "All right ladies, here you go," she says as she hands one out to each of them. "If there's something you don't like or can't use, just pass it on."

I watch them dig through and scrutinize all the items inside. Toothpaste, toothbrush, deodorant, shower gel, chips, cookies, granola bars, bottled water, a list of resources and tons of condoms. The one who was tryna holler at me has her nose all turned up, but the gladiator chick stands to her feet.

"Thank you, Darlene," she says as she gives the receptionist a hug. When she does, I notice a tattoo in the space behind her left ear. It's a heart with a crown on top and it looks like something is written inside. *Where have I seen that before?*

"Alright y'all, let's go," she says to the other two. When they walk past, I see that all three of them have the same tattoo. All of a sudden I feel real stupid. *I wonder what their pimp would do if he knew they were here.*

The door across from the case manager's office opens and a bunch of people in suits and casual business clothes make their way out of what looks like a conference room. Most of them are talking and shaking hands and stuff, but a tall, brown-skinned lady with chin-length dreadlocks glances my way a couple of times. She has an intense look, but there's a slight smile on her face. Something tells me that she's the lady I'm supposed to be meeting with. That's confirmed when she heads to the case managers office instead of out the door with everybody else. I can tell they're having a discussion, but it's muffled so I have no idea what they're saying.

The case manager steps into the hallway a few minutes later. "Angelique, come on in."

Once again, I grab my bags and follow her, but this time I'm feeling one-hundred percent confident. I already know how it works. They wouldn't have me sitting here all this time if they weren't about to give me a spot in the program.

When I step into the office, the lady with the dreadlocks is sitting in the chair that I had been in earlier.

"Hi Angelique, my name is Kim Carson," she says as she extends her hand. "I'm the Founder and Executive Director here."

"Hi." I shake her hand and all of a sudden, I start to feel nervous for some reason.

"Have a seat." I put my bags on the floor and take the seat next to her.

221

"We've been going over your paperwork." She gestures and the case manager slides my forms across the desk. Kim flips through the first couple of pages and then looks me dead in the eyes. "It's obvious that you have a lot of skills. You're intelligent, and you know how to take care of business. So, I'm curious, what do you think your problem is?"

Did she really just ask me that? "I'm homeless, remember?" I look at her like she's crazy but she's not even phased.

"Yes, but being homeless isn't the real problem, that's just a consequence of something else." She leans back in the chair and sighs. "All those women you saw out there today were homeless, but their real issues are things like addiction, domestic violence, incarceration and human trafficking. Do you understand what I'm saying?" I think about it and nod my head, but I don't say anything because I don't like where this conversation is headed. "You had a place up until a few days ago," she says. "I wanna know what happened. What's preventing you from keeping stable housing?"

I sit there thinking about it and the longer I think, the harder it is to answer. *Just be honest. At this point, what do you have to lose?* When I try to talk, it feels like a hand is tightening around my throat, and I have a hard time catching my breath. The words won't come, but the tears do.

"I don't have anybody," I finally manage to say, and when I do, the realization of what comes out of my mouth makes me feel empty. "I spent most of my life in foster care just tryna be with my sister—but now she doesn't want anything to do with me." I feel like I'm embarrassing myself but I can't stop talking. "I was in a program, but I let my mom move in with me. I thought I could help her, but the drugs made her crazy. She attacked me and got arrested … I got evicted … and then I found out she drained my bank account." Saying everything out loud makes me feel a hundred times worse, and all I can do is sit there and sob like an idiot.

Kim puts a box of tissues in front of me. I pull out a couple and wipe away the snot that's starting to drip from my nose.

"First of all, do you understand that your mother is sick?" She asks, as if I haven't been hearing it for the past twelve years.

"I know that ..."

"Do you really? Because it sounds to me like you're expecting a dope-sick person to make healthy life choices. And I can tell you from experience—she's not gonna change until *she* is ready." She stares at me and I start to feel even more uncomfortable. "Let me tell you what I see," she says. "What I see is loneliness, and that can be a powerful thing. Sometimes people will do and accept almost anything just to avoid feeling lonely."

I have nothing to say, so I just stare at the pencil holder on the desk in front of me.

"Here's our problem," she sighs. "A lot of women out here need help, but there aren't enough resources to go around. Sometimes we have to make hard choices." A sick feeling starts to form in my stomach and I already know where this is headed. "Do we pick the former crack addict straight outta lock-up with nothing but a little gate money? The domestic violence victim with a toddler and newborn? Or the employed college student who just needs a little help until payday?"

I can't believe this shit! After everything I just told them? After being completely honest and pouring out my damn heart, this chick ain't even tryna let me into the program!

Kim stares at me like she's tryna read me or something, but I don't even bother looking at her. "You don't know *anybody* who might be willing to help you out awhile ... nobody from school or work?"

"I already told you that I don't have anybody." I'm trying my hardest to not cop an attitude with this lady, because I know she has the space, but she's not tryna hear me.

"What about church?"

Goosebumps form on my arms and I honestly can't think of anything to say.

A big smile spreads across Kim's face. "Uh huh, you know somebody," she says with a little bit of attitude.

Maybe I do, but I'm not tryna go there.

"Angelique, I'ma be honest with you." Her smile fades and she gets one of those matter-of-fact looks on her face. "If your main concern is being uncomfortable or embarrassed, then you don't need to be here. The women we help are past all that because they're just tryna survive. Do you hear what I'm saying?" I nod my head slowly. "So, you need to call whoever it was that popped into your head." And then, as if to make sure I do, she reaches across the case manager's desk and pushes the phone towards me. For a minute, I actually think about acting like I deleted the number by mistake, but I already know how people like Kim operate. She'll have me calling the church and hitting up social media to track folks down. That *'I don't have their number'* line doesn't work anymore. *Dang.* As soon as I pick up the receiver, Kim and the case manager start looking at each other and grinning like they just solved some big-ass mystery or something.

41

IT FEELS WEIRD SITTING HERE in Melinda's office. It doesn't look like anything's changed, I mean, her desk is still the color of dark chocolate. She still has those scented candles that make me think about tangerines, and she still has that framed picture of her and her husband in Jamaica. Everything is in the same place, but it doesn't feel welcoming like it used to. When I got here, she was polite and all about business like always, but it's obvious that things are different. Plus, she left me sitting here almost five minutes ago!

She's probably out there telling everybody about how jacked-up I am. About how I messed up a once-in-a-lifetime opportunity that probably won't ever come my way again. How I'm probably gonna end up homeless or dead in some gutter. I know I messed up, but that doesn't mean my whole life is over. Everything happens for a reason. Maybe all this had to happen so I could focus on taking care of me for a change.

When she finally does come back, there's a folder in her hand. She sits at her desk, opens it, and hands me an envelope from inside.

"There you go." She shakes her head and a smile spreads across her face.

Now she's laughing at me? How is she just gonna laugh in my face like this? Maybe I didn't make the best choices when it came to my mom, but that doesn't give her or anybody else the right to make fun of me!

225

My heart starts beating like crazy and I can feel myself getting heated. Melinda's cool and all, but if she wants to test me, I can take this to a whole different level.

"What?" I blurt out, but her smile doesn't go away.

"I'm proud of you," she says. I'm speechless. I look her dead in her eyes and I can tell she's not being funny or sarcastic. She's being one-hundred percent real. As a matter of fact, she's being so real that it makes me even more uncomfortable. "Angelique, I know how hard it was for you to ask for help, but you took a chance and look what happened."

A lump forms in my throat and I have to take a deep breath to keep my emotions in check. "I didn't have anything to lose." I shrug and focus on the envelope in my hand so she doesn't see my eyes tear up. All of a sudden, I realize the craziness of this whole situation and I can't help but laugh. "As a matter of fact, I even prayed a real prayer."

"Well, didn't Brenda say that God was working something out?" She gives me one of those knowing smiles and all I can do is roll my eyes. "Come on, I'll walk you out," she says as she stands and walks toward the door. I follow her feeling a whole lot better than when I first got here. Vanessa's mouth gets all twisted when I walk past her desk, but I don't pay her any attention. I don't pay attention to any of the residents looking at me crazy in the courtyard either.

When we get to the front of the complex, Orlando and Chris are loading up the last of my stuff.

"That's everything," Tony says as he slams the tailgate shut.

This whole situation is surreal. I mean, I'm glad that Brenda and Tony are letting me live with them, but it's weird how everything worked out. Her and Melinda being friends since middle school; Brenda and her husband wanting to be foster parents, them hearing my entire story and still being cool with me; visiting a church that they happen to attend, and now this.

"Alright then Jelly," Orlando jokes as he leans in for a hug. He's ridiculous, but he's actually been a good friend. And now that he showers on a regular basis, I don't have a problem letting him hug on me. After I pull away, I glare at him and put my finger in his face.

"Stay away from grown-ass women," I tell him. He gets a cheesy grin on his face and I can tell he's embarrassed.

It may sound strange, but I'm not really mad at him for being into my mom. Sometimes I think she has some kind of special power over men. Unfortunately, Orlando is just one of a whole string of dudes who got caught-up in her spell. But I still gotta give him a hard time.

When I turn to say bye to Chris, I see him all the way over by the curb on his phone. His back is turned so I have no idea what he's saying, but I can tell that it's intense from his body language. After a few seconds, he turns around and we make eye contact, but it doesn't look like he's tryna end his conversation anytime soon.

Dang, I'm getting ready to leave and he ain't even tryna say bye to me? I tilt my head and look at him like he's crazy, and then it hits me—Ashley. I'm not tryna get with Chris or anything like that, but I am annoyed that she's always tryna take up his time. *Whatever. She's gonna have to wait.* I walk over and stand right in front of him with my arms crossed.

"Lemme call you back," he says and hangs up.

Yeah, that's what I thought, I smile. All of a sudden he's looking at me like I'm a piece of trash or something.

"I can't believe you doin' this," he says catching me completely off guard. "After all the shit we talked about, you just bonin' out?"

I stand there like an idiot with my mouth hanging open, because I can't believe that Chris of all people is coming at me like this.

"Are you serious?" I try my best to keep my temper in check, but I feel like I'm starting to boil up inside. "What exactly do you want me to do? I need a place to live—like, right now. Why are you trippin'?"

"Oh, I'm trippin'? I'm not the one going back into foster care," he says like he's tryna accuse me of something. I don't know what the hell his issue is, but he's pissin' me off.

"First off, I'm not going into foster care, I'm going into AB-12."

"What's the difference?"

"The difference is that I finally have a *choice*!"

"Yeah, good luck with that," he says and walks away without so much as a goodbye.

What just happened? Part of me wants to run after him, but I'm not tryna keep Brenda and Tony waiting while I deal with flaky-ass friends. As I walk back over to the truck, I can't help but think that Ashley is the reason that he's acting crazy all of a sudden.

"... If you want, just call the office," Melinda says.

When I look up, her, Brenda and Tony are staring at me.

"Sorry, say that again." *I hate zoning out when people are talking to me. It makes me feel so stupid.*

"Just stay in touch," Melinda says with a smile. She gives me a goodbye hug and I climb into the backseat with Jordan and Kobe.

As Tony pulls out onto the street, I imagine myself running back and begging Melinda to give me another chance. I would never do it, plus I know I can't go back, but the fact that I'm even thinking about it makes me realize that I really did like living at Perdido. Yeah, a lot of people got on my nerves, but it wasn't that bad. I got to know a lot of cool people, I learned a lot, and I had my own apartment. Do I wish I would've done some things differently? Of course, but sometimes that's how life is. Sometimes you don't know how lucky you are until that luck runs out.

42

MY COLLAGE is still the first thing I see when I wake up, but now I have a few more pictures in my collection. Melinda said I could still participate in the Tuesday night group as part of my aftercare services, so that's what I'm doing. I didn't want anybody thinking that I went back to the same life I had before THP-Plus, so I told them everything. I told them about seeing my sister again and about my mom doin' me dirty. I even told them about tryna stay at a sober living house. The crazy thing was, nobody judged me. As a matter of fact, they seemed more supportive than they did when I actually lived here. And when I asked for a group picture for my wall, everybody was down—even Vanessa's janky ass. And then, of course, is my Williams' family portrait. We don't look the same, we don't act the same, and we definitely don't believe in the same things, but it didn't matter.

All those sayings about family sticking together are actually pretty stupid when you think about it. I mean, I ended up in foster care because of family. My bank account got drained because of family, and I ended up losing my housing—all because of family. Sometimes I think it's easier to get along with people you're not related to. There's no history or feelings of obligation. Sometimes you just need to be around folks who'll let you start fresh, and that's exactly what I got from the Williams'.

Angelique
A Transitional Age Youth Novel

Glossary & Character List

Aaron Nelson The Director of Creekside Family Services and a colleague of Melinda Brooks. Angelique talks about her experiences in foster care during one of his foster parent trainings.

AB-12 / AB-212 (Also known as Extended Foster Care) The California law that allows foster youth to stay in, or return to, foster care until the age of 21. To qualify for Extended Foster Care, participants must be enrolled in school, employed at least 80 hours a month, or enrolled in a job readiness program. Youth who are unable to attend school or work due to a disability are also eligible.

Amanda Mills A resident in Perdido's Transitional Housing Program. She and Rodrick are brother and sister.

Angela Bailey Angelique and Bribee's biological mother.

Angelique Lopez (Nickname: Geli or Babygirl) The protagonist or main character of the story. Angelique is a former foster youth and a resident in Perdido's Transitional Housing Program. She attends school at River Beach Community College and works part-time as a youth partner at River Beach Residential Youth Academy.

Ashley Carter A resident in Perdido's Transitional Housing Program.

Aunt Rachel Miss Gavilan's sister. She is married to Uncle Jeff. Craig, Wyatt and Noah are her sons.

Brenda Williams A long-time friend of Melinda Brooks and a member of Calvary Hill Church. She and her husband Tony are training to become foster parents with Creekside Family Services.

Brianna Bailey (Nickname: Bribee) Angelique's younger sister.

Calvary Hill Church A non-denominational church in the city of River Beach. Angelique and Dani attend a service after Dani is invited by her coworker Candace.

Candace Dani's coworker and a member of Calvary Hill Church.

Carrie The Executive Director of the drug treatment program where Angela is sent after her arrest.

Chris Stein A resident in Perdido's Transitional Housing Program. He and Angelique were once in the same foster home.

Cornrows A recently released inmate who seeks help at the women's shelter run by Kim Carson.

CPS (Child Protective Services) A social services agency that investigates allegations of child abuse and neglect. If children are removed from their homes, CPS social workers typically place them into foster homes, group homes or with relatives. Before children are returned to their homes, CPS usually requires parents to participate in programs such as parenting, anger management, drug treatment, domestic violence, counseling, etc. CPS may also provide services to families while the children remain in their homes.

Craig Kimi's older teenage cousin. He is Aunt Rachel and Uncle Jeff's oldest son.

Creekside Family Services A non-profit Foster Family Agency under contract with the County of River Beach to recruit and train foster parents. It is one of many agencies that the County calls when they need to find foster homes for children who are removed by CPS.

Dani Edwards A resident in Perdido's Transitional Housing Program. She and Angelique are best friends.

Darcy Gavilan Angelique and Bribee's third foster mother. Her husband is Robert and their daughters are Kimi and Paige. The family provides a stable home for the girls and attempts to adopt them.

Darlene The receptionist at the women's shelter run by Kim Carson.

EBT (Electronic Benefits Transfer) The plastic debit card that replaced Food Stamps.

EDP (Extreme Dodgeball Players) Members of Calvary Hill Church and the National Dodgeball League. They are extremely competitive and typically perform acrobatic tricks during dodgeball games.

Emancipated (Also known as Aging-Out) No longer under the authority of the foster care system.

Emiliana Tavio's girlfriend and the mother of his son.

Ernesto Chavez A resident in Perdido's Transitional Housing Program.

Former Foster Youth A young adult over the age of 18 who did *not* choose to stay in foster care. Also a young adult who has "aged-out" and is no longer eligible for foster care benefits and services.

Foster Care The system that allows abused or neglected children, or those at risk of abuse or neglect, to be removed from their homes. In foster care, government agencies (ex. the Courts and Social Services) take on the role of parents. Once that occurs, they partner with foster parents or group homes who care for the child on a daily basis. Foster care is the system that replaced orphanages in the U.S.

Franklen A potential resident in Perdido's Transitional Housing Program. He visits a weekly group session to get an idea of how the program operates.

Garrett Marshall Bribee's Adopted father.

Graciella Miss Zarate's daughter. She is a full-time college student. She also helps run her family's home daycare business.

Group A weekly self-help meeting for residents of Perdido's Transitional Housing Program. Participants discuss problems, success stories, and concerns that occur while they are in the program. Residents usually attend group when they are not interested in going to traditional therapy.

Gwen Angelique reaches out to her for a place to stay but she never responds.

Harmony Angelique reaches out to her for a place to stay, but she has moved in with her abusive boyfriend.

Heina Tavio's tricked-out 1984 Chevy El Camino.

Independent Living The ability to live without the long-term help of a program or a caregiver such as foster parents. Independent Living Programs are required to educate foster youth in areas that will help them become more self-reliant. Topics usually include job readiness, job training, money management, housing resources, educational resources, shopping, cooking, cleaning, time management, healthy relationships, transportation, etc.

India Patrick A resident in Perdido's Transitional Housing Program.

Jasmine Angelique reaches out to her for a place to stay, but she is living with her boyfriend.

Jason Bribee's biological father.

Jordan Brenda and Tony's 7 year old daughter.

Kathy The Director at the River Beach Residential Youth Academy.

Kim Carson The Founder and Executive Director of a women's shelter.

Kimi Angelique and Bribee's foster sister.

Kingston Park A park in one of River Beach's high-crime neighborhoods. Criminal activity takes place during the day. At night it becomes a homeless encampment.

Kobe Brenda and Tony's 5 year year old son.

Liz Angelique's case manager at Perdido's Transitional Housing Program.

Luis Vega A resident in Perdido's Transitional Housing Program.

Max A resident at River Beach Residential Youth Academy. She and Angelique have a close relationship.

Melinda Brooks The Director of Perdido's Transitional Housing Program.

Miss Gina The CPS social worker who removed Angelique and Bribee from the home of Mr. and Mrs. Dorsey. She taught the girls how to use a telephone.

Miss King An elderly neighbor who babysat Angelique and Bribee before they went into foster care.

Miss Zarate Angelique and Bribee's second foster mother. She ran a daycare business from her home.

Monet Powell A resident in Perdido's Transitional Housing Program.

Mr. Dorsey Angelique and Bribee's first foster father.

Mrs. Dorsey Angelique and Bribee's first foster mother.

Nadia The social worker who stays after-hours to help Miss Gina find a new foster home for Angelique and Bribee.

Noah Aunt Rachel and Uncle Jeff's youngest son. He and Bribee are close in age.

Non-Minor Dependent (NMD) A young adult over the age of 18 who chooses to stay in, or return to, foster care. Non-minor dependents continue to have an attorney and a social worker.

Omar Alexander A resident in Perdido's Transitional Housing Program.

Orlando Walker A resident in Perdido's Transitional Housing Program.

Paige Kimi's older sister. She attends college in New Mexico.

Pastor Bob McClure The Senior Pastor at Calvary Hill Church.

Pastor Miguel A Pastor at Calvary Hill Church.

Perdido A non-profit agency under contract with the County of River Beach to run a transitional housing program for former foster youth between the ages of 18 and 24 (THP-Plus).

Perry A potential resident in Perdido's Transitional Housing Program. He visits a weekly group session to get an idea of how the program operates.

Professor Lau An Instructor at River Beach Community College.

Quin A member of Calvary Hill Church. He collects super hero action figures.

Resident Advisor (R.A.) A graduate of Perdido's Transitional Housing Program. They are hired to live on-site and serve as mentors and advocates for current residents.

River Beach Community College (RBCC) The two-year junior college that Angelique attends.

River Beach Residential Youth Academy (Also known as The Res or The Youth Academy) A group home for girls between the ages of 11 and 17. Angelique was hired to work there as a Youth Partner.

Robert Gavilan Angelique and Bribee's third foster father. His wife is Darcy Gavilan and their daughters are Kimi and Paige.

Rodrick Mills A resident in Perdido's Transitional Housing Program. He and Amanda are brother and sister.

Section 8 A federal housing voucher program that provides discounted rent to low-income individuals and families. The elderly and the disabled are also eligible.

Sherry Marshall Bribee's Adopted Mother.

Shonda Angelique reaches out to her for a place to stay, but she is pregnant and moving to Atlanta.

Tavio Lopez Angelique's biological father.

Teri Candace's sister and a member of Calvary Hill Church.

Tony Williams The husband of Brenda Williams and a member of Calvary Hill Church. He and his wife are training to become foster parents with Creekside Family Services.

Transitional Age Youth (TAY) Young people between the ages of 16 and 25 who have aged-out, or are preparing to age-out, of foster care, children's mental health services, or the juvenile justice system. After leaving these programs, many struggle with unstable housing, mental illness and fractured support systems. Many also do not have the basic skills that would allow them to live independently.

Transitional Housing Placement Program (THPP) A transitional housing program for *current* foster youth in the state of California. The goal is to prepare youth between the ages of 16 and 18 for emancipation by providing life skills training in apartments or single family dwellings. Participants typically live with a roommate, but special permission may be granted to live alone. An employee of the program may live with the participant or nearby to provide supervision. Foster youth supervised by the Probation Department are also eligible.

Transitional Housing Program-Plus (THP-Plus or THP+)
A two-year transitional housing program for *former* foster
youth in the state of California. The goal is to help young
adults between the ages of 18 and 24 prepare for life after
foster care by providing stable housing, life skills training, and
educational support. Participants may live with a roommate,
alone, or with a Host Family (ex. former foster parents).
Former foster youth supervised by the Probation Department
are also eligible.

Transitional Housing Placement-Plus Foster Care
(THP+FC) A transitional housing program for youth
between the ages of 18 and 21 who chose to stay in, or return
to, foster care. The goal is to provide stable housing and
supportive services to reduce the high rates of homelessness,
unemployment, and incarceration normally experienced when
youth leave foster care. Participants may live with a
roommate, alone, or with a Host Family (ex. former foster
parents). Foster youth supervised by the Probation
Department are also eligible.

Uncle Jeff Aunt Rachel's husband. Craig, Wyatt and Noah
are his sons.

Vanessa One of three Resident Advisors.

Vincent Marks A martial arts expert and a survivor of child
abuse. He speaks about his abusive childhood on the day that
Angelique and Dani visit Calvary Hill Church.

Wyatt Aunt Rachel and Uncle Jeff's middle son. He and
Bribee are close in age.

Youth Partner A part-time position at River Beach
Residential Youth Academy created specifically for former
foster youth. Youth Partners supervise, mentor and advocate
for girls at the group home.

Yvonne Angelique reaches out to her for a place to stay, but she becomes angry because Angelique only called when she wanted something.

Zoila A Counselor at River Beach Residential Youth Academy. She and Angelique are coworkers.

A Transitional Age Youth Novel

Discussion Guide

1. What were Angelique's goals at the beginning of the book? How were her goals helpful? How were her goals harmful? How did her goals change by the end of the book?

2. What were some of Angela's strengths? In what ways was she a good mother? What were some things Angela struggled with? How did her struggles impact the way she cared for her children? What could she have done to properly care for her children?

3. What were some of Tavio's strengths? In what ways was he a good father? What were some things Tavio struggled with? How did his struggles impact the way he cared for his children? What could he have done to properly care for his children?

4. Angelique talks about "foster parents who piled their personal problems on top of ours." What were some of the Dorsey's personal problems?

5. What were some of the cultural factors that may have led to the kids being removed from Mrs. Zarate's home?

6. Angelique admits that she often "thinks the worst" in situations. Why do you think she had such negative thoughts?

7. What were Angelique's favorite foods? Why do you think those foods played such an important role in her life?

8. Why do you think Angelique was so uncomfortable around "church folks"? How did her feelings change? Why do you think her feelings changed?

9. Why do you think Brianna wanted to be left alone?

10. Why do you think Angelique chose to break the rules instead of getting help for her mother? Why do you think she was so angry after she got evicted?

11. What were some of the problems with Perdido's Transitional Housing Program? How do you think those problems could be solved?

12. What were some of the advantages and disadvantages of Perdido's weekly support group?

13. Which character(s) interested you the most? Why?

14. Which character(s) bothered you the most? Why?

15. What advice would you give to young adults like Angelique?

Made in the USA
Lexington, KY
09 June 2017